ADULTERY

ADULTERY

A Novel

RICHARD B. WRIGHT

HarperCollins*PublishersLtd*   A PHYLLIS BRUCE BOOK

HarperCollins books may be purchased for
educational, business, or sales promotional use
through our Special Markets Department.

HarperCollins Publishers Ltd
2 Bloor Street East, 20th Floor,
Toronto, Ontario, Canada,
M4W 1A8

www.harpercollins.ca

Library and Archives Canada Cataloguing in
Publication

Wright, Richard B., 1937–
Adultery / Richard B. Wright. – 1st ed.

"A Phyllis Bruce book".
ISBN 0-00-200586-7

I. Title.

PS8595.R6A64 2004   C813´.54
C2004-903331-X

HC 9 8 7 6 5 4 3 2 1

Printed and bound in the United States
Set in Monotype Fournier

FOR

GERRY SHANTZ

One

After an hour the young policewoman brought Fielding a cup
of coffee and left him alone in the room. Constable Warren
did not approve of him or his story, and in a way he had found
her intimidating with her judgmental silences and her wary
manner of glancing at him from time to time. It was ridiculous, for he doubted that she was even twenty-five. The sergeant was more sympathetic and said that a detective from
Exeter was on his way and would be there within the hour.
Fielding told the two police officers about the man on the
beach with his greying hair pulled into a ponytail, and the
surly, vacant face that had reminded Fielding of a clenched
fist. He didn't use those words; he didn't want them to think
that he was too fanciful or literary. Earlier he had told them
that he was an editor in a book publishing company. In
Toronto, Canada. So he said only that the man looked angry.

What did he mean by that, they had asked and he said that
the man looked troubled and intense, as if something were

bothering him. Had the man said anything to him? No. In fact, when Fielding glanced at him, the fellow had looked away. Denise had hardly noticed him; she was busy talking about being there, walking along the beach and looking out at the grey sea. It was an adventure for her, a new experience and she was excited and drawn in on herself; the passing stranger was not a part of anything that she was interested in that afternoon. But Fielding had been mildly unsettled by the man's look of dedicated grimness, his peculiar, hurried gait. He had watched him coming along the empty beach towards them, his eyes downcast. He was walking at a furious pace. And when, they asked him, had he seen this man on the beach? Fielding wasn't exactly certain, three thirty, perhaps four o'clock. Had he seen the man again after that? No.

Telling them about the sex in the car had been humiliating. The sergeant had barely concealed his smirk, but the pie-faced Constable Warren had listened with stern attention. She had been suspicious from the moment she shone her flashlight in his face in the car park. When she sat beside him as he drove into Glynmouth, she had offered nothing more than directions to the police station, and her silent disapproval of his behaviour had made him feel vaguely unclean. In the rear-view mirror he had watched the lights of the police cruiser driven by the sergeant, and he had felt an enormous despair infecting him. He saw his life turning in an altogether different and uncertain direction, and he sensed that it would now be divided into before and after what was happening on this Saturday night in October.

It was now nearly ten o'clock, and through the window he could see the lights of the big hotel that faced the esplanade. In the rainy darkness it looked like a cruise ship at sea. Ten hours ago he and Denise had walked along the seafront, joking about the elderly tourists and looking for a place to eat lunch. Later they were going to Lyme Regis. Denise wanted to see the town where they had filmed *The French Lieutenant's Woman*. Fielding had been there years before and had not been particularly impressed. He wanted to stay in Glynmouth-on-Sea, for he liked the sleepy little town. There were far prettier villages along the south coast of Devon, but Glynmouth was familiar and comfortable. He and Claire had been here a dozen years ago, their first holiday together since Heather's birth, and Claire had worried about being so far away from the child; every day she had phoned the Burtons. Besides, it was a windy, overcast day and it would almost certainly be raining soon. He and Denise could check into the big white hotel with its blue trim. He foresaw an afternoon in bed and a late dinner in the dining room looking out at a wet dark night. But first Denise wanted to see Lyme Regis.

She was already teasing him about Glynmouth and all the old people. They had lunch at a pub in the centre of town, and she was right about the aging sightseers. Seated at a table by a window that overlooked a cobblestone square, they watched the elderly tourists making their way in and out of tea rooms and souvenir shops, clutching their maps and cameras. Denise was on her second pint of lager.

"Have you ever seen so many old people in one place?" she whispered. "They must make a fortune at these . . . what do you call drugstores over here? Chemists? They must make a fortune peddling Viagra to these old buggers." She was smiling at him, pleased with her mischievous tone, and looking, he had to admit, immensely appealing in her jeans, white cable-knit sweater with the brown suede jacket and the jaunty little peaked cap.

"I can see you in a few years," she said. "Shuffling around places like this in your new walking shoes. One of those white flat caps on your head. A scarf around your throat to keep off the wind. Worrying about the sniffles as you move along to the tour bus."

Then reaching across the table, she had squeezed his hand. "Just kidding, Daniel."

Yet she had a point. In ten years he would be sixty-five, nearly the age of many of those around him in that pub who were shaking pills out of little bottles, or on steady parade to the lavatories. Denise's ribbing was good-natured, but it stung a little, and of course there was no mention of Claire. Her name had not surfaced once during the whole week. It was as if he were not even married. Had no wife or teenaged daughter back in Toronto. In a strange way Fielding was still at a loss as to how he had allowed all this to happen. But of course he had.

Two hours later, on their way back from Lyme Regis, Denise saw the sign *Car Park and Lookout, 1 Mile*, and she asked him to stop. She wanted to take some pictures of the sea. Fielding wanted to get back to Glynmouth and find a place for the night. By then it was midafternoon, and although the rain had still held off, the heavy, lowering sky looked about ready to dump whatever was up there. Fielding was thinking of shelter, but Denise only said, "You worry too much, Daniel. We'll find a place in that pokey little town of yours. It's October, for God's sake. All those pensioners will be on buses now, headed for home and a hot drink. Why fuss about a room? There's always a room somewhere, and sooner or later you find it."

The verb had annoyed him a little. He didn't like to see

himself as someone who fussed, but perhaps she was right; perhaps he was getting a bit like that. In a certain mood Denise could be unsparing. At editorial meetings, she championed her authors and projects with a fierce determination. In a way it was admirable though it could also be irksome. She could wear you down, make you look for more reasons to dislike her. Since her arrival at Houghton & Street in June, there had been a studied formality between them, a kind of dance in which each sidestepped the other, avoiding any major skirmish. She was cordial enough to him, but he sensed that she was amused by his flannels and blazers, his greying, courtly manner, his old-fashioned shyness. It was a surprise to discover over these past few days that those were the very things that attracted her.

That morning at Paddington, she had held onto his arm, tugging him closer.

"Don't look so grim, Daniel," she said. "We're just having a little fun together. It's not the end of the world."

But as the train raced southward through the grey morning, Fielding remained withdrawn. He hadn't really wanted Denise to come to Devon with him for the weekend. Devon was special. It was for Claire and him, and bringing this young woman along seemed especially disloyal. That was perhaps an odd way to feel after cheating on your wife all week in hotels in Frankfurt and London. It made him remorseful and glum to think about it all as he stared out the train window at the brown countryside, at men fishing along the banks of canals, at villages flashing past. Denise had gone to sleep leaning against his shoulder and now and then a man Fielding's age looked over his newspaper at them. His envious look had helped, but not much.

Now, looking out at the night and the big lighted hotel, Fielding felt again the onset of panic he had experienced in the car park when Denise did not return. You read about these things in newspapers, or you watched them on television, briefly pitying those whose ordinary lives were suddenly invaded by upheaval: the sniper's bullet, the house ablaze, the abducted child. In a matter of moments, lives were spoiled forever. He had often wondered how people endured and got on with things. Some, he supposed, were permanently shattered. The loss of a child could surely ruin a life.

He remembered such thoughts passing through him as he stood in the car park with the rain beating on his head and the sound of the sea below. He was shouting Denise's name. But standing there in the rain as he shouted into the darkness, he sensed that his life was changing forever, that he was now a participant in one of those calamities. He remembered the surly-looking man on the beach and he knew at once that he too was a participant. So of course was Denise. The three of them were now joined in chaos, and soon there would be others, family and friends, acquaintances and relatives, all would be affected in some way by this night's events.

For a few moments, he had wondered if perhaps she had just lost her way and fallen. Bad enough, to be sure, but not as bad as the other possibility. He tried to imagine her squatting by the bushes, misjudging the distance, grasping a branch which then broke away; saw her falling backwards down the cliff to the stones along the beach. Yet it seemed unlikely. Denise was far too capable and sure-footed for something like that to happen. Besides, there were two portable toilets in the corner of the car park. Surely she would have headed for one of those. Still, he had hurried down the stairs, grasping the railings, feeling the rough wet wood under his hands, astonished and horrified to find his life unravelling so quickly. Along the beach he looked for her, but he could make out nothing but chunks of sandstone which over the years had broken away from the cliffside. That afternoon they had read the sign that warned of falling rocks.

He had run back up the stairs, arriving breathless at the top, panting on the wooden platform that overlooked the sea. Then he had shouted her name a final time and returned to the car. He was trembling so badly that he had trouble fitting the key into the ignition. Waiting for the car to warm him, he tried to remember the sequence of events. The police would demand a coherent sequence of events, and this was now surely a matter for the police. The woman he was travelling with had vanished. They would want to know what he and Denise were doing in the car park at that hour of the night.

He had sat trembling, trying to put it all together. When they had pulled into the car park in the late afternoon, there was only one other car, an ancient Morris Minor. Denise had remarked on the funny-looking little thing. Fielding could remember seeing others like it on the streets of Toronto in the 1950s when he was a child. On the wooden platform a few minutes later they saw the owners, an elderly couple labouring up the stairs towards them. They looked as comically antiquated as their car: the old fellow tall and thin in a jacket and plus-fours, knitted stockings and walking shoes, a flat tweed cap; his wife short and stout in trousers and a tan safari jacket with numerous pockets. They looked like birdwatchers and when they got closer, Fielding saw the binoculars strapped to their necks. As they passed them, the old man had said only, "Bit of a climb that," and his wife had merely nodded.

Fielding had watched them make their way to the little car. What colour was it? He couldn't remember, though the police would probably want to know. Denise had finished taking pictures and said they should go for a walk along the beach before it rained.

"Come on, Daniel," she said. "It will be good for us. We've been sitting on our butts all day."

She started down the stairs, taking them lightly in her new Reeboks, and he followed, watching the little cap disappear then reappear among the tough bushes that clung to the rock face as the stairway zigzagged to the beach where she was waiting for him. She looked so pretty standing there that he told her so and immediately kissed her. Leaning into him she had said something about the old beast returning to life. He could not recall the exact words, but he could remember thinking at the time that this was a moment of pure elation. The guilt that had dogged him all week was somehow in abeyance, and ahead of them lay the rest of the afternoon and the evening; no one in the world knew they were here. After the walk, they would get a room somewhere in Glynmouth. Denise was right not to worry about such minor concerns. It was foolish. He had kissed her again and then arm-in-arm like honeymooners they had walked along the beach, pausing to read the sign about the falling rocks.

For the first time since Frankfurt, they had talked about work. She was reading a manuscript by one of her young novelists. It was good, but had a terrible title. Something like *All for Tomorrow*, or *All our Tomorrows*.

"Isn't it funny," she said, "how otherwise intelligent writers can come up with such cheesy titles for their books? Do you know what Fitzgerald wanted to call *The Great Gatsby*?"

Fielding had no idea.

"At one point he thought of calling it *The High Bouncing Lover*. Can you imagine? *The High Bouncing Lover*. It was Maxwell Perkins who insisted on *The Great Gatsby*, thank God."

She was excited to be there, walking along the beach and looking out at the sea towards France. After a few moments she said, "I wish I had spent some time in France. Lived there, I mean. I should have spent a year or two living there at some point in my life. It's my only regret so far."

She told him that her mother was French Canadian. She had been a cook on a lake freighter and that was where she met Denise's father, who was an engineer. Years later, Denise, her brother Ray, and her mother spent two weeks each summer aboard the boat. These were among her happiest memories, and she told him that walking near water, even this cold grey stuff, reminded her of childhood summers. It was then that he had seen the distant figure hurriedly closing the space between them, walking like a man whose unruly thoughts consumed him, made him furious with impatience. As he passed, the man had only glanced at them and then again looked downward. Denise took little notice of him, or if she did, she said nothing. She was talking about her young brother and the grief he had caused his parents over the years. But Fielding had wondered about the ponytailed man and as he did so, thought of one of his mother's old expressions. "He didn't look all there."

Not long afterwards, they felt the first drops of rain and turned back. By the time they reached the car, there was a steady drizzle and their clothes were damp. Fielding turned on the engine to warm them up and Denise suggested a drink from the pint of Ballantine's he had bought at the off-licence in Lyme Regis. They had paper cups and bottled water and she made the drinks for them.

"Reminds me of my wicked youth in Bayport," she said. "Saturday nights at the gravel pit outside of town. In those days it was lemon gin and Seven-Up. Or Southern Comfort and Pepsi. My God!"

He thought he could see her in the back seat of somebody's family car, a boy trying to remove her bra, another couple in the front seat necking, music from a ghetto blaster placed on a rock nearby. There were probably several cars parked by that gravel pit on Saturday nights.

But this afternoon, she was with him in a car in the south of England drinking whisky and water. By then it was raining much harder; the late-afternoon air seemed filled with water and the windows of the car were streaming. They decided they would wait for the rain to let up before driving on to Glynmouth.

"Isn't this the coziest arrangement?" Denise had said, nestling in against him. He could remember how excited he was when she touched him. "Why, you naughty old thing," she whispered.

They had kissed and he smelled the perfume behind her ears and along her throat.

"Let's have a quickie, Daniel," she said.

In two deft movements she peeled off the heavy white sweater, and undid her bra. Her sexual boldness and craft! How artful she was and how lightly she carried her erotic gifts. Sex was a comic interlude in an otherwise ponderous drama. It was never to be taken seriously. The car was a British-made mid-sized something or other. He reclined the seat, and after

Denise had manoeuvred herself out of her jeans, she strad-
dled him.

"Just a quickie, Daniel," she repeated.

When he thought about it now, the entire episode seemed
preposterous: fucking in a car in a rainstorm on Saturday afternoon; they must have been in some kind of sexual delirium.

A week ago, almost to the hour, he and Claire and his father-
in-law had been watching Heather play field hockey at St.
Hilda's. A sunlit fall day in Toronto, with the grey stone of the
school against the blue sky and green field, the leaves turning.
He had been happy standing there next to Claire watching
their daughter. It was some kind of tournament and there
were several teams playing on different fields. The air was
filled with the excited cries of teenaged girls and their parents.
Fielding was not athletic, but he was glad that Heather was
like her mother, physically graceful and entirely at ease playing games. Thirty years ago Claire had been an accomplished
athlete at St. Hilda's, and in a small corner of their basement,
there were trophies from her days of competing in volleyball,
field hockey, and track. Without quite knowing why, Fielding
was proud of his wife's athleticism. Claire was an enthusiastic
spectator, shouting encouragement to their daughter and her
teammates. Mildly flushed with excitement, her blonde hair
pulled back into a ponytail, she looked, Fielding thought,
thirty-seven not forty-seven, and he could remember thinking
how lucky he was to be her husband. Beside her, Dr. Moffat
watched his granddaughter's every move. A perfect little family tableau among other privileged Torontonians.

And just a week later, in a car park in Devon, Denise's
short dark hair in his fingers, and beyond her bare shoulders,

a curtain of grey rain. Then they had drifted into sleep. He remembered turning off the car; it was warm then and rank with the smell of sex. They were both tired. On the flight to Frankfurt, Denise had told him that she was an insomniac. He was about to offer his pillow, but she said she didn't sleep well at any time, let alone on a plane. She said she probably inherited it from her father who would stay awake until all hours of the night when he was home for the winter months. As a child she would hear him walking about downstairs, making himself a drink, settling in under the reading lamp with yet another book about the Second World War. Fielding had slept a little on the plane and when he awakened at the announcement for breakfast, Denise was still reading her manuscript, the severely dark reading glasses giving a rather prim cast to her features.

This afternoon, however, she went quickly to sleep in his arms, and he soon followed. Since Thursday night, when he had called Claire, his sleep too had been fitful. Years ago they agreed that on business trips, he would call every other night. And so he had phoned on Tuesday. But that was before anything had happened between him and Denise Crowder. By Thursday night they were lovers, and when he called, he had just returned from Denise's room. The smell of her was still on his fingers, and standing in his hotel room, looking out at the lights of the city, he had felt oddly unbalanced waiting to hear Claire's voice. It was nearly midnight in Frankfurt. Six o'clock in Toronto and she would be waiting for his call, having a glass of wine before her dinner. Fielding was new to adultery. Not in seventeen years had he strayed, and he could remember wondering if Claire would detect any hint of betrayal in his voice. He wondered too if he were being merely naïve. Most of the men and many of the women he knew had done this kind of thing from time to time. Was it not the way of the world anymore? Perhaps. And maybe. And maybe not. Then he heard Claire's voice. She could have been in the next room.

"Well, hi. It *is* you, isn't it? I've been waiting. How is it going?"

"It's going fine," said Fielding. "A couple of promising things. A novel by a young Australian in particular. She's very good. I may have told you about her. I put in a bid."

"Good for you, darling."

"Haven't sold anything yet, unfortunately."

"Well, you will. Who could resist you?"

"Thousands, I expect."

She laughed. "I don't believe it."

There had been an awkward silence and he had panicked a bit.

"The fair has become so big," he said. "In a way it's no longer manageable. You get the sense, well I do anyway, that you are never quite in control of anything. That you're missing out on something important. It's all going on elsewhere."

He was babbling, but he couldn't help himself. Then Claire said, "And how are you getting on with Ms. Crowder?"

She deliberately exaggerated the buzzing of *Ms.* Claire didn't much like Denise, and it was her impression that neither did Fielding. When Denise first arrived at H & S, he had complained over many dinners about her aggressive New York style, her roughshod approach to discussion at editorial meetings. Looking back he could now see that he had overreacted during those first weeks. In fact, Denise had never been quite as difficult and combative as he had portrayed her.

Claire, however, was prepared to dislike her on sight and did so when they met for the first and only time. A cocktail party at the Windsor Arms for an American author who was passing through town on a publicity tour. The room was crowded and the great man was surrounded by admirers. Denise, who had confided to Fielding earlier in the day that she knew the man and that he was a creep, stood next to him wearing a black cocktail dress. Across the room Claire had whispered into Fielding's ear, "She doesn't mind showing off her tits, does she?"

When he introduced them, Claire offered her icy smile, and to Fielding, Denise's wry little grimace seemed to say, "Okay, lady. Whatever."

So to Claire's question on Thursday night, he had said only that, since arriving, he and Denise Crowder had pretty much gone their separate ways. They each had different agendas, different meetings, and, really, they hadn't seen that much of one another. How trippingly the lies had come off his tongue, though duplicity bothered him, and he would brood over it in the days and nights ahead. Claire was talking about a dinner at St. Hilda's. Sometime in November. She was chair of an alumni committee for the development office and the dinner was a fundraiser. It took a while to realize that she was asking him if he wanted to go with her. Finally she said, "Dan, are you still there?"

"Yes. Sorry. I'm here."

"Well, what about it? Is that Saturday all right for you?"

"Yes, of course. It's fine, Claire." He had no idea what Saturday she was talking about; he had missed that part. He was saved by his daughter's voice in the background.

"Is that Daddy?" Then he was speaking to her, or rather

listening to her tell him about an injury to her knee, and how it had happened in a game on Wednesday, and for a few moments he forgot about this new arrangement in his life. All the same, he didn't sleep well that night or the next.

It was hardly surprising then that he too had fallen asleep so quickly in the car this afternoon. How long had they slept in one another's arms? He could remember Denise stirring beside him, struggling into her clothes. Remembered her kissing his cheek and whispering, "I have to pee, Daniel." Her last words to him. He had murmured something, but he was barely awake. The rain had stopped, and it was dark and misty. When Denise opened the door, he could see the fog, like grey smoke curling into the light from the car. Then she closed the door and he went back to sleep. That was unconscionable. He should have stayed awake until she returned. Yet how tired he had been. After the whisky and sex, after the nights of interrupted sleep, his fatigue had been extreme, and he had slept through whatever ordeal she had suffered.

When he finally awakened, he was unsure about how long he had slept. Perhaps it was only a matter of minutes, and so he had adjusted the seat and sat there waiting for her. It was raining again and cold and he started the car. By the light from the instrument panel he looked at his watch, startled to see that it was nearly seven thirty. And looking out at the rain he knew that something was terribly wrong. A woman whom he had lived with for eight years before his marriage once told him that he had the most pessimistic imagination she had ever encountered. Perhaps that was so, but in the car he had thought at once of the man on the beach. Imagined him standing in the rain, peering through the streaming glass at the lovers. Squinting at the blurred window and seeing a woman and her white breasts leaning into a man. The two figures moving in sex. It was horrible to imagine the man in the rain looking in at them like that, but in the minutes after awakening, Fielding could not help himself. In his innermost being he knew that the man had been there all the time; oblivious to the sodden clothes and the lank hair plastered to his skull, he had watched and waited. And then for him a kind of miracle, a dark gift. The car door had opened and the woman got out and she was alone. The next thing Fielding remembered was standing in the rain shouting Denise's name.

From the next room he could now hear voices, and there was a new voice too, a man's voice. Fielding looked at his watch. In another hour he would owe Claire a telephone call. It would be dinnertime in Toronto. Heather might be going to a movie with Allison Harvey or that Khan girl whose first name he could never remember. They would be up in Heather's room listening to music, or talking about boys or teachers or hockey matches. Claire would probably make herself an omelette and a salad. Drink a glass or two of wine. Wait for his call.

When he looked up, a man in a grey suit was standing in the doorway holding a light coat over his arm. He was in his thirties, mesomorphic, with an Irish face and a brush cut, as it was called in Fielding's day.

"Mr. Fielding, is it?"

"Yes," said Fielding, standing up.

"Detective Inspector Kennedy. I've come down from Exeter," he said throwing the coat on the table. He was not as tall as Fielding but heavier, packed tightly into his suit. A former rugby player, thought Fielding, one of those fellows in the scrum who wore a leather helmet, presumably to keep his ears from being ripped off.

"Please sit down," said Kennedy.

The young policewoman had followed Kennedy into the room and sat down at the other end of the table with her notebook.

"You've already met Constable Warren," said Kennedy, who had taken out his own little notebook and pen and placed an envelope on the table.

"Yes," said Fielding.

"Mr. Fielding," said Kennedy. "We're treating all this at the moment as a missing person case. The officers have filled me in on what you told them, but perhaps we can just go over some of that, and see if we can get to the bottom of all this."

He stopped to scratch his chin while he consulted his notes.

"It's a Miss Denise Crowder who is missing. She lives at 3233 Bloor Street West in Toronto, Ontario. She is thirty-two years old and Caucasian. Works as an editor with a publishing company. Is that information correct?" he asked, looking up at Fielding.

"Yes."

Kennedy continued to look at him. It must be part of their training, thought Fielding. Stare people down. Look for signs of tics or flinching.

After a moment the detective took from the envelope Denise's passport and looked at her photograph. Fielding had found the passport in her handbag and given it to one of the officers. Then Kennedy looked again at Fielding.

"And what exactly is your connection to Miss Crowder?"

"We're colleagues," Fielding said. "We spent the week on business in Frankfurt, Germany. They have this big book fair every fall."

Kennedy was again looking at his notebook.

"I've heard of the Frankfurt Book Fair, Mr. Fielding," he said dryly. "And you are both Canadian citizens?"

"Yes."

"So you and Miss Crowder were having a bit of a holiday down here after the book fair?"

"Yes," said Fielding. "We spent the week in Frankfurt and then flew to London yesterday afternoon. I've been to Devon many times . . ." He almost added "with my wife," but realized how absurd that would sound. "I'm fond of the area. I thought I would spend a day or so and then return to London on Sunday. I have . . . we had business there on Monday. Denise decided that she would like to come along. She had never been to this part of England before. We were planning to fly home on Tuesday. I do this trip every year."

Kennedy had leaned back in his chair. "Are you married, Mr. Fielding?"

"Yes, I am. Seventeen years. I have a fifteen-year-old daughter." He stopped. Why was he going on like that? What did they care whether he had one daughter or six? He always offered too much information when asked simple questions. He was too eager to secure the good opinion of others. It was a foible. His father had been like that.

"So I take it," said Kennedy, "that you and Miss Crowder were having a relationship?"

"Yes," said Fielding. "We were having an affair. It happened very suddenly in Frankfurt. There was nothing between us before we left Canada. Then it just happened."

The young policewoman had stopped taking notes to watch him.

If Kennedy, who looked like a man who had married his

childhood sweetheart for life, disapproved of Fielding's behaviour, he didn't let on.

"Let's just see if we can go back over your day and piece things together. Would you like some more of whatever you have there? What is it? Tea or coffee?"

"It's coffee, but I'm okay thanks."

"Well, I think I'll have some," said Kennedy. "Constable Warren? Could you get me a cup of tea? Milk and two sugars?"

"Certainly, sir," said the young policewoman, getting up. Fielding felt as if he were in the middle of some British crime drama, the sort he and Claire sometimes watched on Sunday nights.

While Kennedy drank his tea, Fielding recounted the day's events: the train to Exeter, the rental of the car, the lunch in the pub, the drive to Lyme Regis, the stop at the car park, the walk along the beach, the man who passed them. Kennedy listened while the policewoman made notes.

"And when you got to the car park," asked Kennedy, "were there any other cars?"

Fielding told him about the Morris Minor and the elderly birdwatchers.

"So then you and Miss Crowder went for your walk and you saw this man. What did he look like, Mr. Fielding? Describe him for me."

"Late thirties or early forties. Poorly dressed. Scuffed sneakers. I suppose you'd call them training shoes over here. He looked like a man who was living rough. And he walked in an odd manner. Very fast with his head down. But what struck me most about him was his face!"

Kennedy looked up from his notes.

"What about his face?"

"He had this look of anger, almost rage. He just looked very angry, very intense. There was also . . ." Fielding chose his words carefully. "There was also a kind of frightening vacancy in his look."

"A frightening vacancy," said Kennedy with a slight smile. "You mean he didn't look all there."

"Yes. Exactly." His mother's old expression!

"Did he look at you or Miss Crowder as he passed? Did he say anything? Threaten you? Swear at you?"

"No, nothing. He glanced briefly at us, but then looked away as if he were almost afraid to make eye contact. Then he carried on down the beach walking at this rapid pace."

"So he was walking back towards the stairs that led up to the car park?"

"Yes."

"Did you see him climb the stairs?"

"No. We were some distance along the beach by then. Denise and I were talking about work. She had taken little notice of the man."

Kennedy finished his tea in one great swallow. "So then you both returned to the car. What time would that have been?"

"I can't be sure, but I would say close to five o'clock."

"Still light then?"

"Yes, but it was a dark afternoon and raining. That's why we turned back. It had started to rain, and when we got to the car, it was coming down quite hard and so the light was murky. It's the only word I can think of."

"Murky will do," said Kennedy, writing in his notebook, and Fielding began to wonder if Kennedy really believed

him. For the first time it occurred to him that they might think
he was lying. It came as a shock, but why not? From their
perspective he had to be considered a suspect in Denise's dis-
appearance. Cops were by nature suspicious: nearly every
day they dealt with the failings of their fellow mortals, with
their cheating and stealing and murdering, with their ingenious deceits to avoid detection. As far as they were concerned, he might easily have pushed his girlfriend off the cliff
and now was trying to make it look like either an accident or
an abduction.

They didn't know the details of his relationship with the
missing woman. All they knew was that he was an older married man having a dirty weekend with a young woman. Perhaps the affair had been going on for some time and had now
become strained and demanding. One person too many. There
was a motive for murder. It happened all the time. One of the
world's oldest stories. His role of the innocent bystander with
his rather too precise descriptions might sound a bit off to
them. *Frightening vacancy. Murky light.* Such phrases might
strike them as having been especially invented for the occasion. As preposterous as it seemed, it was possible that they
saw him as a murderer. The problem with thinking that way,
of course, was that it made you more nervous than you already were.

Kennedy was asking him about the Morris Minor and
whether it was still there when they had returned to the car
park after their walk.

"No," said Fielding. "It was gone. There were no other
cars."

"Can you be sure that the Morris belonged to the old couple?" asked Kennedy.

"Yes. We saw them earlier opening the doors to put away their things. They were getting ready to leave."

"All right. What happened next?"

Now he would have to mention the sex. Why was he so reticent? These things happen all the time. Cops heard all kinds of stories, tales far more salacious than anything he could relate. He was living in an age of pornography, so why the prudish reluctance? He had felt this way earlier with the police officers. Perhaps it was the young female constable. Kennedy had on his beetle-browed look, a man puzzling out another question.

"You had sex in the car?"

"Yes."

At the other end of the table Constable Warren's round, plain face looked up at him briefly. Then she returned to her writing. Kennedy seemed to be considering the scene in the car park. Fielding could hear the squawk of a radio from the next room as he watched a light go out in one of the windows of the hotel. Some lucky person's head was touching a pillow, or a hand was reaching across to another. Plans were being set in place for tomorrow. Kennedy was looking over his notes as if unhappy with what he saw there.

"All right. Then what?"

"Then we fell asleep," said Fielding. "It was raining hard and we decided to wait out the storm. The next thing I remember was Denise waking up. She told me she had to urinate, and so she got out of the car and I went back to sleep. When I woke up, I thought I'd just slept a few minutes and she'd soon be back. Then I looked at my watch and I could see it was nearly seven thirty. It didn't seem right. I waited another few minutes and then I got out of the car and looked around. I called her name several times. I suppose I was in a bit of a panic. I ran down the stairs to the beach thinking maybe she had lost her way in the dark or had just stumbled and fallen. But I was also thinking of the man on the beach."

"Why would you think she had fallen?" asked Kennedy. "Did she have a lot to drink? Was she intoxicated when she left the car?"

"No, no . . . not at all. I thought . . . Well, I don't know what I thought, to tell you the truth." Fielding tried to sound reasonable. "I imagined her, well, squatting down to urinate and I don't know, maybe losing her balance and falling backwards over the cliff side. I . . . don't know."

Kennedy seemed not to be listening. He had turned to ask over his shoulder, "Aren't there portable toilets in those car parks, Constable?"

"Yes, sir," said Constable Warren. "There are two at that particular location."

Kennedy turned to look at Fielding.

"Why wouldn't she use one of those?"

"I don't know," said Fielding.

"So you looked for Miss Crowder," said Kennedy. "Called her name. Went down the stairs to the beach and back up to the car park. What did you think happened to her?"

"I thought that the man had somehow abducted her. I wondered if he had been watching us all the time. Had seen . . . what went on in the car and had waited." Fielding hesitated. "I remember thinking that if this man had tried to harm her, he would have had to strike her from behind. Denise was . . ." He was aware of having already consigned her to oblivion. "Denise is a strong young woman. Very fit. If she'd had any warning at all, she would have put up a fight. So he must have attacked her from behind. Knocked her out or something." He shook his head at the miserable image of it all happening nearby while he slept.

"And you heard nothing?" said Kennedy. "No screams? No sound of a car engine?"

"No, absolutely nothing."

"So then you called us?"

"Yes. I got in the car and tried my cell phone, but it wouldn't work. The battery was dead. So I looked in Denise's handbag and found her phone. I kept trying 911 before I realized that you must have a different emergency number over here, and then I finally found the information on the inside of the glovebox. So I dialed 999."

Would he ever forget those moments? The dryness in his throat as he wiped his glasses with the crumpled tissues Denise had used after the sex. They were on the floor of the car. Then pushing the tiny buttons of her cell phone with an unsteady hand. Listening to the rain on the roof of the car. Seeing his world coming apart at the seams.

Kennedy was again consulting his notes.

"Your call came in at 7:42 and Sergeant Dickens and Constable Warren arrived at the car park at 8:03. You stayed in the car all that time?"

"Yes, I did."

Kennedy continued to read his notes as if testifying in court.

"Sergeant Dickens then went down the stairs to the beach. Had a bit of a look. Too dark to see anything, according to him. Then you drove back here with Constable Warren while Dickens followed. Then you gave a brief statement to both of them."

"Yes."

"You're sure you didn't have a quarrel with Miss Crowder and she just walked out of the car."

"No, nothing like that happened. She was fine when she left the car. She gave me a kiss," he added.

Kennedy regarded him with a steady, level gaze that was surely meant to intimidate. He was daring him to blink.

"Is there anything you've left out, Mr. Fielding?"

"No, nothing."

Kennedy glanced at his watch, a large silver thing, the biggest wristwatch Fielding had ever seen.

"Well, it's getting on," he said. "We've fixed you up with a room at the Royal. That's it across there," he added, nodding at the window. "You'll have to pay for it, of course. It's a little pricey, but I expect you're on a business account. We could have put you up at one of the B & Bs, but the landladies can be a little too curious. No one will bother you at the Royal and you'll be comfortable. It's four stars. You can get out of those damp clothes and have a drink of that whisky you carry around in the car."

It was a little jibe, but Fielding supposed that such things went hand in hand with their suspicion of people like him who appear with their strange and muddled stories. He could now see only a hotel room, its anonymity and privacy. A hot bath and, yes, a drink too, damn it.

"What happens now?" he asked.

Kennedy was putting his notebook into his suit-coat pocket.

"We can't do much tonight. Tomorrow we'll comb the area. Get the dogs out. Do you have anything of Miss Crowder's, by the way?"

"Yes, her things are in the car."

"Good. I'll get something tomorrow from you, a sweater or

gloves. I'd also like you to come up to Exeter in the morning and look at some pictures for me. We don't really know yet what happened. As I said earlier, Miss Crowder is still just a missing person, but if this man you saw is involved, well, it could be something else."

He stood up and reached for his coat. "I'll walk you to your car."

Constable Warren had gathered her notes and gone into the other room. Kennedy's raincoat fit him snugly as a wrapper, and Fielding followed his broad, olive-coloured back through to the other room towards a side door that led to the parking area. As he passed them, the police officers stopped talking to look at him.

It was just drizzling now, but blustery, the wind slamming into their faces as they walked towards a cluster of cars. Kennedy moved quickly, his collar up and his hands in the pockets of his raincoat, the bristly head bent into the weather. At the car he stopped.

"This is yours, right?"

"Yes."

Opening the trunk, Fielding took out his garment bag, trying not to look in the corner at Denise's overnight case. They had left the rest of their things in the hotel storage in London. He also wanted her handbag from the back seat, for he was thinking of addresses and phone numbers in Canada. With each passing hour it was growing more difficult to dismiss the conviction that before long he was going to have to deliver unspeakable news. Looking in the car he said to Kennedy, "I suppose this will bring out the local media."

Kennedy shrugged. "Probably. We don't need to say much

until we find out what's really happened. But they'll be sniffing around. You can count on it."

He looked away, squinting into the rain and wind.

"I don't think it's anything to interest the London press yet, but you never know. The fact that you're Canadians and that you were in the car when Miss Crowder disappeared . . ." He shrugged again and looked at Fielding. "It's the kind of slant they like. They've got stringers down here so if they come around, be careful what you say. Saying nothing is probably best until we know what's really happened to Miss Crowder."

"Right. I can see that," said Fielding.

"Good," said Kennedy, turning towards the hotel. "Well, that's it over there. Just across the road and through the car park. Hard to miss, isn't it? I'll give you a call around ten tomorrow. We should have things well underway by then. If we haven't found her, we'll want a piece of her clothing, a sweater, a blouse, something she's worn. Something we can use with the dogs. If it comes to that. And then we'll go up to Exeter and look at those pictures."

"Fine. I'll be ready."

"Good. I'll take the keys to your car, Mr. Fielding. You can pick them up in the morning at the station."

Fielding handed him the keys and Kennedy nodded and walked quickly away towards the station. When all was said and done, thought Fielding, he was not such a bad fellow. Blunt to be sure. A bit of a bruiser. But he was just doing his job. And there was at least a small measure of relief in knowing that a process was underway, that people like Kennedy who were trained for this kind of work were now on the job of finding out what happened to Denise. There was no reason to resent any of them for being suspicious of him. They had to suspect everybody. In time they would get to the bottom of this.

Folding the garment bag across one arm, he crossed the road to the car park and found a flagstone pathway that led to the hotel veranda. On the wide front lawn a Union Jack atop an immense flagpole was snapping in the wind. By the front steps he stopped for a moment and looked towards the seafront road where a car was passing. Another time he would have enjoyed a walk in this weather. He and Claire used to do such things. They both enjoyed the darkness and mystery of a strange village late at night, whether in England or Italy, Ireland or Spain. Wondering as they walked what kind of lives were being lived behind the walls and shuttered windows. Thinking of their own room and the erotic appeal of a hotel bed. He had to wonder if such experiences were over now. Could he and Claire ever travel to villages like Glynmouth without remembering this weekend? For that matter, would he and Claire ever again travel anywhere together?

At the front desk a young woman in a white blouse and dark skirt was talking on a cell phone. She nodded to Fielding as he approached, gently pushing a registration card across the desk towards him. She was hurrying to finish her conversation.

"Yes, yes. I'll be there by noon. Not to worry. Bye now."

She smiled at him. "You must be Mr. Fielding. We've been expecting you."

Fielding nodded. "Good."

Leaning against the desk he filled out the form with the gold-trimmed pen that lay across the white card. A genuine fountain pen! He hadn't used one in years. Around him was a great deal of polished white wood, a huge vase of fresh flowers, and on the wall a picture of a shipwreck in a storm. Behind the desk a clock quietly ticked away the seconds. It all looked restful and rich and would probably cost the earth. Sy Hollis would certainly finger this extravagance, but at the moment, Sy Hollis was the least of his worries. He sensed that the young woman in her crisp white blouse would consider it bad form if he inquired about the rates. In any case, what was the point? This was where the police wanted him, and for that matter where else could he go at this hour? After he completed the form, the young woman returned his credit card and Fielding took the elevator to the third and final floor.

Unsurprisingly his room was large and comfortable, and he didn't mind that it overlooked the car park. From his window he could see across to the police station with its tiny blue light, and the rented car. When he raised the window a few inches, he could smell the sea and hear faintly the snapping of the flag. It was twenty minutes to midnight. He would have to call Claire within the hour or she would worry. He was already forty minutes late, but the thought of telling her what had happened, what he had been up to these past few days, filled him with an almost dizzying sense of unreality and dread. He wondered about his blood pressure and what danger zone it was now ascending through. And what of Denise's family? Her father was dead, but there was her mother and brother in that little Ontario town. Bayview? Bayport? They would have to be told, of course, but there was no point in doing any of that until he knew for certain what had happened.

Sitting on the edge of the bed he felt like weeping. Felt the onset of another panic attack. What a mess it all was and what in God's name had happened to her? Yet he could see it unfolding. The man out there in the darkness, filled with rage, stepping from behind a tree as Denise made her way across the

car park to the toilets. A choke hold from behind or a piece of
rope across her throat. The fearful shock of it as he carried her
off like an animal with its prey. Fielding knew, had known for
a long while, that there were absolutely no limits to human
depravity. Imagine the worst thing that someone can inflict
upon another, then multiply it by a hundred, and you can con-
clude that it's already been done and will be done again and
again, and again after that. It really came down to opportunity,
to an unlucky choice, to happenstance. Yet it made him shud-
der there on the bed to imagine her lying somewhere in a
laneway, bruised and naked, abandoned.

In the bathroom he leaned across the big tub and turned on
the faucets. Poured a large drink and eased himself into the
tub. After sipping some whisky he unwrapped a little scented
medallion of soap and lay back. Less than a week ago he was
packing for this trip. Arranging his socks and underwear
neatly in the suitcase, wondering about the weather in Frankfurt. From the doorway of their bedroom, Claire had looked
in, reminding him not to forget the hydrochlorothiazide, and
without looking up he saluted her, for indeed he had nearly
forgotten. His mild hypertension had been discovered only
two weeks before by Janet Lieberman during his annual medical. He was still not used to taking the little pill every day.

The last thing on his mind a week ago was an affair with
Denise Crowder. An affair! Even the word sounded quaint. A
term from the 1950s. He could remember as a child overhear-
ing his parents in the next room discussing an affair someone
was having. Another nurse at the hospital where his mother

worked. He had wondered what the word meant. Had looked it up in the dictionary. But in all the years of his marriage, he had never felt the need for casual romance. Had never suffered those spells of boredom and longing that sometimes afflict middle-aged men and send them careening off on hazardous paths to disruption and heartbreak. He had no sense of missing any parade, and he was reasonably certain that Claire felt the same way. Besides, he was twenty-three years older than Denise Crowder. Still presentable, yes, but hardly someone to attract the attention of young women.

Fielding had often wondered how women saw him. A tall, slender man in a suit jacket in which one could still see the outlines of his shoulder blades. Tightly curled hair turning grey. Rimless glasses. A serious face. On the street he often imagined that on passing him an intelligent woman might take him for an academic, say a history professor, or perhaps a classical musician, a man who played the clarinet in a symphony orchestra and gave lessons on Saturday mornings. In a word, harmless. At a party once a few years ago, a pretty woman in her thirties, a little drunk and belligerent, had pinned him against the wall of a terribly crowded room.

"Are you married?"

"Yes," he replied. "I am."

She had then poked him sharply in the chest with a forefinger.

"Well, you don't look married," she said, and wandered away to mingle with other guests. She had made it sound as if it were his fault for looking the way he did, and he was left to wonder if she had given him a kind of involuntary compliment.

Friends often remarked on how well he and Claire looked together. Last December at Elena Burton's forty-seventh birthday party, Elena had taken pictures of everyone; her husband, Garth, had given her an expensive new camera and she was trying it out. A few days later, a Saturday, she dropped off the pictures while Fielding was at the office working into the early afternoon. When he came in, Elena had left and Claire was seated at the dining-room table. She was listening to Bach's *Christmas Oratorio* and writing cards. Before her on the table, propped against a bowl of oranges, was a photograph in which Claire was smiling slyly, amused by something Elena had said. Next to her Fielding looked pleasantly solemn, but then he always looked that way in photographs.

He had leaned down from behind her as she worked at her cards, resting his chin on her shoulder.

"Why is that picture there?" he asked, pointing a finger past her eye at the photograph.

She shivered a little. "Your face is cold."

"Sorry." But he hadn't moved.

"I was just looking at us," she said. "Damn it all, Dan, we're still a good-looking couple, aren't we?"

"Indeed we are," he said, reaching down to touch her breasts. "When is Heather coming back?"

"Not until suppertime," she said, laughing. "And stop groping me while I'm listening to Bach. It's disrespectful."

"We're the finest-looking WASPs in the land," Fielding murmured, kissing her hair.

She had tried to shrug him off. "What's come over you, anyway?"

"A spell. You've cast a spell over me, Claire. Here, on this Saturday afternoon with Heather away for hours. Doing your Christmas cards with old Bach. I'll bet he was always corking his wife between cantatas. How many children did they have anyway? Twenty? Twenty-one?"

"Dan, you're getting me all flustered. Now I've ruined this card to the Ellisons. Look. I've written 'God rushes' instead of 'Good wishes.'" She was laughing. "Will you stop that?"

"No."

"Saturday-afternoon sex. What will he think of next?"

"Who's thinking?"

"I thought it had to be raining or miserable. It's a bright cold day out there."

"That's all right."

She laughed again. "Maybe you should carry me upstairs?"

"I can no longer carry you. You're too big a girl."

"You could never carry me, Dan, and you know it."

"Alas, it's true."

Claire was still a terrific-looking woman. And she kept fit. Loved playing squash and tennis with old girlfriends in the courts of St. Hilda's. Now and then she would compete in a tennis tournament for older women and he would go over to watch on a Saturday morning in the summer. Other husbands were there too, most of them in the money business, stockbrokers, financial consultants, portfolio managers. Their talk, as they absently watched their wives play, was filled with the jargon of their trade: leverage options, market volatility, negative economic environments. Mostly, Fielding stood apart from them, admiring the arc of Claire's bare arm as she reached skyward to deliver her serve. He also liked the way she flexed her knees waiting for a set to begin. After a match, she always came over and gave him a kiss before going off to the shower.

She didn't seem to mind that, apart from walking, Fielding

did no exercise whatsoever. He wasn't fat, she said, and that was all that mattered.

"I don't want a porker for a husband, Dan. You're a lucky man with your metabolism."

That was true. Except for the stiff, uncombable hair and a certain wryness in his smile, both of which he got from his late mother, the fiery little Scottish nurse, Jean Muir, his body could have been Ted Fielding's. When he died, his father still weighed a hundred and sixty pounds and he was a tall man for his time, six feet with a mild stoop in his shoulders. With his grey indoor look, you could see that he wasn't much for nature walks or sitting in those sloping cloth chairs of the day, soaking up the sun.

Fielding spent only one year in his father's classroom, managing to avoid him as a teacher until his matriculation year when he had no choice. That year, his father was the only teacher of Senior History, and so Fielding had sat at the back of the room. He was self-conscious and oddly divided in his loyalties between the spare, melancholy figure at the blackboard in the sweater coat and grey flannels, outlining the origins of the American Revolution, and his classmates with their whispered jokes about the dandruff on the sweater coat (girls), and the utter absence of buttocks in Mr. Fielding's trousers (boys). How Fielding had hated that sweater coat and those baggy grey pants hanging from his father's hips as he prepared them for the 1965 Departmentals, the warmth of the June air filling the room from the open windows. Not once did Fielding say a word all year, nor did his father ask him a single question about the *Stamp Act*. Perhaps they had unwittingly entered a pact in which neither would attempt to exceed the embarrassment they both felt at sharing the classroom. After school, driving home in the little bustlebacked Dodge his father had owned for fifteen years, they felt completely at ease with one another and talked of many things, none of which he could recall.

Now, in this bathtub in this seaside town in the south of England, Fielding could see his father in his own unspectacular but serviceable body. See him too in the way he approached doorways, tilting his head slightly. In the way he always pushed ill-fitting glasses against the bridge of his nose. And in the absent-minded humming that accompanied small tasks. It used to quietly enrage him to be near his father when the man was wrapping tape around a leaking garden hose, or setting up Christmas tree lights. Always with that droning hum in the background, a faint buzzing. Now he did the same thing. Only a week or so ago while unwinding Silas's leash, which had become entangled around a tree in the garden, he had been at this humming business with Heather saying finally, "Daddy, why are you making that sound? It is *so* annoying."

It was strange, mysterious, what we were given from those who sired or bore us.

As he dried himself with the heavy, soft towel, he wondered again what he would say to Claire. What could he say? That he hadn't really wanted any of this to happen? That was lame and anyway it did happen. But how had it all come to pass? It seemed to have happened so quickly and effortlessly. When Sy Hollis told him six weeks ago that Denise Crowder would be accompanying Fielding to Frankfurt, he was not particularly surprised. She had been to the book fair many times while working out of New York. As Hollis told him, "Denise has important contacts and will be useful. You can see how people take to her."

Which was perhaps another way of saying that people didn't take to Fielding, nor was he especially useful. Lying in bed that night he decided that Hollis was up to something, and that perhaps this was a sign that his days at Houghton & Street were numbered. Yet, when he thought of it, did he really care?

After thirty-two years in publishing, he was weary of the whole business and perhaps it was beginning to show. He was tired of the relentless pace, of the constant pressure to find new books, of the effort to placate writers. If the truth were told, he was tired of writers, period: tired of their emotional neediness, their whining about money, their childish vanities. J.J. Balsam came to mind with his drunken 2 a.m. phone calls. Yes, he had grown sick of all that, and he seriously doubted whether he now had the energy and enthusiasm to be an effective editor. This manuscript he was lugging around Europe, for example, *A History of Water*. Without a doubt, an important book. According to Tom Lundgren, large parts of the planet were quietly running out of water. The major conflicts of the next hundred years would all be about water or the lack of it. Professor Lundgren had everything documented in 348 pages. Yet, after several tries, Fielding was only on page 32, his mind spinning around irrigation mismanagement and diminished aquifers. It was comforting to imagine passing *A History of Water* on to someone else. Why not?

For the past couple of years, Claire had been urging him to consider retirement. Get out while they were both still young enough to enjoy leisure and travel. As she put it, "Before the first heart attack or cancer scare."

Claire's medical school experience had left her an unrepentant realist. If he felt like it, she said, he could do some freelance editing. Have some business cards printed. *Dan Fielding. Editorial Consultant.* He could work at home in his own study and on his own time. They could travel when they felt like it. Spend six months in Italy or in Greece. Heather could board for a while at St. Hilda's; she might resist the idea at first, but she could be persuaded. There were so many good things to enjoy in life while they still had time and health on their side. These delightful plans were often celebrated over the third glass of wine at Sunday dinner, particularly if Heather were visiting a friend. Best of all, money was not a problem. Clarie's paternal grandfather, a urologist who had made a fortune in Toronto real estate back in the 1950s, had left her a comfortable legacy, and there would be more money for both her and Heather when Claire's father, the redoubtable Dr. Moffat, concluded his days on the planet.

"I wish you'd get over your puritanical hang-ups about money, Dan," Claire once said to him. "We've got enough. The minute you get tired of working for Hollis, quit. It's as simple as that."

He had almost done it too, a few months after Hollis was brought in as president by an elderly and ailing Jim Houghton. But then Fielding had felt that, at fifty-two, he was far too young to retire. It was odd that now, only three years later, its appeal seemed to have grown exponentially.

So, on the plane last Saturday night, Fielding had felt a certain lightness of heart; he saw this trip as probably his last to Frankfurt. Ahead and perhaps not too far ahead lay an agreeable turning in his life. Beside him, Denise Crowder, with her manuscript and her old-fashioned reading glasses, looked as chaste as a convent girl. How then had he ended up in a hotel bed with her?

Looking back, he could see now that there were signs. He supposed that in these circumstances there were always signs if you looked for them. But what night had they first had sex? Tuesday? No, it was Wednesday night.

They had checked into the InterContinental on Wilhelm-Leuschner Strasse late Sunday morning and Fielding had gone at once to his room to pull off his shoes. This was an old habit. He and Claire always began visits to Europe with an hour or two of rest. It was still too early to call her and so after drawing the curtains across the glass wall of his room twelve stories above the grey streets, he lay on the bed in the darkened room. Under a reading lamp he held the manuscript of *A History of Water* and waited for his fatigue to give way to sleep. Awakened by the ringing telephone, he was startled to hear Denise asking him where he wanted to have dinner. Did he wish to visit the red-light district? She sounded cheerily alert while he felt drugged with sleep, still on Toronto time.

He hated the thought of showering, of changing clothes, of studying a foreign menu. All he wanted was a glass of wine and a sandwich in his room and so he had begged off. Ordered his little meal from room service and talked to Claire while waiting for it. Feeling a little guilty the next morning, he had been quick to phone Denise about breakfast though he soon discovered that she wasn't in the least offended about Sunday night's dinner. On Monday she had dinner with friends from New York, while he met Tony Anderson and they talked about his upcoming London visit after the fair. And Tuesday? Tuesday had been a near miss. He could see that now.

They had dinner in a noisy cellar restaurant with an American agent named Leah Barry, a tall, funny woman who had the horsey face of a television comedienne from the seventies whose name Fielding could no longer recall. She and Denise had known each other in New York and talked about business, or gossiped about people they knew in publishing who were yet again changing jobs or being fired. Fielding smiled and nodded from time to time, bemused by the notion that none of this probably mattered any longer. It might soon be behind him and thankfully forgotten.

He had spent a good part of that dinner Tuesday night watching an American writer who was at the bar across the room, seated next to a blonde woman whom Fielding had met once. She was an editor with a Swedish publishing house. The writer was a handsome, dark-haired man in his forties with a high, sloping brow. He was also something of a literary celebrity; his adroitly crafted tales of American white-collar disappointment with life had won a Pulitzer Prize, and according to Denise his new novel had just earned a high six-figure advance. The blonde woman had swivelled on her stool to face him so that their knees were now touching. In his corduroy jacket and open-necked shirt, his slacks and loafers, the writer looked relaxed and pleased with this kind of female adoration that perhaps he now claimed as one of his dues in life. Fielding imagined that the American writer and the blonde Swedish woman would soon be together in a hotel room nearby, on a firm German mattress bucking and moaning with pleasure.

Around him the noise in that rathskeller had been relentlessly assaultive; there was accordion music and a great deal of jabbering and laughter. So much loud laughter. Christ, the Germans were a noisy lot when they'd had a drink or two. The place was altogether too turbulent, though he tried not to let it bother him. Now and then Denise brought him back from his reveries like a dutiful wife who didn't want him to feel neglected or appear dull-witted to guests. There was a kind of proprietary affection surrounding all that. He remembered her at one point smiling and saying, "Daniel, Leah has now asked you the same question twice this evening."

So he turned and leaned in against the checkered tablecloth, folding his hands together in a purposely droll manner.

"May I apologize, ladies. I have indeed been daydreaming through this nightmare."

He hadn't intended the words to come out that way; it was a rushed response. But far from seeing it as a slight to their company, they had immediately laughed. He offered them an apologetic shrug, but they continued to laugh, shaking their heads at him. Both women liked him, he could see that. His self-effacing, old-fashioned courtliness surprisingly had its own appeal. Soon afterwards, Leah Barry excused herself; she had an early appointment next day and so he and Denise were left by themselves to finish the wine. But not for long.

A heavy-set man with a shaven head, a wrestler in a suit, appeared at their table, bending down to hug Denise.

"My little Denise," he growled into her ear. He offered Fielding a handshake that was surprisingly gentle. Alexi somebody or other—he didn't catch the complicated surname, and the man wasn't a German, as Fielding had supposed, but a Russian who owned a small publishing house. He and Denise were old friends who had done business together. His large, bald head was like a kind of weapon and put Fielding in mind of Chaucer's miller, who "could heave any door off hinge and post/ Or take a run and break it with his head."

"And now you are back in Canada, I hear?" said Alexi, his

hand resting on her shoulder. "Well good for you, my dear. I am sure it will be much safer for you there."

He seemed to be waiting for an invitation to sit down, but Denise only smiled up at him, somewhat demurely, Fielding thought. What was going through her mind? Was she ashamed of knowing the Russian? After a while Alexi had taken the hint and giving Denise another hug he said, "Well I must join my friends again. Nice to see you, Denise, and a pleasure to meet you, sir."

The "sir" had made him feel rather elderly, though he didn't think the Russian was that much younger. When the waiter brought a bottle of champagne in the customary ice bucket, they had both looked across the room at the table where Alexi was seated with several other men. In their terrible suits, they looked like gangsters. Alexi had waved to them, and while the waiter fussed with the label and cork Fielding said, "What do we do about this?"

"We'll leave it," she said.

"Your friend will be offended."

"Fuck him," she said. "He's a bozo. Let's get out of here."

When they returned to the hotel, it was nearly midnight, and as they made their way along the hallway, fishing room cards out of purse and pocket, Denise asked him if he felt like a nightcap. She had a bottle of duty-free Glenlivet in her room.

"Like a nip before beddy-byes, Daniel?" They had stopped at her door and she had looked up at him with a quizzical smile.

He wondered now if that smile had been in response to his expression. How *had* he looked to her there in the hallway outside her door last Tuesday night? Confused? Hesitant? Fearful? Perhaps he hadn't looked like any of that. All he could remember thinking was that if he followed her into the room, they would spend the night together. How had he worded his reply? "Thanks, but it's late" or "I had better not, it's late." Yes, he had said something like that, and his phrase *I better not* might have provoked the smile.

"It was just a thought," she said, and reaching up had kissed his cheek. "You're such a gent, Daniel," she said. "I think that's why I like you. You're a serious man, but you're also quite a funny guy in your own way. I hope you don't mind my calling you Daniel. You've never struck me as a Dan or a Danny."

He said he didn't mind, and he also said he admired her use of the gerundial phrase. You didn't hear it much anymore. She had laughed and kissed him again on the cheek. They were like teenagers flirting in the first week of school.

"Have a good sleep, Daniel."

In his room he had stood by the glass wall looking out at the lights of the city and second-guessing himself. Yet when he picked up the phone and called Claire, spoke to her, listened to her voice, he felt only relief.

Still, he was wavering and perhaps had been all along. Something was going on between them, and surely it was the intimation of sex. They were attracted to one another and they were three thousand miles from home. Nobody in the German city knew or cared what they did; moreover, in a matter of months he would very likely have another kind of life and Denise Crowder would be just a memory, a woman he knew briefly in publishing. Nor was she the sort to tell tales— he felt he knew that much about her. Was that how he had looked at things? Probably, or at least something very like it, for at breakfast on Wednesday morning, he knew that if she asked him into her room again, he would go.

That evening they had dinner alone in a café near the hotel. Denise was talkative, exuberant with wine, and she told him about her family in the little town on the shores of Lake Huron: her mother, Lucille, who had always seemed more like a big sister than a mother; her younger brother, Ray, with his cars and the drinking, his road accidents and scrapes with the law, a ten-year headache for his mother though he seemed at last to be settling down. Had a new girlfriend, an ex-stripper of all things, but sound-hearted and sensible in her own way. The woman was raising an eight-year-old daughter. Denise had talked about her dead father too and his life on the Great Lakes as an engineer, his winter nights at home when he sat up late, drinking Canadian Club and reading histories of the Second World War and biographies of Churchill and Stalin. She talked about growing up in that town, and of how she couldn't wait to get out, of how she lost herself in books and came to value literature for the truths it revealed about human experience. When the waiter brought their coffees, Fielding could scarcely wait for the check, and by ten o'clock he was in her bed.

Now, in another hotel room, he unpacked the garment bag. Stretched his damp jeans across the top of the big cream-coloured radiator and hung up trousers and jacket for the next day. Put on his pyjamas. The pyjamas he had never worn with Denise. She had looked at them and laughed. Was that Thursday night?

"PJs, Daniel! They look adorable!"

She was wearing only a New York Yankees T-shirt to bed.

Sitting by the phone, Fielding sipped at his second drink. He had to call Claire now. It was ten minutes to one. Nearly eight o'clock in Toronto. She would be waiting, wondering why he was late. The rain had started again. He could hear it against the windows and he could hear too the snapping of the flag at the front of the hotel. He tried not to think of the pony-tailed man carrying Denise's body across a field to the woods. Leaving her face down in the wet undergrowth. Hurrying away in that strange, robotic gait.

He pushed the buttons and waited, listening to the silence and then the steady ringing of his home number, trying to imagine the pressure on his racing heart, the turmoil within the darkness of his body. Taking another gulp of the whisky, he waited and then heard Claire's "Hello." Always that slight upward curl of the last syllable.

"Hi."

He thought his voice a mere croak, a barely whispered acknowledgment of his presence on the line. Claire's voice rose a little.

"Dan? Is that you?"

"Yes."

"Well, it's about time. What have you been up to? Are you down in Devon now?"

"Yes. In Glynmouth. How are you, Claire? How is Heather?"

She laughed. Seemed mildly amused by the intensity in his voice.

"We're fine. We're all right. What were you expecting, Dan? An outbreak of typhoid?"

"No, of course not."

"Heather's gone to the movies. She just went out the door

with Allison Harvey and Nadina Khan. Told me to say hello, of course. They had supper here. God, how they talk! Three fifteen-year-olds together. The quiet in the house now seems heavenly. I've got my feet up. Silas is here to protect me. They're showing one of your old favourites on TVO tonight. *Double Indemnity*. Wish you were here to watch it with me."

"I wish I were too, believe me."

"I've been looking at the weather section of the *Globe*. There's rain everywhere in Western Europe."

"Yes, it's been miserable here, I'm afraid."

"Poor darling. You can't have been doing much hiking then?"

"Not really, no."

"Sitting around in the pubs all day I bet. Where are you staying anyway?"

"I'm at the Royal."

"Is that the big white place that overlooks the walkway along the sea?"

"Yes."

She laughed again. "Aren't we grand, though? You never put us up there when we stayed in Glynmouth. I had to make do with Mrs. Irons and the potty down the hall. You treat yourself pretty well when you're on your own."

"It was all I could get, Claire. I got in late, you see, and most of the places were filled." He was floundering. When would he get to it?

"Never mind, I was only joking. Enjoy yourself, for goodness' sake. Nobody's begrudging you. There in the lap of luxury. I can just see you in some enormous claw-footed tub with a drink in hand. And there's a bed big enough to sleep four. It's raining like hell and you're inside snug and cozy. That's right up your alley, isn't it? How you love those rainy nights in bed. Well, enjoy it, darling. I just wish I were there with you."

"I wish you were too, Claire." Did his voice really sound that weak and anguished? He wasn't weeping; that would be despicable, but he knew he wasn't far from it and now she heard something in his voice.

"What's the matter, Dan? You don't sound right. Is something wrong?"

He could picture her on the sofa in the den, sitting up now, attentive and alert, back straightened and feet on the floor next to the dog.

"Yes," he said. "Something is very wrong."

"Dan, what is it? Are you all right? Have you been in an accident? A car accident?"

He could not reply. He seemed to be dumbfounded by the enormity of what he had to tell her.

"Have you hurt someone in another car?" she asked. "Is that it? Was it a car accident?"

"No, nothing like that," he said. "But Claire, something terrible has happened, and I'm begging you to try to understand."

"Begging me?"

"I am really asking for your understanding, Claire."

"Just tell me what happened, Dan, please."

There was now a hint of irritation in her voice as if she were arming herself for a peculiar kind of unwelcome news. Fielding wished he had brought the little whisky bottle to the bedside table. There was still one more good drink in it.

"All right, Claire," he said. "Here it is. I came down here with Denise Crowder."

He waited, counting silently to four, and then she said,

"You are in Glynmouth with Denise Crowder? What are you saying anyway? That you're sleeping with that woman? Is that what you're trying to tell me? That you are in this fancy hotel shacked up with this woman you told me you couldn't stand. Christ! This is a funny goddamn time to call your wife and tell her you're fucking another woman. And what do you find so terrible about it anyway? Are you drunk?"

"No, I'm not drunk. Listen to me, Claire, it's much worse than you imagine. Denise has disappeared."

"Disappeared? Do you mean she walked out on you? She didn't like the sex or something? Couldn't you get it up?"

He had to make allowance for her anger. She was devastated. Why wouldn't she be? "Claire, this is very serious. Denise may be dead."

"What the hell are you talking about?"

"Just listen to me, Claire. Please. I know it sounds bad, but you have to listen. This afternoon we parked at a lookout site about ten miles from here. We went for a walk along the beach and then it started to rain so we went back to the car. It was raining hard by then and we decided to wait it out. We fell asleep." He couldn't tell her about the sex. She would hang up on him. "At one point, Denise woke up and got out of the car. She had to relieve herself." He stopped, bothered somehow by his prudish euphemism. Imagining Claire's frown as she listened, trying to make sense of what he was telling her. "She never came back," he said. "There was a man around. We saw him earlier on the beach. He looked a bit odd, disturbed in some way. I think he abducted Denise. When she left the car . . ."

"Have you talked to the police about this?" She sounded impatient now, exasperated.

"Yes," he said. "I've spent three hours at the police station. They brought a detective down from Exeter and I told him everything. He wants me to go up there in the morning and look at some pictures. Something horrible has happened to her, Claire."

He waited and then she said, "Yes. Perhaps it has. And you've got yourself into quite a mess, haven't you?"

"I have," he admitted. "And I'm sorry. If only . . ."

"Yes, yes," she said quickly. "If only etc., etc. The old 'if only.'"

In the silence that followed he understood how things would never again be quite the same between them. A fault line had opened beneath their marriage and it would always have to be reckoned with in one way or another. This came as no surprise to him; from the moment Denise vanished, he knew this was coming. How could it be otherwise? Yet its inevitability still shocked him.

"So what are you going to do now?" she asked.

"I don't know," he said. "Wait until the morning to see what happens. It's all I can do. They're going to search the area as soon as it's light. It's possible she could have fallen down the cliffside, though it seems unlikely to me."

"Dan," she said. "I'm going to hang up in a minute because I have to think about what you've told me. But just let me see if I got this much straight. You went down to Devon with Denise Crowder, so I suppose that means that you've been fucking her all week. Maybe even before this week for all I know."

"Claire, no."

"Then you go for a walk and she disappears. And you think some guy you saw on the beach abducted her."

"Yes, but after the walk. It started to rain, and we went back to the car."

Claire's voice rose sharply. "Well, what in God's name were you doing all that time? How could you allow such a thing to happen?"

"I was asleep, Claire."

"Asleep? In a car park in the country at night?"

"Yes. We both fell asleep waiting for the rain to let up. And then she woke up. It was dark. She had to go. She left the car and I went back to sleep. And when I woke up a couple of hours later, she was gone. She just vanished."

He could hear the impatient intake of breath. "It sounds incredible. Do the police believe you?"

"I think they do. I hope so because it's the truth. Why would I lie? At least they didn't lock me up. They even arranged this hotel room. I told them everything. That man got hold of her and took her away. I'm convinced of it."

"I'm going to hang up now, Dan," she said. "I have to think about all this. Christ, what a mess you've made for yourself with your dirty little weekend in the country! And what can I say to Heather? What am I supposed to tell your daughter when she comes home from the movies and asks about you? What am I supposed to say to her?"

"You'll have to tell her, Claire."

"And what's going to happen when the newspapers get hold of this? Your name and picture will be in every fucking tabloid in Britain. It'll happen here too. We'll have reporters at the door. At Heather's school. Jesus, this is so awful. Cheating on me with that little cunt. You didn't even like her. You told me so." She was now weeping.

"Claire, please," he said.

But she had hung up on him.

For a moment he sat holding the dead phone. It had been an awful conversation, but at least it was over. Now Claire knew, and she would have to assimilate all this into a different reality, a new way of looking at their lives together. Or apart, as the case might be. Suddenly everything would look terribly skewed to her, outrageous and chaotic, complicated. She would need time to sort it out. Still, the rage and disappointment in her voice had been chilling. He imagined her pouring a glass of wine and phoning Elena Burton or perhaps her father, though that call would probably wait for morning. She would be in no mood tonight to hear her judgment in a husband called into question yet again.

When Heather arrived home from the movies, Claire would be waiting for her in the living room. While Heather kicked off her shoes and unbuttoned her coat under the hallway light, Claire would call out to her, and Heather would enter the room with that skeptical look of hers, a little frightened by the tone of her mother's voice. Like him, Heather was a pessimist.

"What is it? Has something happened? Is Daddy all right?"

Imagining this, Fielding found it hard to fight the despair that was surrounding him.

Yet what of Denise's mother, the widow in Bayport, Ontario? Now enjoying a Saturday evening at home. Perhaps looking forward to cooking Sunday dinner for her errant son and his girlfriend who would bring along the little girl with her bears and dolls. How could he reach Lucille Crowder? Standing over the bed, he emptied the contents of Denise's handbag: wallet, Kleenex, a condom, lipstick, mints, compact, address book, glasses, tampons, a pair of panties strewn with tiny stars and moons and fishes—a mere handful of cloth that might fit a child; her cell phone with a trace of perfume lingering near the mouthpiece. A paperback copy of *The Wings of the Dove* with the bookmark halfway. She had told him she was re-reading Henry James. "Why?" he had asked. "Isn't once enough?" But she had only looked at him with mock sternness. "Now don't sound like a barbarian, Daniel. Actually, I would have expected more from you."

Fielding looked through the little directory, squinting at the numbers and initials. Would she have bothered to record her mother's number? Surely she knew it by memory. But there was an L.C. and a 519 area code. That was Western Ontario and L.C. was probably Lucille Crowder. But he decided the call could wait. There was no point in spoiling the woman's Saturday evening. He would telephone in the morning when he had more definite news.

Opening the wallet, he looked past the money and credit cards to a small envelope of photographs. Studied a picture of Denise with her arms around two women, one of whom was surely Lucille Crowder, an older version of Denise, still pretty enough with her short dark hair and trim figure. She did look more like Denise's older sister than her mother. The third woman was also in her fifties, sturdy-looking with a pleasant, open face. All three were wearing halters and shorts and laughing at the camera on a summer day. Behind them were trees, a picnic table, a glimpse of water. The picture might have been taken at a cottage or in the backyard of someone's house near a lake. There was also a photograph of Denise with her brother, who had a smirk on his handsome face. Again Denise was laughing, looking up at her brother triumphantly as if she had finally coaxed a kind of smile out of

him. Fielding put everything back in the handbag, and after
turning out the light, got into bed. His body felt suddenly
leaden, overused, the whisky souring in his stomach. He lay
there listening to the rain against the windows and the faint
sound of the flag snapping in the wind.

In the dining room of the Royal Hotel, Fielding sipped his
second cup of coffee and looked at his watch. It was five minutes past nine and the dining room was surprisingly lively,
nearly filled with people his age or older, prosperous-looking
retired couples enjoying their rashers and eggs, taking a little
holiday from diet and cholesterol worries. The pretty young
hostess in her dark skirt and white blouse had smiled as she
gave him the last window seat, so that he could look out at the
rain-washed promenade where a man was now holding onto
his hat as he walked his terrier. The storm had passed and the
morning was bright with sunshine. Across the blue sky,
shreds of cloud raced seaward ahead of a strong westerly. It
was a fine autumn morning and Fielding briefly imagined
what it would be like sitting there with Denise, planning their
day: dropping off the car at the rental depot, taking the train
up to London, eating dinner in the hotel, spending another
night together.

Throughout breakfast he had been watching a couple
across the room at a corner table. The big man was Fielding's
age, even older perhaps by a few years. He looked like a
wealthy yachtsman in his navy blazer and grey trousers. His
face was tanned and he had a large head of abundant silvery
hair. The young blonde woman smiled at him from time to

time and reached across the table to touch his arm. Was she a new, young wife or a mistress, Fielding wondered? Probably the latter, he thought. There was in both their faces that look of cunning self-regard and satisfaction; they had planned this weekend together and they were getting away with it. He knew these thoughts were unworthy, even base. What did their little affair matter to him? Denise had probably died in a horrible way only a few hours ago, and soon he would have to tell her mother. When the waitress asked him if he would like more coffee, he shook his head, thinking that by tomorrow or the next day, she would be showing friends and family his picture in a local newspaper. "Why, he was in the dining room Sunday morning. I served him breakfast." It was all doubtless inevitable.

When he returned to his room, he noticed at once the red message light blinking on the bedside telephone, and he felt a surge of adrenalin flooding through him, a tightness in his throat. Another step had been arrived at and he prepared himself for the worst. In the bathroom he swallowed the diuretic with a glass of water. When he picked up the receiver and pressed the message button he listened to the disembodied voice say, "Good morning. You have two messages. To listen to your messages, please press one." He pressed one. "Mr. Fielding? It's Mark Kennedy at Exeter CID. It's now eight forty a.m." There was a pause and Fielding waited. "We've found her, Mr. Fielding. I'm very sorry, but I'm afraid she's dead. That's the worst possible news I can give you, and I'm sorry I have to." There was another pause. "If it's any consolation, there is better news at least. We have the man responsible in custody. If you could give me a call as soon as possible, I'd appreciate it. I think you have my number, but if you mislaid it, it's 008452 777 444. Extension 215." Again he heard the disembodied voice. "Second message." And then Claire was on the line.

"Dan. It's me. I can't seem to get to sleep. It's about four o'clock here now. Give me a call when you have a minute." He had just missed her.

He put down the receiver and sat on the edge of the bed. Claire still sounded cross and wary, but at least she had called him back. And so Denise was now officially dead. He was not surprised; all along he had sensed it. Yet confronting the fact was something else again. Now he was going to have to tell her mother who was sleeping in her Ontario village. The man who murdered Denise had already been caught. How had they caught him so quickly, he wondered? Fielding punched in the numbers that Kennedy had given him.

"Mark Kennedy here."

"It's Dan Fielding, Inspector. I was down at breakfast when you called."

"Mr. Fielding. Yes. Well, as I said on my message, I'm sorry it's turned out this way, but at least we have the man responsible."

"How can you be so sure?" asked Fielding. "Isn't it a little early for certainty?"

"Oh, the man has confessed. He told us he did it. Took us to her body."

Kennedy sounded almost buoyant. But why shouldn't he sound like that, thought Fielding. A Canadian had been murdered, but the killer had been captured and confessed to the crime. The media would be off his back. It was probably the best time in a cop's life.

"His brother-in-law brought him in this morning at five

o'clock. The man, his name is Woodley, George Allan Wood-ley, is known to us. He's spent time in prison."

"Was he out on parole or something? Aren't these people supervised?"

Kennedy caught the note of resentment; he was used to the outraged voices of the citizenry.

"Woodley," he said calmly, "served his sentence. Eight years in Dartmoor and he served every minute. He was released last December, around Christmas. Of course we knew of his whereabouts, but we couldn't do much about it. The man had served his sentence. We couldn't keep him under surveillance twenty-four hours a day. He was staying with his sister and working for his brother-in-law who has a small plastering and painting business. Woodley seemed to stay out of trouble all those months and then . . ."

Kennedy hesitated, "His sister and brother-in-law went away for the weekend. Over to Brighton to see friends. When they got back late last night, well, this morning really, about one thirty, they noticed the van was gone. The brother-in-law didn't even think Woodley could drive. He's marginally retarded, you see, doesn't have a licence. The brother-in-law had been worried about him these past few weeks. Said he seemed a bit restless and bad-tempered, but his wife kept insisting that things would be all right. He told us he was going to call us and report the van stolen. He and his wife were hav-ing a bit of a row about that when Woodley came back to the house around three o'clock. The brother-in-law felt some-thing was wrong and after a while he went out to the van and he found some of Miss Crowder's things. Some underclothes, a cap and a sweater. He finally got the truth out of Woodley and phoned us. They came in together about five o'clock this morning and he took us out to where he had left Miss Crowder."

"Where did you find her?"

"About a mile from where you were parked. A wooded area off the main road. He told us how he'd waited outside your car. He said he watched you and Miss Crowder having relations. When she got out of the car, he grabbed her. Struck her. Carried her off to the van, which was parked down a side road. You couldn't have seen it from the car park."

"And so," said Fielding, "after he'd finished with her, he just threw her out on the side of a road."

Kennedy sounded a little weary. "Yes, I suppose you could say that."

"Christ. And he raped her, of course."

"I think we have to assume that, Mr. Fielding. She was naked. He's a convicted sex offender. But we'll have to wait for the coroner's report. And we need a positive ID. I know this is difficult for you, but could you come up and officially identify the body? It's a formality, really, but we have to do it. She's at the Royal Devon Hospital off Wonford Road, but one of the officers in Glynmouth will come along with you."

"Yes, I can do that. When?"

"The sooner the better. The Coroner's Office likes to get these things underway as quickly as possible, and positive ID of the victim is the first step."

"I have a phone call or two to make, but I'll be up within the hour."

"Good. We can phone next of kin if you like, though it would be better coming from someone who knew her. Easier on the other side, I mean."

"I'll do it."

"Good, but let's have the positive ID first. I mean, we're fairly sure it's her, but you never know. Best to be absolutely certain."

"Of course."

"Fine then, Mr. Fielding. I'll see you in a bit." He paused. "Oh, and by the way, we're not saying much to the press at the moment. There's no need really, and we're certainly not identifying the victim until next of kin has been notified. The local press will be after you. I'd say as little as possible if I were you. You don't have to say anything really. You're under no obligation, believe me."

"Right."

"I'll see you then."

Fielding hung up and walked to the window. Directly below him in the hotel car park, the couple from the dining room were putting their luggage into the trunk of a maroon Jaguar. It was gusty and the young woman was wearing a smart-looking belted tan coat. Now and then she would tuck away strands of blonde hair that kept escaping from her kerchief. She was watching the man load the cases into the car, and he was saying something that was making her laugh. His silvery hair was untidy in the wind and it made him look younger. At the window Fielding stood envying them their happiness, while he tried to sort through all the things that would now have to be dealt with. He warned himself not to panic, though it all seemed impossibly complicated: the phone calls, the explanations, the pestering of media people. And how did one get her body back to Canada? Arrange matters at the other end? He supposed there were people at the airline who would know about these details. Tony Anderson in London might help; he would be sympathetic

and nonjudgmental. In Frankfurt they had arranged a meeting for tomorrow at two o'clock. He would have to phone
Tony later in the day with the news. If he could find his home
number somewhere. He felt suddenly flushed and hot under
the arms.

After several deep breaths, he walked across the room,
picked up the phone receiver, and tapped at the numbers of
his home phone. Claire's "Hello" was hoarse and creaky, as
though the call had just awakened her.

"It's me. I was at breakfast when you called earlier."

"Yes."

"Claire, it's the worst possible news. Denise has been murdered. They found her body this morning."

"Jesus Christ, Dan." She was clearing her throat.

"It's awful, believe me. But it's happened and I have to deal
with it."

"Yes, of course."

"I have to call Denise's mother. She lives in some little town
up on Lake Huron. Right now, though, I have to drive up to
Exeter and identify the body."

"Do they know who did this?" she asked. "Was it the man
you saw on the beach?"

"Yes. At least I think so. It has to be. They've got him in custody. He's some halfwit who was released from prison last
year. Did you talk to Heather last night about any of this?"

"No," she said. "I thought I'd wait and see what happened.
I thought it might turn out another way, and she wouldn't
have to know."

"You'll have to tell her now."

"Of course I will."

"It's going to be ugly, Claire, and I'm sorry about that."

There was no response and he hurried on. "I have to let that poor woman know today that her daughter is dead."

"Do what you have to do," she said.

"I'll phone you later. Try to get some sleep."

She didn't answer. He could picture her lying in their bed, frowning into the morning darkness. Now there seemed to be nothing more to say, and so he quietly hung up the phone.

Only seconds later the ringing startled him. "Mr. Fielding? It's Constable Warren. I just had a call from Inspector Kennedy. He wants me to accompany you up to the Royal Devon. When you're ready, I'll see you in the car park. The inspector said he'd meet us at the hospital."

"All right. I'll be there in ten minutes."

"Sorry to hear about Miss Crowder."

"Thank you."

He walked down to the lobby, his footsteps silent on the carpeted stairs. Through the doorway of the dining room he could see people still eating breakfast. The young hostess in her dark skirt and white blouse was still there too, holding a menu against her chest and smiling. On the veranda two old women were buttoning themselves into coats, preparing for a walk. It was a colder day than he had imagined, and especially so when passing clouds obscured the sun and darkened the sea.

Constable Warren was standing by the rental car in her uniform. With her prim little hat and its checkered band she looked as pious as a Salvation Army girl. He asked her if she wanted to drive, and she thought about it for a moment before shaking her head.

"Better not," she said. "The insurance."

A prudent young woman who abided by all the rules. He could see her as a schoolgirl, seated near the front of the class, attentive to the teacher's observations, especially in chemistry and math, perhaps a little puzzled and impatient with art and poetry—"What's all this about then?"

Not yet twenty-five, and already a stiff little Tory.

With curt directions she got them out of the narrow streets of Glynmouth and onto an A road that led directly to the M5. Travelling north on the motorway towards Exeter, he looked out at the glowing day. The sun was a huge yellow eye behind the clouds, emerging now and then to blaze across the hills and farmhouses and the slowly moving cattle. Constable Warren sat very still looking out her window, and Fielding wondered if she were uncomfortable sitting in the car where only hours ago, a young woman, now dead, had sex. He would not easily forget the young constable's look of disdain when he told Kennedy about the sex. He knew it didn't really matter. Yet it had made him feel shabby to be regarded with such contempt, even by a stranger.

At the hospital car park, Kennedy was waiting for them, his compact frame wrapped tightly in his topcoat. He told Constable Warren to go into the canteen and get herself a cup of tea, and then he shook hands with Fielding, and together they went into the hospital, taking an elevator to the basement and walking along clean, pale corridors to the mortuary. The attendant, a young man with a face scored terribly by acne, was dressed in a green uniform and a surgical cap. He pulled a large tray from the wall and Fielding looked down at Denise's face, thinking that the dead have a pallor all their own. Before the undertaking trade got at them with its cosmetics and unguents, there was this: the incontestable end of lung-breathing, heart-beating existence and so the ash-coloured flesh. Fielding absorbed all this in the few seconds that he took to stare at her face; there was bruising around her throat and a scrape across her cheek. A sharp stone? When he had pushed her to the ground perhaps? A sight to make you howl and shake your fist. Turn you into your own kind of madman.

He nodded to Kennedy and the attendant slid the huge tray back into the wall. Fielding signed some papers for them and then he and Kennedy left.

The policewoman was waiting for them on the main floor near the reception counter and the three of them stepped out into the bright autumn morning and walked to the car park. They stopped by the rented car and Fielding asked, "What now?"

Kennedy told him that the Coroner's Office would get the autopsy underway as quickly as possible. It all depended, of course, on how busy they were. Woodley would be arraigned, probably tomorrow. The whole machinery of the law, clanking and ponderous, had now been set in motion, thought Fielding. One man creates this enormous disorder and now dozens of others have to set about tidying up the mess. He asked about getting her back to Canada. When could he do that?

Kennedy leaned forward, his hands deep in his coat pockets. Fielding could smell stale coffee breath.

"When were you planning to return?"

Beside him, Constable Warren had set her stolid little self against the wind.

"I'm supposed to go back on Tuesday," said Fielding. "We had business scheduled in London tomorrow, Denise and I." He paused. "I'd like to get home as soon as possible."

Kennedy nodded. "That's understandable. I think you can

get out by Tuesday, Mr. Fielding. We have your statement. If you get in touch with your airline and explain the situation, you'll find them helpful. They know what to do. Every week foreign travellers get into difficulties. Car accidents, heart attacks, strokes. Mostly elderly folk. The airlines know how to look after these things. As soon as the Coroner's Office has done its work, they'll release the body into your care. All you have to do then is give me the particulars. We'll see that Miss Crowder's remains get on your flight. I don't see why you shouldn't get home on Tuesday."

"How will I know when to do all this?"

"I'll let you know as soon as I hear from the Coroner's Office. I'd advise you to go up to London today and get into your hotel. Let me know where you're staying."

"I'm staying at the Russell."

"That's fine then," said Kennedy.

"What happens to Woodley now?"

Kennedy shrugged. "Looks like being a straightforward case. Summary conviction likely. He didn't contest the facts and they had a solicitor with them. We'll have to wait and see though. They may change their minds about things. It'll take a while."

"Yes, I expect it will," said Fielding.

Kennedy looked away, across the half-empty car park.

"We aren't telling the press much at the moment," he said. "We're just telling them that a Canadian woman has been murdered and we have a suspect in custody." He looked at Fielding. "As soon as you notify Miss Crowder's next of kin, we'll release her name."

"I'm phoning her mother as soon as I get back to the hotel."

"Good. Give me a call after you do that. Then we can give the press a statement. You can expect the story to appear tomorrow. There'll be stringers for the London papers hanging about, so you might want to let your publishing friends in London know about this today. It could be a nasty shock if they find out about it in tomorrow's papers or on the telly tonight."

The detective's narrow blue eyes seemed to be appraising Fielding. "They'll be looking for you too, Mr. Fielding. But as I said on the phone earlier, you needn't feel obliged to tell them anything."

A cell phone began to beep, and as if he had been holding onto it all along, Kennedy withdrew it immediately from his coat pocket.

"I'll be on my way then, Inspector," said Fielding.

Kennedy nodded and absently shook Fielding's hand; he was already listening to his caller. Constable Warren got into the car and Fielding climbed in behind the wheel. When he looked in the rear-view mirror, he could see Kennedy walking slowly across the car park listening to his call.

Traffic on the streets of Exeter was light and he could faintly hear the oddly irrelevant yet somehow comforting sound of church bells. But after all it was Sunday morning, and some people still went to church. The young policewoman guided him in her clipped manner to the outskirts of the city and the motorway and for fifteen minutes they drove southward in silence. Then he exited onto the A road to Glynmouth and a few minutes later the constable startled him by saying, "Why are you driving on the wrong side of the road?"

"Christ," muttered Fielding, quickly moving back to the left side.

"Sorry," he said. "I had a little memory lapse. We drive on the other side in Canada."

"It's a good thing there wasn't anybody coming." She sounded vexed and sullen. Staring ahead at the road and trees. Glancing at her he chose his words slowly and carefully.

"If someone had been coming, I would have seen him. The fact that the highway is empty is the reason I temporarily forgot. Allow me again to apologize."

It sounded like the kind of silly domestic quarrel that a couple might have on a holiday, but he was astonished at how angry he felt. The young woman put him in mind of his own mother and the quiet rage she used to inspire with her disapproving remarks. So many years ago but he would never forget those rebukes against cherished totems. Playing those early Beatles recordings in his room. "That's All Right," "Ticket to Ride," "She Loves You." Hearing his mother's voice outside his door. "Why do you have to listen to that rubbish? It's just noise."

Opening the door so she could really get an earful. "Well, I know it's not Guy Lombardo, Mother."

"No. It's certainly not Guy Lombardo." Her little Scottish face creased with irritation. "It's not anything. It's just hooligan noise, and I'm on nights this week in case you didn't know."

That was a red herring. It was late afternoon and she'd been up for hours.

"Oh yes. Hooligan noise. And the world is going to hell in a handbasket. Why not say so? I haven't heard that yet today."

"Don't you take that tone with me, you little smart alec." Though at sixteen he already towered over her.

It was odd how this glum little copper in another land evoked his own mother and her reproachful manner.

"Where are you from, Constable Warren?" he asked.

She looked across at him. "What?"

"Where were you born? Where did you grow up?"

"Near Newcastle," she said. "Why?"

"Just wondered."

His inquiry puzzled her; he could see that, and he was glad. He wasn't proud of being glad, but he was still glad.

By the time they arrived in Glynmouth, the sky had filled again with clouds. After she got out of the car, Constable Warren shut her door with more force than was strictly necessary, and left without a word. The same to you, thought Fielding, watching her walk briskly towards the police station. Turning towards the hotel he saw at once another young woman get out of a car. She was wearing slacks and a turtleneck sweater and a light jacket. What did they call it over here? An anorak? Yes. Curious name for something worn in England. The young woman drew near.

"Sir?"

Up close she looked not much older than his daughter.

"Yes?"

"Janet Russo," she said. "I'm with the *Echo*. Could I have a word with you?"

Light rain was now spattering the roofs of cars, and Janet Russo pulled up the hood of her jacket. With her pale, serious face inside the hood, she looked more like a child from a school paper. Fielding was grateful for the rain. It was an excuse to get away from her. He began to walk towards the hotel, reflecting on how many car parks he had crossed in the last two days. He wondered too how the press knew where he was staying. The local cops must have given them the information. Maybe Constable Warren and this Janet Russo were friends. Maybe more than friends. The girl was hurrying to keep up to Fielding's purposeful strides.

"Just a word about what happened, sir," she said.

"I have nothing to say at the moment," Fielding said. He was following a porter who was carrying luggage along the walkway.

"Could you tell me how old the victim was?" she asked.

He stopped by the veranda and watched the middle-aged porter struggle up the steps with the heavy bags.

"Why?" he asked.

"I understand she was quite a bit younger than you," said Janet Russo, looking up at him.

"What's that got to do with anything?" he asked.

He was hostile and sounded it. Taking out his anger on Janet Russo and her idiotic questions. She looked uneasy. A couple coming up the front walk smiled at them as they passed. The man was shaking the rain from his umbrella and chortling about the vagaries of coastal weather.

"If you don't mind," whispered Fielding, "I would like to be by myself at the present time."

Janet Russo offered him a weak smile. "Of course. I can see that. Thank you, sir."

She turned from him and walked towards the car park. Very likely working for her first newspaper, he thought. Perhaps she was still a student on a practicum. Small city newspapers used such people to keep down costs. But looking at the youthful, upturned face in the hooded anorak, he had known that Janet Russo was in the wrong profession. Far too timid and tender-hearted to make it in that game. The professionals would be in London and Toronto. He followed the couple into the hotel.

Lunch was now being served and the dining room was busy, the young hostess still carrying her menus as she showed her guests to their tables. Everything, thought Fielding as he climbed the stairs, was normal for those around him. Only his life seemed touched by this new and frightening strangeness. For others, happenstance and chaos were merely morbid considerations, briefly attended to in the wake of the highway accident, the grisly murder of a child, the airplane filled with people that falls into the sea. For him it was now immediate, close to hand, and soon he would unravel a woman's life with the worst news imaginable.

He had thought of going to the lounge bar for a drink before this call, but decided that it was cowardly. It was now twenty-five minutes past eleven. Nearly six thirty on a Sunday morning in Ontario. Heather would still be sleeping, but Claire might be up and have fed the dog; she would now be sitting in the kitchen drinking coffee, her elbows on the table and the mug in both hands. Staring tiredly out the window at the dark garden with its oak tree and leaf-covered lawn. Wondering what all this would mean in the days and months ahead. As for Lucille Crowder?

Fielding waited for the call to go through, listening to the shrieks of gulls beyond the windows. A small card on the bedside table informed him that checkout time was 1 p.m. He wondered about the next London train from Exeter. Then he heard a woman say, "Hello."

"Mrs. Crowder?"

"Yes."

"My name is Dan Fielding. I'm a friend of Denise's."

"Denise isn't here this weekend. She's in Germany right now. She phoned last week and told me she was going to some book conference in Germany."

There were traces of Denise in the light and girlish voice.

"I'm calling from England, Mrs. Crowder. I've been with Denise."

"I thought she was in Germany."

"Well, yes. We both attended the Frankfurt Book Fair. Then we had to come to England on business."

"I'm sorry, but what did you say your name was?"

"Fielding. Dan Fielding. I work with Denise at Houghton & Street."

"Oh, Mr. Fielding, yes. She's mentioned your name many times. I didn't catch your name at first. I'm sorry. What can I do for you, Mr. Fielding?"

"Mrs. Crowder, I have some really terrible news."

There was quiet and he imagined that across the thousands of miles of ocean floor he could hear Lucille Crowder breathing.

"Has something happened to Dee? Has she been in an accident?"

"Mrs. Crowder," he said. "Denise is dead. She was murdered. I'm sorry to have to tell you this."

There was now an intake of breath. He heard that. "Murdered? My God, what are you telling me? How could that happen?"

"She was attacked by a man and he killed her. The police have arrested the man who did it."

There was a further silence and then she said, "My God! Where exactly are you calling from, sir?"

"I'm in Devon, Mrs. Crowder. In a little town called Glynmouth."

"When did all this happen?"

"It happened last night."

"I thought she was in Germany at this conference."

"Well, we were in Frankfurt, but we had to come to London on business."

"But you're not in London now? I'm trying to make sense of all this, sir."

"No, I'm in Devon. In the south of England. We came down here for the weekend."

"I see," she said. "And how did she die? Where were you when it happened?"

Her voice was breaking.

"I've got to bring her back, Mrs. Crowder," he said. "Probably Tuesday." He stopped. Jesus, this was so awful. She was now crying. "Could you give me the name of someone in your town? A funeral director? So he could be at the airport to meet the plane?"

Her voice was tiny now, as though fading away. "I'll talk to someone at Gladstone's. How was she killed? She isn't cut up or anything, is she? She isn't mutilated?"

"No, nothing like that, Mrs. Crowder."

"You've seen her then? Are you sure it's Dee?"

"Yes, I'm sure."

"I don't understand any of this. Where were you when it happened?"

"I was sleeping, Mrs. Crowder."

"Did she go out on her own then?"

"We were in a car in a parking lot. In the country. At one point she left the car and the man abducted her." He stopped. The story sounded crazy. Unreal. It would take an hour to explain things.

"I think you can expect people to be calling you, Mrs. Crowder. Reporters. It's going to be on the news. In the papers and on television."

"Yes," she said. "I suppose it will."

"Maybe you should call your son. You need to be with someone."

"Yes," she said. "I'll call Ray. Ray and Kelly will come over."

"I have to go now. I'm sorry. I have to check out of my hotel."

"My God! Dee murdered. I can't believe it."

"I'm going up to London today," he said. "Do you want me to give you the number of my hotel? I'll be there later this afternoon."

"I don't want any numbers," said Lucille Crowder. "I don't want anything. I have to phone Ray and Kelly."

"I'll be at the Russell Hotel if you or your son want to get back to me," he said. "I'll be there in a few hours."

"Yes. All right. Thank you, sir."

Fielding heard the click and carefully put down the receiver, staring at a framed print on the wall. A tavern scene by a Flemish painter. Stout and smiling burghers eating oysters and drinking ale. Servant girls in aprons and caps. Fielding turned away from the picture and looked out at a patch of grey sky framed by the window. He thought he could see himself in the years ahead on another Sunday in October, an elderly man walking through a park in Toronto, remembering the details of this Sunday morning: the crying of the gulls, the couple in the maroon Jaguar, the mark on Denise's cheek, the sound of Lucille Crowder's faint and dazed voice as she thanked him for delivering his wretched news.

Two

As British Airways flight 0098 climbed steeply through the clouds, Fielding felt the terrible thrust of the engines, suffering with like-minded souls around him the thirty seconds or so during which he imagined that the enormously complicated interconnectedness of the physics involved in liftoff was most likely to fail. Every rivet in the cabin appeared to be rattling and loosening as they soared. Somewhere below him in the hold of the plane lay Denise's body in a cardboard coffin. That, Rosemary Spencer of British Airways had told him, was how they transported the dead. Listening to her, Fielding had to believe it was an art to have a voice and manner so pleasingly sympathetic. He had expected it all to be difficult, mired in bureaucratic complexities, but in fact everything had been handled with courteous dispatch, and George Gladstone of Gladstone and Sons would be waiting in Toronto. Yesterday morning Fielding had picked up the phone in his London hotel and heard the friendly, calm voice of a fellow Canadian.

"Mr. Fielding?"

"Yes."

"George Gladstone here. Calling from Bayport, Ontario. Mrs. Crowder has informed us of her loss, and we'll be looking after the arrangements here." He then asked about the airline and flight number, the anticipated arrival time. "My son and I will be there to meet the plane, Mr. Fielding. We'll look after everything at this end."

Glancing sunlight struck the windows of the cabin as the plane broke through the clouds to blue sky. Soon the seat-belt sign would be turned off, and the young, gay steward would be taking drink orders and serving lunch. Fielding briefly considered the wisdom of mixing alcohol and diazepam. Before boarding he had taken another of the half-dozen yellow pills that Fiona Anderson had given him the night before as he was leaving their home in Holland Park. She had wrapped them in a tissue and pressed them into his hand at the door. The taxi was waiting by the curb.

"These will help you to sleep over the next few nights, Dan. I must say you really do look awfully tired."

Behind her, Tony's rumpled figure, the large, cherubic face. He looked like the medieval scholar that, in fact, he had once been. They had known one another for years. And what a godsend the Andersons had been yesterday! Keeping the press away from him. Inviting him for dinner.

The London tabloids were all carrying the story and there were pictures of George Allan Woodley, the same one in each paper, a stark police photo. There were also photographs of him and of Denise; his had been taken nearly ten years ago and had accompanied a *Globe* interview on the role of editors in book publishing. Denise's was much more recent, a shot of her at the Windsor Arms cocktail party in late August. Staring at it Fielding remembered Claire's whispered comment that evening. "She doesn't mind showing off her tits, does she?" And standing next to the visiting writer in her little black dress, Denise did look sexy and glamorous. The headlines were predictable. "Canadian Woman Murdered in Devon," "Weekend Tryst Ends in Tragedy," "Raped and Strangled in Devon Car Park." Fielding was variously described as *a middle-aged married colleague, an older man whom the victim had accompanied to the Frankfurt Book Fair, the father of a teenager in Toronto.* Tony had been terrific through it all, handling telephone messages from Canadian Press, the *Globe and Mail,* the *Toronto Star,* the *Sun,* the *National Post,* even as Fielding sat in his office yesterday afternoon. The papers were clamouring for more pictures of Denise and of him. At dinner last night, Tony, flushed with wine, described them as jackals. In the end Fielding had eluded them, and at the airport Rosemary Spencer had whisked him into a VIP lounge and then into Business Class. But as he sipped a Ballantine's and ice, Fielding knew that it was really all ahead of him. He had phoned home last night and Heather had answered. She and her mother were eating supper. His picture, she told him, was on the television news and on the front page of the *Star.*

"And a picture of the woman you were with."

They spoke only briefly and he couldn't yet discern what she thought. When Claire came on the phone, she asked him how he was, and then said, "Do you want me to meet you at the airport?"

"Better not," he said. "There'll be reporters, television cameras. Why get yourself into all that? I'll take a taxi."

She didn't protest. In fact, she seemed impassive. They had had nothing much to say to one another last night.

Now, watching the young man put a chicken dinner and a tiny bottle of French Bordeaux on his tray, he wondered how the media got their pictures. Most likely from Houghton & Street. Sy Hollis would have seen to it. Fielding had called him on Sunday, his last call before leaving Glynmouth. Hollis was sleeping and sounded groggy and irritable. When Fielding told him as concisely as he could just what had happened, Hollis said, "Jesus, Dan, what the hell were you doing down there with Denise Crowder?"

He calmed down after the initial outburst, but his tone remained aggrieved and he gave Fielding a bit of a scolding. What had he been thinking of carrying on like that? Had he not considered how unprofessional it was? How was this going to play out in the media? Not a word about Denise from the sanctimonious prick, a man whose philandering had been industry gossip for years. He had even made a play for Denise. She told Fielding about it on one of their nights together. Hollis had suggested a trip to New York. "A business trip, of course," he added with his smirk. She knew what was on his mind. Well, it was another complication. For the past two years Fielding and Hollis had affected a kind of functional collegiality, but when all was said and done, he didn't think that they really liked one another.

The plane was not full on this Tuesday noon hour, and the seat beside him was empty. Fielding wanted to believe (and perhaps it was true) that the people at British Airways, mindful of his state, his need not to be pestered by some chatty neighbour, had left the seat unoccupied. Of course it might have been different if the flight had been sold out. He connected the wire to the console on his armrest and tuned in the classical station. Old chestnuts, but better than the drone of the engines, a constant wearing background noise to those who noticed. As he ate lunch, he listened to the larghetto movement of Beethoven's Violin Concerto. One of his father's favourites. The Isaac Stern version. An old Columbia recording with the violinist's round face on the cover. He had seen the LP on the stack of records in the front room a thousand times, and such music would always remind him of Sunday afternoons with his father lying on the sofa. Ted Fielding enjoyed either the large surges of romantic feeling that could be found in Beethoven, or the poignant wistfulness in piano pieces by Mendelssohn or Chopin. He kept the door closed because Fielding's mother did not like that kind of music any more than she liked the Beatles. She preferred the show tunes of Rodgers and Hammerstein. "If I Loved You," "Some Enchanted Evening," "The Surrey with the Fringe on Top." When Ted Fielding held his private little Sunday-afternoon concerts, she often chose to work a shift at the hospital. The twelve-year-old Fielding would make supper, heating canned soup and making grilled cheese sandwiches or scrambled eggs. He and his father would eat together in the front room, watching *The Wonderful World of Disney*.

There was an unspoken sadness in his parents' lives, a melancholy that infused the air of the little bungalow in Leaside. The Beethoven or Schubert on Sunday afternoons usually followed some minor disagreement out of which emerged long periods in which Ted and Jean Fielding ceased speaking to one another. The normal business of the household was conducted without words: meals were eaten in silence and his parents would move around one another, wary and polite, but wordless, until one day, perhaps weeks later, when his father would ask a question that demanded a reply.

"Do you want to play cards at the Hamiltons' tomorrow night? Doris asked me this afternoon at the library."

It was enough. She could now answer. As a child, how relieved he was when they were speaking again. He blamed his mother for those gloomy intervals. It was in her nature to hold grudges, and she was temperamentally incapable of apologizing for anything. It always had to be his father or him who broke the ice. Yet when he thought of it now, how emotionally restrained people were back in the 1950s.

He could remember a family, the Websters, who rented a house across the street and lived there for most of one year. As renters, they were regarded with considerable suspicion by their neighbours. Mrs. Webster looked young, almost like a teenager. She was pale and blonde and so were her three children, all under six, two girls and a boy. They were too young for school and the family seemed to live entirely indoors. The glare of their television in the front room could be seen day and night. When they did appear to go to the shopping mall on a Friday night, they looked like little creatures who had been living underground. All except Mr. Webster, who was a different physical type altogether, dark-haired and stocky, and several years older than his wife.

"He's not the real father of those children," Fielding's mother once said. "You can see that clearly enough." She made it sound like a reproach, a mark against the man's character. Fielding's father wanted to know why any of that should matter; he was looking after them all, wasn't he? It had set off another one of their arguments.

What absorbed twelve-year-old Fielding, however, was the

Websters' morning routine. Of all the husbands on the street who were going off to work each day, it was Mr. Webster alone who embraced his wife on the doorstep. Every weekday morning, Mrs. Webster would follow him out onto the little cement stoop, dishevelled and pallid in her housecoat, her white feet in mules. Standing there she would kiss her husband as if he were about to embark on a long journey. You didn't see much of that in those days. Only once had Fielding seen his parents display any kind of physical affection outside of whatever occurred in their bedroom.

A winter Saturday at the end of one of their long silent spells. His mother was stirring something on the stove and, for no apparent reason, Fielding's father approached her and, putting his arm around her shoulders, bent down to plant a kiss on top of her head. Later in his life when he thought about that scene, Fielding wondered what had happened that day. Had they surprised themselves by making love that afternoon while he was out with friends?

How astonished people like his parents would be at today's world, where personal feelings were constantly on display. Where tears of contrition were part of the entertainment package. Those caught out were now expected to behave in essentially the same manner as small children. No matter how odious the misdeed, the offender was expected to present himself as a suffering fellow human pleading for understanding and forgiveness from the public: the politician who squandered millions of tax dollars; the athlete caught in the motel with the fourteen-year-old; the CEO who embezzled the life savings of thousands. All felt the need to stand before the television camera with tears in their eyes. Perhaps, thought Fielding, it was the modern equivalent of medieval stocks.

Instead of being humiliated in the village square in front of neighbours, you made a fool of yourself in front of millions.

He, for example, would doubtless be perceived as an unsympathetic character in this story. He was the older man who took advantage of a younger woman on a business trip, persuading her to accompany him on a weekend of sex in the English countryside. Perhaps he had even used his more senior position in the company to inveigle her into accompanying him. The British tabloids had already, more or less, assumed that he was culpable. He was *a married middle-aged colleague, the father of a teenager in Toronto.* All true, of course, but the slant clearly suggested moral irresponsibility. Not to mention the fact that he was cheating on his wife. Nothing new there; it was done all the time, wasn't it? But he had been caught out by a terrible event, and now he must be judged accordingly. He had taken her down there for his own pleasure. What in heaven's name were they doing in that car in the countryside after dark? You didn't have to guess hard to arrive at the answer. No, he wasn't a criminal. They caught the criminal, apparently. But the man was a damn fool. An aging lecher. Taking a young woman off like that. He should be ashamed of himself.

In response to such judgments, he would be expected to express some kind of feeling before the cameras and the newspaper people. Ordinary sadness at the strange turnings life can take was no longer enough. Many would look for a more heartfelt reaction. Tears would be proof of a contrite heart. But what exactly did he feel about all this? A young woman he didn't really know all that well was dead. Who could not feel sorrow for someone whose life had been so brutally stopped? Who could not sympathize with Lucille Crowder and her son, who even now were absorbing Denise's death into their own lives.

There were also, of course, feelings surrounding his marriage. Perhaps as the weekend papers sometimes claimed, it was all changing and people nowadays took adultery in stride. It was now the way of the world. Get used to it. Yet Fielding suspected that most people of whatever age have difficulty with the idea of sharing someone they love with others. And when it happens it has to be hurtful. Last night he had lain in bed, waiting for one of the little yellow pills to do its job, listening to the arrival and departure of taxis near the hotel entrance on the street below. He had wondered how *he* would feel if it had been Claire and not him.

Why might it not be? Three or four times a year she attended conferences on fundraising for independent schools. Only last June she had gone to Boston. Later she told him how much she enjoyed meeting people from the American schools. How the speakers they had brought in to advise delegates had been so inspiring. How many worthwhile ideas she had shared with others. Suppose, he had thought, in his London hotel room last night, she met a man at one of these conferences. A tall, good-looking man in his early forties, the father of a boy who was already attending his dad's old school. Like Claire, the man was very proud of his school; he was a volunteer on the fundraising committee for a new gymnasium. It was a project close to his heart because he had played varsity basketball for the school. That was interesting to Claire, for she too had played the game at St. Hilda's. She and the man, who introduces himself as Dr. David Forsberg, discover they have a great deal in common. Both enjoyed sports as young people and both have continued to do so in a modified fashion into their middle years. Both are interested in medicine although she doesn't tell him yet that she spent nearly two years in pre-med before abandoning her ambition to be a doctor. They learn some things about one another as they chat that first morning during the coffee break between sessions. He has even been to Muskoka for a summer visit with friends, to the same lake where her best friend Elena Burton and her husband have a cottage. What a small world it is!

During the afternoon panel discussion in the auditorium, they sit together taking notes. He suggests they have dinner that evening. A Boston friend recommended a little Thai restaurant, only a ten-minute walk from the hotel. Does she like Thai food? Yes, she does, but she declines, citing another engagement, though that is only partly true. She is not really committed. She had breakfast that morning with two women her age from Memphis, jovial types who despite their talkativeness were a lot of fun. They said that if she had no other plans, she should join them for dinner. They would meet in the Skyroom bar of the hotel at six o'clock for cocktails. But they were very casual about it.

"Only if you don't get a better offer," one of them laughed. And David Forsberg is definitely a better offer. Yet, the truth is, she is afraid to be alone with this attractive man who seems to like her so much. That evening she doesn't feel like sharing the company of the ladies from Tennessee, and so she watches television and has a club sandwich and a glass of Chardonnay in her room. Afterwards, she phones Toronto.

The next day is the last day of the conference and there is a dinner at the hotel for delegates. She feels she has been delivered from temptation, but David Forsberg chooses to sit beside her and she doesn't object; in fact, she would have been disappointed had he not. After the coffee and dessert, while people are heading for the washrooms before the speeches, he

quietly suggests a walk along the river. It's rude to leave
before the speeches, and it challenges her sense of duty, but
she agrees finally and they leave the banquet hall with its white
tablecloths and empty wine bottles, its side plates of half-eaten
dinner rolls being gathered up by the waiters.

An early summer evening in another city and she feels
happy walking along the river with David Forsberg. Other
couples, mostly younger, are strolling by arm-in-arm, the
girls pretty in their summer dresses. She too feels younger and
says nothing when he takes her hand. As darkness seeps into
the sky, she watches the lights of the city reflected on the
water, wondering if something radically different is about to
occur in her life. It's rather exciting to think so, but does she
really want it to happen? Yet if it does, will anyone but she and
this man ever know?

David Forsberg is easy to talk to, and she tells him about her
father who so badly wanted her to become a doctor. She tells
him how she spent nearly two years in pre-med before abandoning her studies. The whole enterprise seemed beyond her;
she was no longer interested, perhaps never had been. How
disappointed her father was. It was a depressing time in her
life. Beside her, David Forsberg, a dark, tall figure, nods as he
listens attentively to her tale.

When he invites her for a nightcap in his hotel suite, she hes-
itates, looking out across the river at the lights. Then she
smiles at him and says all right. It will, of course, be more than
just a drink, and both of them now know this. She can feel the
slight pressure of his fingers in her hand. In the bedroom of
his suite minutes later, they are soon naked on the bed, the
covers thrown back. The ecstatic abandonment of it all.
Fielding could remember lying in his bed last night, drowsy at

last from the drug in his bloodstream, but still trying to imagine how those secret moments in a Boston hotel room could become public information.

In his mind, he saw a twenty-year-old man, an American version of Woodley. Dressed in maintenance coveralls, his head fizzing with crack, he prowls the corridors. Has a girlfriend who is a head case, a college student in hotel management, her third or fourth attempt at a career. She is working at the front desk for the summer and has given him copies of several plastic room keys. The young man intends to find what he can in those rooms while their occupants are downstairs in the banquet hall listening to some boring speech. In a sheath strapped to his belt is a hunting knife with a four-inch blade, once owned by his stepfather, a man he had often dreamed of murdering with that very knife.

The young man has already rifled several rooms, picking up some trinkets, a ring or two, a necklace, and five hundred dollars in twenties concealed in a drawer of ladies' underwear. Some stupid old woman's idea of a hiding place for money. This will be his last room and then he and his girlfriend will split. Boost a car and get away from this fucking city. They have talked about it. They'll go up to Canada. Or maybe down to Louisiana or Arizona. Mexico. Wherever. He inserts the plastic into the slot of David Forsberg's door, and seconds later is surprised by the pale figure approaching him through the darkness.

In the bedroom she listens, petrified. She hadn't wanted him to leave the bedroom. Had whispered to his back as he sat on the bed putting on his underpants.

"Phone the desk." But he was insistent. He was fit and unafraid. Angered in his own quiet way by the intrusion. She hears the sounds of struggle, the muffled grunts of two men fighting in a dark room, and then something is overturned, perhaps a floor lamp. With shaking hands she calls the front desk. She cannot, of course, hear the dying groans of David Forsberg as again and again the hunting knife slashes through the muscles and organs, severs veins and arteries. The newspapers will make much of the grisly *mise en scène*, the blood-splattered walls, etc. And of the young murderer, of course, wild-eyed and smeared with gore, trapped in a stairwell and shot dead by a hotel detective.

Suppose something like that had happened to Claire, he thought last night, before drifting into sleep. And suppose that while all that was taking place, he was watching television on Kendal Avenue—an old movie from the forties with one of his favourite actresses, Ida Lupino. Eating a slice of leftover pizza from the supper he had shared with Heather. Waiting for Claire's call. But oddly enough it doesn't come until he is asleep, and then he awakens, startled by the sound, squinting at the bedside clock. How would he feel as he listens to her improbable story at two o'clock in the morning? What degree of disappointment or outrage would he experience? And as the whole sordid business unfolds, where amid the detritus—the scandalous publicity, the averted eyes of friends, the teenaged daughter's shame, the cuckold's humiliation—would forgiveness lie and how might it be unearthed?

The Beethoven was over, and someone was yakking about the next development in the history of the concerto as a musical form. "Take Tchaikovsky, for example."

—

Fielding removed the headphones and looked across the aisle at the hands of a young woman who was working on her note-book computer. Her fingernails were painted a brilliant red. He could just make out the larger letters of the page heading. *Project Outcomes.* Around him several others were likewise engaged. The patter of computer keys was now a common-place in air travel. People, he thought, used to relax a bit on these transatlantic flights. He could remember his first busi-ness trip to Britain twenty years ago with Jim Houghton. They talked and drank. Had a couple of meals, flirted with the stewardesses. Slept a few hours and awakened, ready to go. Now everyone seemed to work nonstop. Not a minute to lose. A driven look to so many of the younger ones. The woman across the aisle looked about twenty-five. She was frowning in concentration as she worked, the scarlet fingernails flashing across the keyboard. His own briefcase in the luggage rack overhead was filled with unfinished business: contracts unsigned, galleys unread, expense accounts not yet tallied. *A History of Water* lay on the seat beside him, but he doubted whether he had the heart to tackle it.

On the television monitors, the tiny image of their airplane was inching its way west of Ireland. Digital lettering on the screen informed him that they were now travelling at 532 miles or 856 kilometres an hour. Fielding tried to get his mind around the fundamental absurdity of moving at such veloc-ity. He considered the notion that it wasn't really travelling at all; it was more like being hurled through space. Looking out his window at this space, he thought of a song his mother used to sing when he was a child. "Beyond the Blue Horizon." But, of course, it wasn't blue. Space was black in its nothing-ness. And below him somewhere Denise was now lying in her cardboard container. *Refrigerated Air Freight* was the term used by Rosemary Spencer when he asked.

"I know it sounds awful, Mr. Fielding," she added, "but it's necessary, as I'm sure you can appreciate."

"Of course."

He wondered if he should have another cognac. Another drink and he might manage to get two or three hours' sleep. This lunchtime extravagance needed no justifying today. The media hounds would be waiting for him at the airport; Claire would be watching for him at home. The ginger-haired steward was hurrying down the aisle and Fielding held up an empty glass.

"Another, sir? Certainly."

Was it just another urban myth that airports arranged for three or four jumbo jets to land within minutes of each other? It always seemed that way to Fielding when he found himself shuffling forward in these lineups for immigration and customs inspection. Ahead of him an elderly man was complaining about the unattended wickets. Another example, the man declared, of public service ineptitude. He was staring ahead as he voiced his opinion and didn't notice his wife's look of distaste. Fielding imagined that it telegraphed her wish that he shut up, that she'd had a lifetime of listening to this kind of thing.

It was easy to become discontented and whiny, however, when surrounded by hundreds of other weary, sour-bottomed travellers at the end of a long flight, though for once Fielding didn't actually mind. He was in no hurry to step through the

door to Arrivals, and this queue he regarded as just another
step to wherever he was headed. There would be many steps
awaiting him in the next few days. When you were facing a
complicated situation, you broke things down into steps.
They were called something or other. Some jargon phrase.
Manageable components. That was it. Waiting with all these
people was just another manageable component of a far more
complex problem.

What nonsense those speakers talked, even if some of it
was partly true. Most of it, of course, was common sense in
fancy language. Mutton dressed as lamb, as his mother might
have put it. For a year or two after taking over, Sy Hollis was
keen on motivational seminars. Monday mornings in hotels
out near this very airport. The sound of the big planes could
be faintly heard behind the plate glass of the hotel windows.
Coffee in rooms where the tables were covered in green
cloth. There were folding metal chairs and at the front next
to the microphone were the large white sheets of paper on an
easel with words like *Commitment* and *Planning* in bold
Magic Marker script. The speaker was usually a Patty or a
Polly, a little blonde from California or one of the southern
states. Full of pep and gab and the slick bossiness of those in
command.

"And that's what I mean by meeting your targets, folks, and
don't you forget it."

He and Linda McNulty used to make fun of it all. Like high
school kids they sat at the back of the room and drew faces on
their yellow legal pads. Traded jokes as they watched others,
mostly younger people in sales and marketing, take notes,
colouring key phrases with their highlighters. A woman in a
tangerine-coloured pantsuit had talked about complicated

problems and the need to break them down into manageable components.

Fielding watched the woman with the bright red fingernails lean into the wicket ahead of him and offer her credentials for admission to the country. He fingered his own passport and customs declaration, listening absently to the grumbling of the old man in front of him, wondering if the Gladstones were now going about their business. Father and son lifting the cardboard container and carrying it to the hearse. The father signing papers to take delivery while the son closed the heavy rear door. He would take the wheel for the drive to Bayport, and soon they would be moving westward along the expressway, past the suburbs and industrial parks, the Cadillac a long dark shape moving swiftly in the outside lane, everyone affording them room, for they were on serious business and entitled to respect and privilege. In an hour or so, they would travel on narrower roads, passing villages and small towns and brown cropped fields. Falling leaves from woodlots would be scattered across the highway and George Gladstone's son would turn on the lights of the big car. By early evening they would reach Bayport where Lucille Crowder would be waiting for her daughter's body. Friends and neighbours, relatives, the minister or priest, all would have now been notified. Everything would soon be in place for mourning.

When the Arrivals door opened, the familiarity of it all startled him, he had seen it so many times on television: cameras on the shoulders of men in plaid shirts and jeans, the nest of microphones in outstretched hands, the people behind the barrier awaiting friends and loved ones, but staring now at a stranger. Then the flash of a photographer's camera, and a

microphone thrust towards him by a young woman determined to ignore the pushing of others.

"Mr. Fielding? Can you tell us anything about what happened last Saturday night? Where were you when Ms. Crowder
was attacked?" She was almost shouting and to him the words
seemed jagged, torn from any context. Just out there, noise in
the booming corridor of the airport. He was trying to move
past them, shouldering his way along with the luggage, saying
nothing, remembering Mark Kennedy's words, "You are not
obliged to say anything to them."

He recognized a woman in the middle of the pack; he had
seen her face countless times on a late-evening newscast. She
too was shouting her question.

"Was Miss Crowder's body on your flight, Mr. Fielding?"

He was moving quickly, but he was being jostled, and he
looked, he supposed, grim and uncooperative as he headed for
the glass doors to the taxi ramp. But how crazy it all was! Seen
from above, it must have looked like some writhing organism
spreading across the floor of the airport.

One of the cameramen was walking backwards quickly,
trying to keep Fielding in focus. The man was no longer
young; there was grey in the hair around the red bandana and
he was sweating. He looked totally used up, decrepit as an old
rock star, and Fielding wondered how much the camera on his
shoulder weighed. The automatic doors slid open, and the
newspeople with their cumbersome paraphernalia followed
him outside where the air seemed exhausted, choked with
fumes from idling taxis. Fielding signalled to the next car in
line and it moved forward, driven by a young Sikh, bearded
and fierce-looking. Ignoring the questions, Fielding stuffed
his bags into the back seat and climbed into the car. After

giving his address, he looked out through the glass at the aging cameraman, at his perspiring brow and ridiculous headband. The camera's red light was still on as the Sikh put the car in gear and Fielding leaned back. Another step completed.

They left the airport and joined the traffic flowing southward on Highway 427 towards the lake, passing apartment buildings and small factories, the strip malls; if you let it, the heartlessness of it all could get to you. The Sikh's turban, like a large black beehive, partly obscured Fielding's view of the road, and now and then he would lock eyes with the man when he glanced in the rear-view mirror. Doubtless he was wondering what his passenger had done to deserve such public attention. Still, he was gravely courteous and said nothing, moving them expertly through the traffic, eastward along the Queen Elizabeth Way to the Gardiner Expressway. Fielding stared out at Lake Ontario, an expanse of grey water under a toxic sky on this mild, overcast day. Ahead through the soiled windshield he could see the towers and office buildings of Toronto. Soon they were travelling north on Spadina Avenue past the Chinese restaurants and markets, taking the long curve north of College Street by the old Borden's Dairy buildings (he could remember their home-delivery service) to Bloor Street. Then left to Kendal Avenue and soon they were in front of his house.

After climbing the veranda steps, he set down his bags and paused. He knew Claire would be home waiting for him, but he almost wished that she weren't, that she was playing squash with Elena Burton, or at one of her alumni meetings. What he really wanted was the house to himself for an hour. Before he could speak to her about what had happened, he wanted to sit alone at the kitchen table eating a sandwich. Or slowly unpack his clothes while looking out the bedroom window at the garden. But he knew she was home, for he could hear piano music. Chopin or Liszt. She was probably listening to CBC Two or the public radio station out of Buffalo. When he opened the door, he heard Silas's low single bark and soon the big retriever was padding along the hallway towards him. No doubt he had been sleeping near the French doors that led to the garden; now he was eager to welcome the traveller home with wagging tail and long handsome face turned upwards. An old friend to whom infidelity in a distant land meant nothing. Fielding knelt to give the dog a hug, calling out, "Hi. It's me." The words sounded odd somehow, misplaced and cheerily false. Or was that only his imagination? But he had to say something.

She was upstairs and a moment later the radio was turned off. Then he heard her footsteps overhead, and watched her coming down the stairs in a white sweatshirt and jeans, her sockless feet in old blue runners she used around the house. As she descended, she said "Hi" without quite looking at him. This was the precise moment he had been dreading, and he knew he had to make the first move. She could accept it or resist it, but he had to be the one to offer, and so he opened his arms to her and they embraced; it seemed more formal than affectionate, the hug of old friends who meet after a long absence.

"Claire," he whispered, "I'm sorry about all this."

She withdrew from his arms. "Yes. Well." Her voice seemed unnaturally low as if she had a problem with her throat.

"How was your flight?" She was looking past him as they stood in the hallway. Seventeen years of marriage and now this terrible awkwardness. But how could it be otherwise? She was very angry. He could see that.

"The flight," he said, "was fine, but the airport was hideous. Unbelievable. I'll be on the news tonight, I'm afraid."

She had already turned towards the kitchen, speaking as she left him.

"There were phone calls for you. Sy Hollis wants you to get in touch with him as soon as possible. A man at the *Sun* would like five minutes of your time. Those were his words. A woman named Sandra or Sandy called from New York. She left her number and would like you to call her." He and the dog followed her into the kitchen.

"Do you want something to eat?" she asked. "Some coffee? Tea?"

"Yes," he said. "A cup of tea would be nice."

The phone began to ring and they both listened to it for a moment before he said, "It's okay, Claire. Let it ring. I can't talk to anyone now. They can leave a message."

She shrugged and then said sharply, "Silas, get out of the kitchen, you're in the way."

The big dog retreated to the hallway while Fielding sat at the kitchen table counting the rings of the telephone. When they stopped he asked, "How's Heather?"

"Heather is fine," Claire said. "She's playing this afternoon at Havergal."

He was looking at her back as she stood at the counter running tap water and filling the electric kettle, plugging it into the socket above the counter. He had always enjoyed watching her perform tasks. Maladroit himself, Fielding admired the brisk economy of his wife's handiwork. Everything was done with such dexterous authority, whether it was hoeing the base of a peony bush or plaiting their daughter's hair. Claire had the skilful hands of her surgeon father. He watched her spooning tea into the warmed pot.

"Will Heather be back for dinner?" he asked.

"Of course. Why wouldn't she be?" said Claire, opening the refrigerator door and taking out the milk. "Do you want anything else with this?"

"No, nothing else, thanks," he said. "Aren't you going to have anything?"

"No," she said, placing the cup and milk jug, the teapot, on the woven reed mat at the centre of the table.

Fielding busied himself pouring tea. Beyond the window, through the branches of the trees and over the rooftops of the houses, was the pale light of the afternoon sky. On another kind of day he would have enjoyed the silence of the old house and this pallid autumn light seeping through the window. Claire had returned to the counter and was putting things away, speaking as she worked.

"Elena says you can use the cottage for a few days if you want to. If you can get away from the office. Until all this dies down." He thought about what she said. The Burtons' cottage in Muskoka. A spacious and peaceful retreat from impending commotion. If he could take some work up with him? It was tempting. Of course, there was Denise's funeral to attend.

"What about you and Heather?" he asked. "Would you come along?"

"No," she said quickly. "Heather can't afford to take any time off school. You know that. It wouldn't work."

What she really meant, he imagined, was that the three of them alone in such a quiet place would be hard. This whole business would fill the empty spaces of the cottage. They would get on one another's nerves. Unforgivable things might be said. To get away, each would take long walks alone. Yet if he went by himself, he would feel somehow imprisoned by all that empty space. A fugitive in hiding. In summers past when they visited the Burtons, he was a wary and reluctant guest. After a few days, he grew tired of the morning swims and boat rides, the glaring sunlight on the rocks and the water, the wearisome evening board games. By week's end, he was always restless and anxious to leave. He supposed he was really a city man.

"I don't think so, Claire," he said. "In any case, I have to go to the funeral."

He had scarcely touched his tea and now no longer wanted it. She was running water in the sink.

"When is the funeral?" she asked.

"I don't know. Probably Friday or Saturday. I'll have to phone Bayport."

"Where exactly is that?" she asked over her shoulder.

"It's up on Lake Huron. North of Goderich."

"That will be another circus," she said.

"It can't be helped. I have to go."

"I didn't say you shouldn't go." She spoke deliberately and slowly, directing the words at the cupboards in front of her. "I just said it would be another circus."

He paused. "Well, I'm sure you're right about that."

He was searching for a way to break through. But it was far too soon. He could see that. She had to get used to him being there in the house again. To see him around so she could hate him for a while. Hopefully just for a while. He was prepared to accept that he deserved her hatred. But how deep was the wound he had inflicted? That, of course, was what he didn't yet know. They had endured many arguments over the years. What couple doesn't have disagreements? And often they were followed by periods of bitter silence, always ended by him. It was not lost on Fielding that he had married a woman whose nature in some important ways was very like his own mother's.

"I'm going into the office tomorrow," he said. "I'm already far behind."

She turned then and frowned at him.

"Have you made a fool out of me before?" she asked. "Have you done this kind of thing on other business trips?"

"No," he said. "I haven't. Over the years there have been close calls. Who isn't tempted now and then?" She leaned back against the counter and crossed her arms.

"I don't believe you," she said.

"Well, it's true. This was the only time, Claire, and I've already said I'm sorry." He stopped. "Denise was murdered and . . . we have to . . ."

"But she wouldn't have been, would she," Claire said, "if you hadn't taken her down to Glynmouth and fucked her in a car in some godforsaken place in the middle of nowhere? If you hadn't done that, she'd still be alive and walking around, wouldn't she? If you had just acted your age instead of behaving like some horny teenager."

Her vehemence was infectious and he could feel his temper rising. There were so many things wrong in her imaginary account of what happened. Yet what was the point of explaining any of that now?

"Yes, I was stupid," he said. "I admit that. But what do you want me to do? Grovel?" Claire shrugged as she headed for the basement door.

"I don't give a fuck what you do, Dan. Do what you like. I've got some laundry to finish."

He heard the basement door slam and moments later the water storming through the pipes, then the steady churning sound of the machine. Her rage was overdue and necessary, and there could be more on the way though he doubted it. Claire was not the histrionic type. She had now made her anger clear to him, and all he could do was wait for a time when she might listen to his version of what happened. But why, when he thought of it, would his version be any more forgivable? Suppose he did tell her that Denise had been the one who initiated everything? Claire had already guessed that. He could hear her saying, "So what? You could have always said no, we're not going to do this." She would also tell him that it was contemptible to blame a dead woman for what happened, and she would be right. Anyway, as far as Claire was concerned, it might not matter one way or the other. For all he knew, she was already thinking of a visit to a lawyer. Yet their marriage had always been so stable. Divorced friends often remarked on it; of course, to live together successfully for nearly twenty years was now regarded by many as something of a feat. But he still loved her, and surely this time last week she had still loved him. Could all this change in a matter of days?

In the bedroom, he was joined by Silas, who had followed him up the stairs and was now lying on the floor watching him unpack. As Fielding threw his socks and wrinkled shirts into the clothes hamper, he felt oddly calmed. Simple tasks could be seen as a beginning of sorts, a step towards some distant Monday or Thursday when a kind of normality would return to his life. On the rug, the dog looked up at him with eyes that appealed for a walk.

"Not now, Silas, old son," Fielding muttered. "I have things to do."

When he phoned the office, Imogene Banks welcomed him back in her low, thrilling voice, a voice Fielding had once ignobly imagined could have earned its owner a fortune in the phone-sex trade. The refined and stately Imogene would have been horrified at such a thought. It was said she had once been a Tutsi princess in Rwanda, though she was now the wife of an academic as well as a receptionist at Houghton & Street.

"How are you managing, Dan? What a dreadful business this is!"

"Yes, it is, Imogene. Could I speak to Sy, please?"

"In an executive meeting, I'm afraid."

Fielding told her he would be in the office the next morning and to pass along the news to Hollis. He then deleted the *Sun* reporter's message and phoned the New York number. Listened to the broadened vowels of a New Yorker's voice.

"Sandra Levine's office."

"It's Dan Fielding in Toronto. I'm returning Ms. Levine's call."

"Of course, Mr. Fielding. Mrs. Levine has been anxious to reach you. One moment, please."

He tried to picture Sandra Levine in her office high above some narrow street or broad avenue in Manhattan. The delivery trucks and yellow taxis, the sidewalks filled with people hurrying through the late afternoon to catch subways and commuter trains.

"Dan Fielding? Thanks so much for getting back to me. You must have a lot on your plate right now."

The confident voice was a little husky and he imagined a smoker.

"I hope you don't mind my reaching you at home," she said. "I know it's a bit of an imposition."

"Not at all, Mrs. Levine."

"It's Sandy, please. I know what's happened, Dan, and I'm totally devastated. Denise meant the world to me. She was a very special person in my life. She was like a kid sister really."

He asked how she had found out.

"Well, Lucille phoned me right away. On Sunday morning after she talked to you." Sandy Levine paused as if indeed she was taking a drag from a cigarette. "Denise's murder made yesterday's *Post* too. Just a small item, but I suppose the fact that she worked down here for the past six years made her newsworthy." She paused again. "I talked to her on Friday night. She called from London and said that you two were going down to Cornwall for the weekend."

"Devon, actually."

"Devon, right. Anyway, I thought, well okay she was with a guy she liked and admired, so I didn't think anything more about it. She told me all about you. She thought highly of you. Said you were a terrific guy to work with."

"Yes, well . . ." He did not know what to say.

"It's so overwhelming. It must be awful for you too."

"I have been thinking of Denise's mother," said Fielding. "How is she handling it?"

"Well, it's a mother's nightmare, isn't it? I'm not a mother, but I can imagine the anguish. A daughter murdered like that? It's just a terrible blow for Lucille. And she's a widow too. I don't know if you knew that. Her husband passed away a few years ago. There is a son, Ray, who lives in town. I'm so anxious to see her. We only met last summer when Denise and I spent a week up there. We just had a terrific week together, the three of us. I'm glad that we had that week."

Fielding now remembered the picture in Denise's wallet: Denise and her mother and a third woman, laughing at the camera on a summer day.

"We became so close during that week," said Sandy Levine. "It was as if I'd know Lucille for years. She is such a good person and this is such a rotten thing to happen to her."

"Yes," said Fielding. "It is."

"I talked to Lucille again last night, just to see how she was getting on, and she asked about you. The point is, Dan, she'd like to talk to you, but she's too shy to ask."

"Talk to me about what?" he asked. "About what happened to Denise, you mean?"

"I suppose so, though she didn't exactly say. I think she'd like to get to know you a little bit. After all, you were with her daughter on the last weekend of her life."

"Well, of course I'll talk to her."

"The funeral is on Friday at two o'clock, and you can imagine what that day is going to be like for her."

"I think I can, yes."

"She wondered if you could go up the day before and maybe have dinner with her and the family. I'm going to be there too."

Fielding quickly considered the idea. Hollis wouldn't mind; he probably wanted him out of the office over the next few days. But Claire and Heather? They would want to know why he was leaving a day early—after all, he'd just come home. On the other hand, maybe Claire would welcome his absence. But all that aside, Lucille Crowder wanted to talk to him undistracted by the media commotion that would doubtless surround the funeral. Didn't he at the very least owe her that?

"I think I can manage it," he said.

"It would mean the world to Lucille," said Sandy Levine, hesitating. Then she said, "This is going to sound awfully opportunistic, but can I get a ride with you?"

"Sure."

"Believe it or not, I have no driver's licence. I'm a big-city girl, and I've never felt the need to drive. But that little town is difficult to get to without a car. Lucille said Ray would pick me up, but I hate to bother the man the day before the funeral. He should be with his mother. I was going to take the bus from Toronto, but it's complicated. You need two or three buses, and it takes most of the day. In August we rented a car and Denise drove."

"Well, don't worry about getting there. You can come along with me."

"Are you sure this isn't putting you out?"

"No, of course not. You'll be company on the drive up."

"That's wonderful," she said. "I'm very grateful. I'm flying on Air Canada. Flight 683. It arrives at Terminal Two at 7:55 a.m. on Thursday."

"Fine. I'll be there. How will I recognize you?"

"I'm not hard to spot," she said. "Too plump for my own good. Dark hair with too much grey in it now. Think Jewish princess who went to seed years ago. Tell you what. I'll carry a copy of *Daisy Miller*. It was one of Denise's favourite books."

"I'll see you on Thursday morning then," he said.

"Yes. Goodbye, Dan, and thanks again."

Fielding lay on the bed and looked at his watch, squinting upwards in the fading afternoon light. He was still on British time and it was now nearly ten o'clock. Taking the watch off his wrist, he held it close to his eyes and reset it at ten minutes to five. He felt exhausted, the circuits of his system over-loaded and threatening to shut down. The past few days had aged him. When he'd looked in the bathroom mirror of the hotel this morning, he was sure he looked older than he had a week ago. The travel fatigue, the booze, the bad food and those little pills, perhaps even his own fear, had drained the energy from his body. Claire was furious with him, but what did he expect? A warm and welcoming embrace? Yet a part of him felt resentful. He knew it was unreasonable, but neverthe-less he felt it.

The first time in seventeen years that he had been unfaith-ful, and it wasn't as if there hadn't been opportunities. He thought of the tall redhead who worked for the *Star* a few years ago, Jane somebody or other. Now and then they met at readings and launch parties. She told him she was writing a novel. In her late thirties and twice divorced with two chil-dren, she was an edgily ambitious woman who liked to make disparaging remarks about those reading from their books or being interviewed; but really she longed, Fielding always felt, to be up there too, expounding into a microphone or talking about her work habits. In spite of which she was an enticing creature, and around her Fielding always felt vulnerable, imagining how easy it would be to fall into her spiky and dis-ordered life where torrid sex and no end of trouble doubtless awaited him. When he heard that she'd accepted a job out West, he was saddened, but also relieved.

Then there was Samantha Chapman, whose book of deft and

gritty short stories he had published just two years ago. All of twenty-six, Samantha was understandably exultant at her success, and her enthusiasm made her a favourite for interviews. Journalists often used "refreshing" to describe her. And one night in a Queen Street bar after a reading, she propositioned Fielding. This happened in the hallway near the washrooms from which they had both emerged at the same time.

"My editor, my hero," Samantha exclaimed, falling into his arms. They had leaned against the wall for a moment or two, listening to the hideous bar music while Samantha suggested they go back to her room. She had been drinking stingers all night, and she'd also smoked a joint or two. It was just a matter of getting her out of the place, and hailing a taxi to the hotel where her room was paid for by his employer. But he plaintively made the case for professional conduct, pointing out that although it was bound to happen now and then, as a rule, a responsible editor didn't fuck his authors. In the hallway, Samantha heard him out, tendering the little verbal shrugs of the age.

"No big deal." "Whatever." "No problem." But no one likes to be turned down, and she was miffed. For the rest of the night she ignored him, leaving finally with the young poet who had shared the stage with her.

Now she was holed up in a cabin in Northern Ontario writing her second book. From time to time she sent him droll little e-mails outlining her progress. In the last one, she mentioned her sex life, which, she said, was now confined solely to pornographic enticements from "lost souls" around the globe. Her *nom de plume* was Sexy Sam, which Fielding considered somewhat prosaic for Samantha, though it probably struck just the right note for the bond trader in Tokyo or the high school kid in Kansas. In his last reply to her, Fielding wished her well but hoped that her new book wasn't about cybersex.

If it came down to serious adultery, he could, he supposed, have lived like a Frenchman all these years, like a Paris businessman with a wife at home and a mistress in another *arrondissement*. For years, Ann Costello had been inviting him back to her bed after their business lunches. After they had cleared away the more bothersome contractual details for one of her authors, and Ann was on her second glass of wine, she would suggest that they "knock off for the afternoon." She still used the 1940s parlance of her tough-talking union boss father. When she and Fielding lived together back in the late seventies and early eighties, Ann used to talk about growing up after the war in Windsor, Ontario, in a house often filled with auto workers and union hall organizers. Their kitchen was crowded with these guys who had suffered on the picket lines of the 1930s. She told him these men were like her father, smart, rough, and profane and they liked nothing better than drinking beer at the kitchen table and talking about how things were going to change. Now that the war was over they were going to insist on a better deal from the bosses. She told him that Jimmy Hoffa had once been a guest in their home. As a girl, she helped her mother make sandwiches for these men. She opened their bottles of beer and she listened to their talk.

"So, old chum," she would say after one of their lunches, "what do you say we spend an hour together? Just for the hell of it."

After all these years, she was still fond of him and he of her. Until a few years ago there was often a young man in her life, but none of them, according to Ann was a "keeper." She would complain about how "dumb" they were.

"It's unbelievable, Dan. They don't know much. They've all been to university. They've found jobs in publishing, bookselling, advertising, government. But they're totally clueless. After the sex, they can't talk about anything except cars or sports or the dumb TV shows they watch. Is this the most clueless generation in history or what?"

Ann liked to rant, but she would suddenly grin and take his hand across the table.

"Not like you, precious. You were such a sweetie when you were a young guy. So full of questions about everything. Remember the list of books you asked me for when you first moved in? 'What should I read?' you asked. I can't imagine a young man asking a question like that anymore. And we talked about everything, remember?"

He remembered. He also remembered the arguments. Long bitter arguments with bags packed and then unpacked the following morning. He would remind her of their fiercely held positions on any number of subjects.

"I had all those opinions," he said. "And all that hair. Do you remember the Afro? My God, I must have looked grotesque. Those bell-bottomed pants and all that hair."

"Nonsense," Ann would say. "You're far too hard on yourself. I always thought you looked cute with that hair and those owlish eyeglasses."

He supposed he would always miss her laughter and her witty, misanthropic thrusts at everything gormless and absurd in the passing scene. She had certainly been fun to live with, but a devil too during those eight years, obdurate and quarrelsome, a stubborn negotiator even at the breakfast table. They had not had lunch for several months and he had heard that she was winding things down at her agency, looking for a buyer.

Just a week before Frankfurt, he had seen her at a party, a noisy affair in a converted brewery near the waterfront. It was filled with people half his age drinking white wine, and he could remember thinking how tired he was of these "events" as they were now labelled on the invitations. At one point he saw Ann. She was standing next to a man who had turned to face her as he talked, anchoring himself by the palm of his hand on the scrubbed brick wall behind him. She offered the man only her profile as she looked out at the large, restored space and sipped her wine. From her expression, Fielding could imagine what she was thinking: "They should still be making beer in this fucking joint." She was wearing a cocktail dress that was far too short for her thin legs, and her hair was now cropped too close to her small skull. He hated to think it, but she now looked like a little old lady, one of those sharp-tongued Dorothy Parker types who are continually exasperated with the folly they encounter each day. And she had been such a vivacious woman when he moved in with her twenty-five years ago.

How many afternoons could they have spent together? But nobody gets little gold stars in his book for resisting temptation. You are expected to be faithful. What had he promised on that September afternoon seventeen years ago in front of the white-gowned rector, watching the dust rise in the sunlight towards the window with its stained-glass portrayal of the kneeling apostles by the Christ figure? "And forsaking all others keep thee only unto her as long as ye both shall live." A tall order, especially nowadays, but that was the deal.

Being out of the country, of course, makes it easier. You have time to get used to the idea. To rehearse your lines. Unless you are a congenital liar, you need time and space to hone deceit. To look her in the eye and say the trip was just fine. To tell her all the things you didn't do in the evenings and on weekend afternoons. Nor are there any worries about lipstick smears or the lingering scent of another. The scratch marks on the shoulder blades have time to heal. He wondered now if he had thought about that last Wednesday night when all this began.

He lay in his own bed listening to the faint throb of the washing machine, picturing the clothes sloshing through the soapy water. An analogy for his own soiled thoughts and feelings as they tumbled within him. He could hear the traffic blare from Dupont Street and the cries of children in the playground at the corner. On the floor, Silas groaned, an old dog's mutter as he entered dreamland. It felt strange to be in his bedroom at this hour of the day, listening to these ordinary sounds. Maybe this was what it was like when you retired. You snoozed in the afternoon with the dog beside you and let the rest of the world fast-forward in its hectic way. It was an appealing idea and Fielding felt himself moving into his own dark space. At one point he thought he heard footsteps on the stairs, the opening of drawers, the shower running. But it didn't matter. He slept and dreamt. He dreamt of Siena and a small hotel near the Campo. He was standing on a balcony that overlooked a narrow street enclosed in shadows. A shaft of sunlight fell across the paving stones beneath him. The remains of his breakfast were on a glass tray on the little wrought-iron table: an empty coffee pitcher and cup, a piece of bread, some fruit rinds. Claire had gone out to visit a church, and before she left, she told him that she would e-mail Heather from one of the cafés in the square. When he stood and leaned out over the railing, he could see the blue sky between the buildings and he felt happy.

Then he awakened and the sky beyond his bedroom window had darkened. He could hear the voices of his wife and daughter. The dog had already got to his feet and padded across the room to the half-open door where he hesitated for a moment before going down to greet Heather. A moment later he heard them both on the stairs, Heather taking the steps two at a time, and the dog now climbing slowly after her. For a dozen years, he had heard these familiar sounds. At one time the dog had arrived at his bed with the Saturday *Globe* in his mouth. Heather had taught him to do this and she was proud of her accomplishment. But now Fielding closed his eyes and feigned sleep; he didn't want his daughter to approach him while he stank like this with his airplane odours, the stale socks and sour breath, the dried sweat from his own anxiety. He could hear her near the door peering in and whispering to the dog.

"Silas, get back. He's still sleeping." He listened as she closed the door.

A few moments later they were downstairs again and he was safely under the shower, lathering himself and letting the hot needles of water rinse away his grime. Then brushing his teeth and running the blow-dryer over the springy hair that over the years had receded to form a kind of greying nimbus above his brow. After half a century you should have come to terms with what your ancestry had given you, but Fielding still hated his stiffly coiling hair, recalcitrant and untrainable, forever resisting comb and brush as it sprang back at once to where it was rooted. It was his mother's hair and, from about the age of fifteen, he had always thought of it like some kind of tough, coarse grass, stubbornly flourishing on some windswept moor in Scotland. By the merciful intervention of

Claire's DNA, Heather now had lustrous, dark straight hair, a genetic compromise that Fielding secretly counted as one of his daughter's serious blessings.

She was waiting for him in the kitchen, sitting on a stool by the counter where they sometimes ate breakfast while looking out at the garden. She was eating ice cream and reading a novel called *The Wars*. Still wearing her school uniform with its grey kilt and maroon sweater and the St. Hilda's gold crest. One of her knees was covered with a band-aid and her face was still reddened from the field hockey game, her dark hair held in place by a headband. She offered him a solemn smile.

"Hi."

"Hi, yourself," he said, hugging her and kissing the top of her head. "What are you doing in the dark? You'll ruin your eyes reading like that."

He had reached for the light switch on the wall, but stopped when she said, "I like it like this, Daddy." Her voice had been sharp, abrupt, but she then added, "It's not that dark. Really." She smiled again. Heather couldn't bear to hurt his feelings. To disagree with him for very long on anything. Even as a little girl she had always tried to appease him although he had often encouraged her to take a different position. She seemed, however, temperamentally incapable of doing so. With her mother, on the other hand, it was often all-out war. Fielding sat on a stool and looked at her.

"How was the game?"

She shrugged. "We lost two to one. They scored in the final minute. It really sucked. It was an easy shot too. Buckley should have had it. It was sooo easy. I could have stopped it."

She closed the book and regarded him with her steady gaze. She had her mother's bones and the wonderful green eyes.

Heather would be a striking young woman one day. Now she was a little gawky and unformed, but in time she would turn heads. Not perhaps as conventionally beautiful as her mother, but she had an interesting off-centre attractiveness that would entice only the most intelligent and discerning suitors. Fielding smiled and this provoked a frown.

"What's so funny, Daddy?"

"Nothing much," he said. "I was just admiring you. If a father may be permitted to do so."

"Admiring me? Why?"

"It's nothing, Heather, nothing, only a father's harmless indulgence."

She was staring at him with her serious look.

"So how are you anyway, Daddy?" she asked. "Your picture is in all the papers. It's a really old picture."

"I haven't seen the papers," he said. "I don't even know where they got the picture."

"They kept phoning Mom here, but she wouldn't give them any pictures."

"Good for Mom," he said. "Well, there'll be a new one in tomorrow's paper. And I'll be on television tonight."

"You're going to be on TV?"

"Oh, yes," he said. "They were all over me at the airport."

"That will be on the early news," she said.

"I guess."

"Poor Daddy."

He smiled. "Not poor Daddy, Heather. Poor Miss Crowder. And her family. They're the ones who deserve our sympathy."

Heather was frowning again and he could see that she didn't want to think about that now. As far as his daughter was concerned, Denise was the other woman. The home wrecker.

Even dead, she was an enemy and a threat. It was best to move on.

"Where is your mother, by the way?"

"She's gone out to dinner with the Burtons. Well, probably just with Mrs. Burton. She left when you were taking your shower." Beyond the window the light had bled entirely from the sky and they were now sitting together in almost total darkness. What was she thinking of him, he wondered, this child of his who loved him so much, and who must now be disappointed in him. A fifteen-year-old girl might giggle at a dirty joke or watch porn sites with friends, but when it came to the conduct of parents, she could be as righteous as a seventeenth-century Puritan. Fielding got up and switched on the light and they stared at one another under its stark whiteness.

"Does all this mean you guys are going to break up?" she asked. "Get a divorce?"

"I hope not," he said. "I still love your mother very much, but I don't know how she feels about me right now. She's very upset and that's understandable. I'm in the wrong. You know that. And because of it all, a terrible thing has happened. I'm hoping your mother and I can get past this, but it won't be easy."

"She's really pissed at you."

"Yes, I can see that."

"Mom holds grudges. She's like that."

"Yes, perhaps she does, but I've hurt her badly," he said. "Humiliated her. She's entitled to be pissed off with me."

Heather was looking at their reflections in the dark glass.

"Yeah, I guess so. But you must have had a rough time over there too. Like it must have been very hard after you found out what happened to that woman. I mean, with the police and all that."

"Not as rough as it was for Denise," he said. Heather had picked up the spoon and was idly stirring the milky dregs in the ice cream dish. "It's terrible what men do to us," she said. "Really scary. We have talks at school about this all the time. Only a week ago we had this policewoman in for gym class. She talked about streetproofing ourselves. You know, learning how to be safe out on the streets. It's such a downer." She was trying to make conversation, trying to neutralize things and make him feel comfortable now that he was home.

"Has this been tough on you at school?" he asked. "All this stuff?"

She shrugged. "It's okay. Everybody's been pretty good. You know, sympathetic. I can tell though that some people are glad it's happened to me. They come up to me at my locker and say, 'Gee, I'm sorry to hear about your dad, Heather,' but I can tell they're not. They're just gloating. I don't care. Allison and Nadina have been great. They're the only ones I care about anyway."

Fielding said, "I hope that you will believe me when I say I'm sorry that all this has happened."

"I believe you, Daddy." When emotional, her voice got a little squeaky and now the tears were not far away. He felt the need to explain.

"I was cheating on your mother, but it really had nothing to do with my feelings towards her. I mean, it just happened. It was one of those things that happens and I'm sorry that it did. What I am trying to say, Heather, is that I didn't do it to spite your mother. I wasn't in love with Miss Crowder or anything like that."

"It was just a fling, right?" she said, wiping her eyes with her sleeve. He hadn't seen her do this since she was seven or eight and the sight of it wrenched him. Jesus, he thought, I'm going to bawl too.

"Yes," he said.

Heather sniffed and looked thoughtful. "It's going to take time, Daddy. Mom's had this look on her face ever since you called on Sunday. The only person she seems to want to talk to is Mrs. Burton. They're always on the phone talking. Doesn't Mrs. Burton like you?"

"I don't know," he said. "I never really thought that."

In fact, all things considered, they had gotten along fairly well in the nearly twenty years that he had known Elena and her likeable, placid husband, Garth. But perhaps he was wrong. Elena could be sly and covert behind her high, beautiful cheekbones, and over the years she may have stored a measure of resentment over Fielding's satirical tongue, his occasional three-drink mockeries of private school alumni with their clubbiness and insufferable nostalgia—middle-aged women who still called themselves "old girls" and reminisced about pranks and volleyball games of a quarter century ago. For a while, early in his marriage, he had gone in for that kind of talk at dinner parties, and now and then it still surfaced. Claire always took his remarks in stride, even recognizing the merits of his criticism. Still, she refused to be drawn into any rebuttal. Her position was both simple and sensible; she and Elena and others like them were probably snobs, but so what? There were all kinds of snobs in the world. Art snobs, music snobs, money snobs. He himself was something of a literary snob, so get off it. Invariably she would follow that with a kiss on his cheek or a nibble at his ear. That was irresistible and he always shut up.

Elena, however, could not joke about St. Hilda's College. The school meant too much to her. Because of it she had met people who "mattered" and she had also met, at a dance for Upper Canada College boys and St. Hilda's girls, her future husband and tax-lawyer-to-be, Garth Burton. Elena Nagy had perhaps not been as socially sure of herself as Claire Moffat, whose father, like his father before him, was one of Toronto's leading urologists. Elena's father was a Hungarian immigrant who came to Canada in 1957 and made his living repairing television sets. Within a dozen years he was a millionaire with a chain of appliance stores throughout the province. So even now, perhaps in some King Street restaurant, it might be payback time and Elena could be handing Claire a list of the half-dozen best divorce lawyers in the city.

"What did your mother say to you?" Fielding asked. They were both still looking out the dark kitchen window at themselves. "What did she say happened in England?"

Heather made a face that suggested she didn't want to be drawn into the details of whatever had occurred over there.

"She said you took this woman you worked with down to this place where you used to spend holidays together. Mom said that part of England was a favourite place of hers and that really seemed to bother her. The fact that you took this other person down to where you two had so much fun together."

"Yes," he said. "I thought she'd feel like that."

"She said it was a mean thing to do. That and the cheating part."

Yes, the cheating part. He wondered how a fifteen-year-old girl would make sense of this. He was fairly certain that unless she was conducting an intensely private relationship with some pimpled youth, his daughter was still a virgin. Yet she was surrounded by sex. It was everywhere now, on television and in music and movies, newspapers, magazines, the Internet. What girl Heather's age hadn't already sniffed the breath of the pornographer and gaped at a hundred copulations? So, what might she imagine happened between her father and Denise Crowder? Could she even picture him as a sexual being, naked and enraptured? Her father "doing it" with a young woman. How might she feel about all that? But it was impossible to imagine; it was too elusive, unknowable.

"What time is it now for you, Daddy?" she asked. "You must still be on English time."

He looked at his watch and counted ahead. "Yes, it's about eleven o'clock now for me."

"Are you hungry?" she asked. "Mom said there are leftovers in the fridge, or I could heat a couple of TV dinners. They're not bad. Sometimes when you're away, Mom and I have them and watch TV."

Heather was singularly inept in the kitchen; she hated preparing anything, and so he appreciated the gesture. "I'm not crazy about those things," he said. "Why don't I open a can of soup and make some grilled cheese sandwiches. You used to like that."

"Cool. And we can watch the news. I want to see what you look like on TV."

What he looked like on TV was a man fleeing from the responsibility of revealing all to his fellow citizens as he made his way through the airport, carrying off his bundle of secrets like a thief. He might just as well have pulled up his coat to shield his face like some investment scam artist or shyster lawyer caught with his fingers in the public till. Who could trust such a bewildered and shifty-looking character? Fielding sat beside his daughter in his study, watching himself being pursued across the Arrivals lobby, shouldering his way through the doors to the taxi stand. There was a final shot of him peering up at the camera from behind the glass of the taxi window, while the blonde woman's brassy voice mentioned Denise Crowder's funeral on Friday at St. John's Anglican Church in Bayport, Ontario.

Fielding turned off the television, and the retriever, as though awakened by the absence of noise, arose and stretched, before settling his big silky head on Heather's lap.

"You looked okay, Daddy," she said, stroking the dog's ears.

"No, I didn't," he said. "I looked guilty as hell."

"I'm glad you didn't say anything," she said. "You know, like stand there and be cross-examined by that blonde bitch."

He was surprised by her vehemence. "You don't think it made me look aloof and uncaring?"

"Not necessarily, but what if it did? Sometimes it's better to say nothing. Besides, it's not really your fault that Miss Crowder was killed. I mean, it just happened, didn't it? She was in the wrong place at the wrong time. The man who murdered her is in a jail in England, isn't he?"

"Yes," said Fielding.

"That TV reporter and those newspaper people who are after you, they just want gossip. It's all they want, Daddy."

The phone began to ring.

"I'll get it," said Heather, springing to her feet and startling the dog who retreated a few steps. "Sorry, Silas," Heather said, rushing from the room. Fielding called to her as she ran.

"If it's for me, tell them I've gone to bed. Jet lag and so on."

"Sure, Daddy. No problem."

He listened to her talking on the hall phone. What a comfort she was turning out to be in the midst of all this! A few moments later she was in the doorway to the study, looking in at him as he stared at the blank screen of the television set and the shelves of books.

"That was some man from the *Sun*," she said. "I told him just what you said. You had jet lag and went to bed."

"Thanks," he said, without turning around.

"Can I get you anything?" she asked. "A cup of tea or something?"

He had to smile. Sitting there he must appear to her somewhat pathetic, a lonely old figure in need of pity. But it would be a sorry cup of tea she prepared. He knew that.

"No, thanks. I'm going up to bed soon."

"You're sure?"

"Positive."

"I've got a ton of homework to do."

"Fine. You better get on with it."

He heard her talking to the dog as they climbed the stairs together. Sitting there, he felt abruptly unsettled at the thought of facing people the next day: the sympathetic nods from some, the questioning glances of others. People couldn't help being curious. What the hell was he doing with Denise Crowder in a car park in the English countryside? Who would have thought it? Dan Fielding and Denise Crowder doing the tango. Of course, you never know about people, even people you see day in and day out. People can do the damnedest things.

As he turned out the study light, he decided that the main thing now was to get as much sleep as he could. There was no

point in waiting up for Claire. At the moment she was in no
mood to talk about any of this, and for that matter, neither was
he. He still had three of Fiona Anderson's pills and he supposed that now was as a good a time as any to wash one down
with a large Scotch. That was surely against all medical
advice, but it hadn't hurt him in England and anyway, desperate times call for desperate measures. In the kitchen, he put the
supper things into the dishwasher, and after leaving the hall
light on for Claire, climbed the stairs. Standing outside
Heather's door, he could faintly hear the thumping bass notes
from the music on her Walkman. Rapping on the door he
waited for her "Come in, Daddy."

She was at her desk typing into the notebook computer that
St. Hilda's girls were now obliged to lug around. Here were all
the accoutrements of the middle-class kid preparing for the
world beyond her bedroom walls. Without quite knowing
why, it worried him a bit, all this electronic stuff, but how
could it be avoided? It was now the way of the world. At least
until the lights went out. Bending over, he kissed the top of her
head. She had turned off her Walkman.

"I stink, don't I?" she said. "I haven't had a chance to take a
shower. I have to get this stuff done." He said he hadn't
noticed, though he had. She told him there was a biology test
tomorrow and a quiz on three chapters of the novel and a major
history project due on Friday. The teachers never stopped, and
with the classes she'd missed because of hockey, there was
always catching up to do. And there was a tournament in Port
Hope next week and then the playoffs. Fielding enjoyed this
grumbling; it grounded him in the quotidian where a school
assignment was a big deal and worth complaining about. The
scale of it was human and familiar, comforting. In a few years,

she would be gone and all this—the movie star posters, the rock music, the clothes scattered across the bed and floor—would be gone too. She wanted to be a doctor, a pediatrician helping out kids in Third World countries. Youthful idealism perhaps, but it was a noble dream just the same and she'd felt this way since she was ten years old. Her math and science marks were strong, though of course it was a long, tough haul and her mother had faltered along the same path. About all he could do was offer encouragement and the hope that it might happen for her one day.

Yet would he be a part of it? His marriage had suffered a huge stress fracture this week, and he had to wonder if he would even be in this house a year from now. Or would his life be chopped up by divorce lawyers into an apartment somewhere in town and weekend outings with his daughter? Starting over again in his middle fifties with stand-up meals at the kitchen counter and the laundromat on Sunday mornings, the awkward courting of divorcees and widows. He knew men who lived this way.

"I think I'll go to bed now. Maybe read a bit," he said, kissing her head again. "Don't stay up too late."

"Don't worry, Daddy," she said switching on her music. "And I'll take Silas out for his pee in a little while."

In his bedroom, Fielding lay wondering but only idly what Claire and Elena Burton were saying about him over dinner. On the bedside table was the manuscript of *A History of Water* and he supposed he should get at that and make some notes. Yet there in his own bed he felt exhausted by the burdensome demands of consciousness, the sheer tedium of staying awake and coping with things. The idea of unconsciousness was irresistible and so he slept, awakening only when he heard a rustling sound in the room and smelled the alcohol. The bed-side clock said twelve thirty. By the light from the hallway he could see Claire in her stocking feet. She was taking a night-gown and bathrobe from the closet. As she moved towards the doorway he whispered, "Where are you going, Claire?"

He had risen on an elbow to watch her. She stopped by the doorway to look back at him and said, "I am sleeping in the other room." The sentence came out oddly stilted, the words too carefully arranged and delivered. Claire wasn't much of a drinker, but Fielding could swear she was tight.

"Oh, come on, Claire," he said. "Is that really necessary? Come to bed. Sleep here." She continued to stare at him, hold-ing the nightclothes against her chest.

"I do *not* want to sleep there. All right? Is that all right with you, Buster?"

Buster. She had never called him such a name in her life. She *was* drunk.

"I will sleep," she said, "where I feel like sleeping. If it's all the same to you."

A few minutes later he heard the toilet flushing and the tap water flowing. Then the hall light went out and he lay in dark-ness, groggy but awake too, wondering if he could now get back to sleep. Turning his head he looked at the manuscript on the table. He had carried it across the Atlantic Ocean and back, and he was still no further than two chapters into it. Perhaps if he read for an hour or two. But he knew he couldn't do justice to the book now; it wouldn't be fair to Tom Lundgren. He would take it with him to Bayport on Thursday.

She'd had too much wine for dinner. Called him *Buster.* "Is that all right with you, Buster?" It was like a line from a 1930s gangster movie. Comical in a way but sad too, her standing there by the doorway in her stocking feet, holding her night-clothes. He hadn't seen her drunk since the night they went skating at Nathan Phillips Square more than seventeen years ago. Afterwards they ate hamburgers at a joint on Yonge Street where she drank too much beer. They talked about themselves and she cried that night, right there in the booth of the restaurant. Fielding was astonished. Tears were hardly what he expected from this tall blonde emblem of composure and confidence.

They had met a week before at a party for one of his authors, a fitness guru named Amy Hampton whose TV show back in the eighties had attracted a following among young women. Fielding had edited or, more precisely, rewritten her book on exercise and diet for teenaged girls. Hampton was an effervescent little gym teacher, and H & S arranged a reception at the Inn on the Park for phys ed teachers throughout the city and neighbouring suburbs. Fielding and a few colleagues and media types were surrounded by three hundred women with high-energy levels. As his father might have said, there was plenty of pep in the room. One of the exceptions to the giddy majority was Claire Moffat who, he discovered later, had been dragged along by a fellow teacher. Fielding could not help noticing this tall woman with her honey-coloured hair and the rather disdainful look. She seemed to stand apart from the others as she helped herself to the crackers and shrimp cocktail. They began to talk and she told him that she didn't much care for Hampton's TV show and didn't intend to buy her book, and she hoped that he wouldn't find that too upsetting. There was plenty of good-natured sarcasm in her regal manner, and he didn't think she really meant any harm. She was nearly as tall as he was, and looked him directly in the eye when she talked. He felt he was being appraised but not unkindly, and her green eyes were remarkable. He could remember thinking that this beauty must already be spoken for. How could such a lovely woman not be?

"I don't get out much these days," Claire Moffat said, narrowing her eyes at the author who was surrounded by her fans. "She doesn't look all that fit to me. She looks more like a little cookie monster."

Fielding couldn't help laughing and she joined him.

"I'm awful, aren't I?"

"Yes," he said, "but I don't care. I'd like to see you again. That is, if you're not involved with someone."

"How gallant of you to ask," she said, regarding him carefully. "Maybe I've had too much wine, but your glasses look a little crooked to me." She had reached up and straightened them and he felt the warmth of her hand on his face. "Do you skate?" she asked.

"Skate?"

"Yes, you know. Blades on the bottoms of boots and you put them on and go across frozen water. Swish, swish. That's what it sounds like. Good heavens, you're a Canadian, aren't you? Everyone in Canada knows about skating."

He could remember feeling a little flustered. "Well, of course, yes. Sure I can skate." He hadn't skated in twenty-five years, and had never been very good at it.

"I've been wanting to go skating all winter and now it's nearly the end of February and I still haven't managed." She accepted another glass of wine from a passing waiter. "Take me skating some night down at City Hall."

"What about this Friday?"

"Why not?" she said. "You're not married, are you?"

"No," he said.

"Well, that's fine then, neither am I."

She had then leaned into him and whispered, "Are you really the editor of that little squirt's book?"

"I am," he said, laughing.

How opportune it all was! Light after darkness, in the coldest month of the year. Over Christmas he had moved out of Ann's apartment. After eight years he was again on his own and miserable. At thirty-eight, with a receding hairline and the beginning of a perceptible stoop, he had often lain awake wondering if he would ever find another woman to love him. Would he ever be a father?

At the skating rink that Friday night, he wobbled around on a pair of used skates he had bought that afternoon. Claire found his efforts hilarious.

"You said you could skate," she laughed. "Why, you can hardly stand on the damn things."

He was struggling to catch up to her. "I suppose," he said, "you even played hockey."

"Of course," she said, deftly turning around to skate backwards so he would see her laughing at him. "I'm a red-blooded Canadian girl. Don't forget that."

"You did this to humiliate me," he said. "You hate men. This is an act of revenge."

She applauded with her mittened hands. "You didn't have to come. You could have said no."

"I was afraid I might not see you again," he shouted. He had felt an intense happiness there at the skating rink with her that evening. He remembered holding onto her arm as they circled the ice and thinking, she likes me. I can tell she likes me. I am going to marry this woman. What a lucky bastard I am!

In the restaurant they drank beer and exchanged histories. He told her about growing up in Leaside and attending the University of Toronto as a wimpy arts student. Then the brief forays into journalism and advertising before he settled on publishing. He didn't go into details about Ann Costello; he didn't mention that the affair had eaten up eight years of his life. It sounded too much like failure. Claire talked about her mother's death from breast cancer and how she'd had to deal with all that at sixteen and how St. Hilda's College had been good for her at the time. She boarded that year, and it helped having other girls around, especially in the evenings and on weekends when her father was often away at conferences. She talked about her father, the renowned urologist, and how disappointed he was when she gave up her medical studies.

"I don't think he's over it yet," she said, "but I wasn't smart enough for medicine. Or maybe I just got fed up with it all."

She had gone instead to teachers' college and for the past several years had been employed by one of the big inner-city schools. But she had grown tired of the sullen kids who didn't want to push themselves at anything. It took constant nagging to get them to move their bodies. She was sick of their yawning and their gazing out the windows during hygiene classes. Claire had mimicked one of her Grade 10 students.

"Me and my boyfriend don't like condoms, ma'am. We don't get the same sensation." The predictable titters from the rest of the class. She also taught two biology courses and they were all right, but she confessed to feeling demoralized by the sour notion that her future might only hold more of the same. She'd thought of taking a year off and going somewhere, Europe maybe. But what would she do over there? Listening to her, he had still found it difficult to believe that there wasn't a man somewhere in her life.

One evening a few years later, on an anniversary, they talked about that first date and he told her how amazed he had been by her tears.

"Yes," she said. "I was a little drunk and teary that night, wasn't I?"

"You were."

"And you didn't think I was the weepy type, did you?"

"I did not."

"Well, that night I was still trying to get over something and that's why the soppy display."

"Oh, come now," he said, "you weren't that bad." She then told him about her many years with Michael, a guy she'd met in university. Remarkably enough, they too had broken up over the Christmas holidays.

"That's why I was so maudlin and goofy that night. I still wasn't sure whether I'd made a terrible mistake. And there you were, and I was starting to like you." He asked her why she and Michael had parted ways.

"I don't know," she said, "but there was something missing. There'd been something missing all along, and I suppose I always felt it but didn't want to deal with it. I guess what it came right down to was the realization that after all those years, I still didn't love him. Oh, I liked him. I liked him a lot. But I didn't love him. He had graduated in medicine and was going off to California. He asked me to marry him but that was nothing new. He'd been asking me to marry him for years. But that Christmas, the one before we met, he gave me an ultimatum. Marry me and come out to California, or I'm going alone. It's funny. We were often happy, and we had some great times together. God, how all my girlfriends envied me. Elena thought I was mad not to marry him. You have to understand that Michael was almost too good to be true. Handsome enough to model clothes when he was in university even though he didn't need the money. His parents were rich. He'd gone to Upper Canada College. He was athletic and he was smart. A golden boy. Women were crazy about him. Yet for years he just wanted me."

"Maybe," said Fielding, "you missed the golden boat. You could now be sailing off the coast of California with your three golden-haired children."

"Perhaps," Claire smiled, "but I'm a happy camper here in Toronto with you and Heather."

They were sitting in the garden drinking cognac after dinner, both very happy. A September evening and dusk had settled over the city; between the houses there was still light in the sky, but the trees and shrubbery were only dark shapes. At one point, Claire got up and came over to sit on his lap and put her arms around him.

"That night we went skating," she said. "I was really confused. The thing is, I liked you, Dan, but I didn't love you yet. How could I? We'd just met. But I do remember thinking, I don't want this guy to get away. I think I could live with this guy."

"Such a ringing endorsement. Thanks very much."

"No, no, you don't get it," she said. He could smell the brandy on her breath, but now she was just a dark shape pressed against him.

"The way I felt with you that evening was different from the way I felt with Michael, even after all those years. As long as Michael and I were out with people, it was fine. We had loads of fun. Skiing trips. A weekend on a friend's boat. A football game. It was great, but we never seemed to go anywhere by ourselves. In all those years, we never took a holiday together. It was always with another couple or two couples. A gang at somebody's cottage. And when we were alone, I sometimes felt as if I didn't really know who Michael was, and he didn't really know me and wasn't interested in finding out. He probably thought he already knew me, but really he didn't. Whereas with you, I could tell right away that you were interested in who I was, what kind of person I was. So I think I must have been really fucked up in my head that night you took me skating. I'm glad you put up with me."

Fielding was sitting on a plastic lawn chair and Claire was heavy on his lap, a big lovely handful of a woman with her arms around him and her warm breath on his neck. He was expecting the chair to collapse and spill them onto the grass. In a way, he hoped it would happen so that her sombre reflections could be lightened by comedy, and they could go into the house and enjoy some playful lovemaking.

Lying now in the darkness, Fielding recalled that that was exactly what happened. Perhaps he had made it happen by leaning sideways in the chair to ease the weight of her. In any case, they had toppled onto the grass laughing and then gone upstairs. He tried to remember what anniversary they had been celebrating. The third? Or was it the fourth? Heather was then a dark-haired little girl of two or three, asleep in her crib. They had looked in on her before going to bed.

—

The serene and elegant Imogene Banks was already at her desk, her high polished brow shiny under the fluorescent light. This morning she was wearing an emerald green dress, though it didn't really matter; whatever she wore, Imogene afforded visitors a spectacular introduction to Houghton & Street. Fielding always thought she was the closest thing to Cleopatra he would ever meet. She smiled at him as he entered, shaking the rain from his umbrella.

"Good morning, Dan. Welcome back."

"Thanks," he said. "How are you, Imogene?"

"I am well."

"That's good."

From Imogene you expected nothing less than perfect tact and restraint with no lingering curiosity in her heavy-lidded gaze. She had already returned her attention to the sheaf of papers she had been reading. Imogene seemed always above the fray. Answering the telephone at H & S was only a diversion; she was married to a professor of astronomy who toiled at his theorems and equations only a few blocks away. Sometimes Fielding saw them standing together in the luncheon lineup at the Swiss Chalet on Bloor Street and he wondered what they talked about, this Rwandan princess and her fifty-year-old astronomer.

The office was still empty except for Jack Perkins, who was standing with his back to the doorway, arms on his hips as he studied jacket designs laid out on a display board. The art director was a prickly man, especially in the mornings, tolerated only because he was so talented. Either he didn't hear Fielding passing in the hallway, or he chose to ignore him. The door to Denise's office was closed and Fielding opened it, looking in for a moment. It was just as she left it, with a pile of manuscripts on a shelf, a coffee mug with Henry James's face on it, her radio, a pair of scuffed loafers by the desk. She liked to slip them on when she was working. Fielding closed the door and went to his office and stood by the window, watching the traffic below on Avenue Road, the brake lights flashing along the wide street. People with umbrellas were carrying cups of coffee and shoulder-strapping notebook computers as they hurried through the rain.

His airport picture was on the front page of both the *Star* and the *Sun*; he had seen it while passing a newsstand. The *Globe and Mail*, which he had picked up on his own veranda and left on the hallway table, had relegated him to page 7, but it was the same picture. There he was, looking up from behind the taxicab window, a frightened, evasive-looking figure, possibly an enemy of the people. There was voice mail and e-mail and stuff in envelopes stacked on his desk. The first telephone message was from his daughter.

"Hi Daddy, it's me. It's seven thirty on Monday morning and I'm heading out for school. I know I will be seeing you before you hear this, but I wanted to say it anyway. Yesterday afternoon Mom told me what happened in England, and I just wanted you to know that I love you, no matter what. Bye."

The next from J.J. Balsam, a man Fielding had given up any hope of ever hearing from again.

"Hey, Dan, you old bastard. It's Jack Balsam. I've been reading all about you. You're probably in deep shit with your old lady, right? Well, I've been there, believe me. Many times. Too bad about the girl. You'll have to tell me the whole story when we meet. Anyway, guess what? I've finished this fucking novel. Had my first drink today in six and a half months. One hundred and ninety-four fucking dry days and so it's celebration time. I'd like to come into Toronto and see you asap. I'll bring the book and you can treat me to a long boozy lunch. I figure you could do with some cheering up. Give me a shout, you horny old bugger."

No novel from J.J. Balsam in almost nine years, and in normal circumstances his call would be welcome. A new novel from a major author for next fall's list. But when Balsam was drinking, whirl was king as the old Greek put it, and the thought of entertaining this wildly unstable man was depleting. Jack Balsam was a gifted writer but he was also egotistical to the point of self-delusion; he probably believed that bringing his new novel would help to make Fielding whole again. But if Balsam was on a bender, the care and feeding required would feel like a week-long migraine. Balsam was a throwback to an older, more jagged generation of writers, men like Richler and Purdy who drank freely and didn't give a damn what others thought. The young writers Fielding sometimes met in Denise's office mostly struck him as careerists, carefully managing their images with appointments to arts committees and profiles by journalist friends. They drank their two glasses of red wine every day and worked out at the gym like young corporate players. To them, Balsam was a dinosaur and so, probably, was an editor like Fielding.

After deleting the next two messages from reporters, he listened to Ann Costello's voice.

"Hi, Dan. It's Tuesday at seven ten p.m." It was the same voice that used to excite him when he was a young man, and they were going to meet for drinks on a Friday evening at the roof bar of the Park Plaza, a prelude to a weekend in her house.

"God, I'm so sorry this has happened. What a desperately awful thing it all is. I just saw you on the news. I'm sorry, Dan, but you looked like a scared rabbit. Who could blame you with all those awful people around you? My God, what a maelstrom you were in."

Maelstrom. It was the very term he had thought of yesterday as he was trying to escape from the media people at the airport. But then he and Ann were often on the same wavelength in the old days. Conjuring up the same word as they sat in bed on Sunday mornings drinking Irish coffee and doing the *New York Times* crossword puzzle. Ann had the big Sunday paper delivered to her door. At twenty-nine, Fielding always felt wonderfully urbane sitting in bed on Sunday morning with this small, quick, erotic woman who was seven years older. Now she was a little old lady; she couldn't have weighed more than a hundred pounds when he saw her in that converted brewery.

"Listen. If you feel like getting away for lunch one day, give me a call. It's not morbid curiosity, Dan. You just looked as if you could use a friend. Give me a call if and when you feel like it. And take care of yourself. Okay?"

He could now hear the voices of colleagues greeting one another, and the editorial assistant, Martha Young, leaned in from his doorway. She was still wearing her raincoat.

"Hi, Dan. Welcome back. You're early."

She gave him a tired look of sympathy.

"Dan, I'm sorry about what happened. It's just terrible. I'm sure you've heard that enough times to be sick of it, but I *am* sorry. Is there anything I can do?"

"Keep the media people away from me until they get tired of asking, or until I am pushed off the front page, which will probably be after the funeral on Friday. I'll be going up to Bayport tomorrow, by the way. Back on Monday."

"Fine, I'll do what I can."

"I just have to avoid meltdown, Mart."

She smiled. "You won't melt. A day at a time."

"Right."

He listened to the bustle of others as people came in to begin another day. Loren Schultz who worked in publicity looked in and waved.

"Nice to have you back, Dan." And Bob Constable, tall and lugubrious, offered him a gentle smile before going to his office and his religious books. Fielding wasn't supposed to close the door against any of this. Sy Hollis didn't like closed doors unless they were absolutely necessary; a confidential chat, say, with an author or an important customer. In Sy's view, a closed door was an act of unfriendliness; you were turning your back on fellow workers. It was, to use his term, *uncollegial.* Fielding had never regarded a closed door in quite that way, and so he didn't strictly adhere to the policy. He felt he'd been at H & S long enough to ignore some of Sy's more asinine notions about office protocol. Sometimes he went along with them, and sometimes he didn't; inconsistency, he felt, was a useful weapon in confusing authority. On the other hand, he didn't want to be seen as a crank who couldn't adjust to new times and conditions.

Scrolling through his e-mail, he opened a note from Tony Anderson. The London papers had already dropped the story and, according to Tony, probably wouldn't revive it until Woodley's trial, and that wouldn't likely be until next spring, maybe even later. He had talked to some people who knew about these things. He and Fiona had a bed for him if ever he wanted some downtime in London during the trial. Glancing through the rest of his e-mail only made Fielding restive; the various claims on his attention seemed trivial and ridiculous in the face of what had happened.

Looking at Denise's office earlier had done something to his head. The Henry James coffee cup. The shoes by her desk. He had felt something like her presence in the darkened air of her office on this rainy October morning. It still shook him how these things happen. They had turned off the road to the car park. They could just as easily have gone on to Glynmouth. Walked along the promenade with the shrieking gulls overhead. Laughed at the old people in their track suits. Gone back to the white hotel with its blue awnings and the Union Jack snapping in the wind. Could have, but didn't. Yet if it came down to the most fundamental "could have but didn't," *the primum mobile*, so to speak—he could have stayed out of Denise Crowder's bed. She would have spent the weekend in London visiting bookshops and museums while he wandered through the back roads of Devon alone. Could have, but didn't.

He felt suddenly restless and unnerved by everything: the letters and e-mails, the pitying looks and expressions of sympathy, the conversations beyond his door. He had taken off his glasses and with his elbows on the desk he leaned forward, pressing the palms of his hands into his eyes.

"Are you all right, Dan?" asked Martha Young. He looked up to see her blurred figure above him. Fielding put his glasses on.

"Yes, I'm fine, Mart. Just a little tired."

"I'm not surprised," she said and added quietly, "Sy's in now, so you can probably expect him to drop by any moment. He's dithering about all this."

"Okay, thanks."

In fact, as she left he could see Hollis talking to the publisher, Linda McNulty, in the hall, glancing from time to time
at Fielding's doorway. As usual, he had his sleeves rolled up.
It was another of Sy's habits, and one that was copied by many
of the younger men, particularly in sales and marketing.
Fielding watched the president of the company make his way
down the hall towards him. He was smiling grimly.

"You free for a second, Dan?"

"Of course," said Fielding, waving him in.

"Mind if I close the door?" Hollis asked.

"Please."

He settled into a seat by Fielding's desk and crossed his legs.
He was marginally older than Fielding, perhaps fifty-seven or
-eight, a numbers man with a background in accounting and
marketing. Most people agreed that he was doing a good job.
He trusted the judgment of his editors and didn't interfere
with their work, even with pet projects that might appear at
first glance a little dubious. The company was making money
now and the people who worked for him, including Fielding,
generally felt comfortable under his leadership. Hollis also
read the books he published, which was probably more than
many others did. Yet there was something calculating and not
quite trustworthy about him; Fielding had felt it from the first
day of Hollis's appointment three years ago.

They looked at one another across the desk. Sy was a heavy-
set man, balding and round-shouldered, and Fielding had
always thought he should have scrapped the union boss look
and hidden those heavy round shoulders in the jackets of his
elegantly tailored suits. There was something of the hustler
about Sy, and Fielding, who enjoyed imagining what people
might have been like when younger, saw Hollis as an earnest,

unathletic 90 percent-er at Harbord or Jarvis Collegiate, un-
blinkingly ambitious and fiercely competitive, driven onwards
by immigrant shopkeeper parents. A man who would cut
corners if necessary and shoulder others out of the queue if the
need arose. Not handsome by any means, but giving off a powerful whiff of virility; he had been a strenuous fornicator over
the years and that might have accounted for Fielding's resentment at the tone of his remarks on the telephone Sunday morning. Rumour had him settling down in the past few years, with
all forgiven by his long-suffering wife, Brenda.

"Well, Dan," he said. "How are you coping with all this?"

"I'm coping, Sy," he said. "I'm coping."

Fielding thought he probably looked flushed. His face had
felt warm against his hands and he wondered if his blood pressure and heart rate were rampaging again.

"And Claire? How is she?" Hollis liked Claire. At parties he
often sought her out and, watching him stand beside her chatting, Fielding always thought Sy looked like a man eager to
please Claire's slightest whim.

"I'm just asking out of concern for you and your family. I
don't mean to be nosey, Dan. This has been a terrible shock for
everyone concerned. For you. For Claire. For Heather."

"They're coping too, Sy," said Fielding. "Everybody is
coping. Coping is what it's all about these days."

He was close to sarcasm, but Hollis didn't seem to mind, or
if he did, he didn't let on. When mildly perplexed, Sy did an
odd thing with his mouth, filling his cheeks with air and then
releasing it with a tiny popping sound. Likely a habit from
childhood, and in its own way, rather endearing. Fielding
could imagine Sy as an overweight seventeen-year-old at the
kitchen table, popping his cheeks as he worked on his calculus.

"I've been thinking about counselling for the staff," said Hollis. "Some of the younger ones have been asking. They expect that kind of thing nowadays. What do you think?" Fielding had no thoughts on the subject that could be remotely construed as positive. He had once turned down a manuscript on grief counselling and he and Claire had also argued about its efficacy following the death of a St. Hilda's student in a snowmobile accident. He saw it as a kind of racket, with its pat formulas and hand-holding, its programmed artificiality.

"Some people need it," Claire had argued, "so why deny them?"

But he remained unconvinced. "I'm not a big fan of grief counselling," he said finally, "but you're the boss." Hollis appeared not even to be listening. He was staring out the streaked window at the grey slanting rain.

"I'm wondering too whether we should close down this Friday. Keep the warehouse open but shut down the office for the day. What do you think?"

"I think we should close," Fielding said. He was trying to take deep breaths. They were supposed to help with anxiety. "Let those who aren't going to the funeral have the day off," he added. "Out of respect for Denise."

Hollis nodded in agreement. "Anyone who wants to go is welcome. We have six or seven people so far who have expressed interest. But we can take others. I'll rent a van if necessary. What are your plans?"

"Actually, I'm driving up tomorrow," said Fielding. "I'm picking up a friend of Denise's at the airport in the morning. She phoned from New York and asked for a ride. It seems she doesn't have a driver's licence. She worked with Denise at YPS."

"Is that so? Who is she, by the way?"

"Her name is Sandy Levine. I think she's one of their senior editors."

Hollis's face brightened. "Of course she is. I know Sandy Levine. I called her when we were hiring Denise. It was Sandy's letter of recommendation that really sold me on the girl. She's very sharp, Sandy. I can arrange for a car to pick her up if you like. I could go myself."

"No, it's fine, Sy," said Fielding. "I think she'd like to talk to me about all this. I gather she was very close to Denise."

"Well, of course she'll want to talk to you about it then," said Hollis. "It's a good idea too. Drive her up and have a talk about Denise. It'll get you away from the city. Do you the world of good." He made another of his popping faces and then said, "In fact, it might not be a bad idea if you took a few days off after the funeral. Maybe go away somewhere until this media stuff settles down."

"It will probably settle down after the funeral on Friday," said Fielding.

"Maybe, maybe not," Hollis said. "Some of those reporters can be persistent. It's a story that pulls their chain, Dan, especially young female journalists. Pretty young woman, older married guy. Tragic death of the pretty young woman. It might not go away for a while. You could take the next week off. Go some place nice, say Bermuda. Take Claire on a little holiday. It would give you both a chance to talk about all this away from the glare. Perhaps Heather could stay with friends."

"I don't think Claire is in any mood to talk to me right now, let alone go on a holiday to Bermuda. And it's one hell of a time to leave Heather."

Hollis shrugged. "Maybe. It was just a thought. Brenda and I once . . . Well, never mind." He now looked uncomfortable and Fielding felt as if the top of his own head might be coming off; his blood pressure had to be in the stratosphere. Could a stroke be readying itself to strike him deaf, dumb, and blind?

Hollis placed his hands on his knees and stared at them for several seconds before standing. "Anything I can do?"

"No, thanks."

"We've sent flowers up to the funeral home."

"That's good."

Hollis stood by the door and looked back at him. "If you change your mind about next week, just let me know, okay?"

"I will."

Fielding rubbed his burning cheeks and left the door closed. He supposed he should have his blood pressure checked. He could go to a Shoppers Drug Mart a few blocks away, but there was usually a lineup, mostly geezers waiting to plug their skinny arms through the sleeve and squint at the monitor to see if they were still on course for survival. But Janet had told him the drugstore machines were often unreliable. He punched in Janet Lieberman's number and got a busy signal. Leaning back in his chair he tried some more deep breathing. All the messages would have to wait for detailed replies; they were simply beyond dealing with at this point in time, to use a much loved expression of the age in which he lived.

He had written a note to Claire about leaving tomorrow instead of Friday. She had been sleeping when he left this morning. Either that or she was lying in the spare room, awake and hungover, waiting for him to leave. The note business was pusillanimous, and he now regretted it. But she was, as Heather might put it, majorly pissed at him, and he had wanted to avoid any more confrontations. Not that she might care one way or the other, but in any case he had filed his intentions in a note, taping it to the morning paper. His entire house seemed to be infected with spores of distrust and hostility. At breakfast even Heather had been moodily quiet, hunched over her cornflakes and biology text.

"Good morning, Dr. Lieberman's office."

"Good morning, Marlene. It's Dan Fielding calling."

"Dan? What's the problem?"

"Blood pressure," he said. "I think my blood pressure is off the screen."

"Are you having dizzy spells?" she asked.

"Not yet. But the top of my head feels as if it's coming off, and I have this headache running down into one side of my face. I don't feel right. Any chance of seeing Janet today?"

"As a matter of fact," said Marlene Glasser, "there is. We've had a cancellation for one o'clock. Can you come in then?"

"I can. You're an angel, Marlene."

"You'd better not drive. Have Claire bring you in or take a cab."

"I will, and thanks." He worked on some e-mail responses to thank the sympathetic, entering pleas for time and space to keep the baying ones off his back for a few days. He was already feeling better. He was dealing with things now, and somehow he would get through it all.

When he came out of Janet Lieberman's office on St. Clair Avenue, the rain had stopped and a powerful westerly was blowing across the city, scattering leaves over the streets and

scouring the air. With the wind behind him, Fielding walked
southward on Avenue Road. He could remember days like
this from high school. Standing on the sidelines at a football
game with his father, watching a punted ball carried aloft in a
gust of wind, travelling an enormous distance to confound the
defenders who watched helplessly as it fell behind them,
bouncing crazily away from their grasp. By halftime Fielding
and his father would both be tired of the game and would
drive home together. Fielding never minded the silence
between them, the unspoken appreciation of a fine day with its
sunlight and its big bracing wind cleansing the city. His father
was interested in weather of all sorts, and like a ship's captain
on a voyage, paid heed to both foul and fair, noting in a small
black book wind direction and barometric pressure, a habit he
claimed to share with his grandfather, an English countryman
who may have had more practical use for such information.

After his father's death in 1983, Fielding discovered scores of
these little black books in the basement, carefully dated, metic-
ulously setting out basic conditions. *Monday, December 13,
1954. Two inches of snow overnight. Temp at 7 a.m. 22F. Winds
light N.NW. Bar Rising 101.47.* He doubted whether his
mother ever knew about the little books, and he was certain
that if she had, she would only have snorted in disdain at the
waste of time and effort required to sustain such a vigil over
all those years. Another example of human foolishness, and
something else about him to belittle. "You can read all that in
the paper or hear it on the radio. Who cares anyway? Weather
is just weather, Ted. Do I wear a raincoat today or not?" She
could never have understood his quiet satisfaction in noting
the various wonders of weather, a daily gift from God. Such
considerations were not in her ken, and Ted Fielding would

have been the first to admit that that was fine too; we were never meant to have the same interests in this life.

It felt good walking down Avenue Road, watching the big ragged clouds sailing before the wind towards the lake, and thinking about his father, who was now in his grave, away from the turmoil of his son's life.

Janet Lieberman had looked him over, her dark hair near his chest as she listened to his heartbeat through the stethoscope. His blood pressure was 160/100. Not as crazy as he had imagined, but still far too high. She allowed for the current stress he was under and gave him a prescription for Lorazepam "to see you through this difficult time." It was her only allusion to what was going on in his life. Janet was a consummate professional; she'd been their family doctor for years, and Claire had known her from student days at St. Hilda's. She was a year or two younger than Claire but they'd played together on basketball and volleyball teams. Janet told Fielding to make another appointment with Marlene.

"Tell her I want to see you within the next couple of weeks, Dan. We'll have a good look at you." He always left her office thankful that this calm, reserved woman was looking after his family's health.

The walk home was salutary and he was feeling better about things until he turned onto his own street and saw the man getting out of a car. He was somewhere in his thirties with streaks of grey in a brown beard. A little stout in baggy corduroys and a bomber jacket. One hand clasped a shoulder strap and case that probably held a camera. Standing on the sidewalk, he was impossible to avoid. He offered a tentative smile.

"Mr. Fielding, Jim Foster. I'm from the *Sun*. I've been trying to reach you. I wonder if I could have a few moments of your time." He was overweight and a smoker. Fielding could smell it on him.

"I know this is a bad time for you, Mr. Fielding, but a few questions."

Asking questions people didn't want to answer. Eating a hamburger in some joint as he sorted through his notes. Cell phone always ringing. Then back to the newsroom to tap the stuff into the computer. Kids at home to support. An estranged wife somewhere. Foster had that look about him.

"Could you tell me where you were and what you were doing when Miss Crowder was abducted?"

"I explained it all to the police in Britain," said Fielding.

"Yes," said Foster, "you were in the car, but you didn't see what happened. Did you hear anything?"

"I heard nothing."

"What were you and Miss Crowder doing in that remote area after dark?" As if he didn't already know.

"Everything will be revealed at the trial."

Foster had removed the camera from its case and was looking down fiddling with it. "Yes, but that won't be until next year according to the British papers."

Fielding shrugged. His sympathy for the man had vanished. "The pangs of dispriz'd love, the law's delay."

Foster looked up. "Come again."

"Never mind. If you'll excuse me, I'd like to get into my house."

Foster had stepped back. "Is it okay if I take a picture or two?"

"You already have my picture. It was on today's front page."

"Another couple won't hurt," said Foster, backing up and

bending his knees to snap away as Fielding climbed the veranda stairs and opened the front door. Through the window he watched the reporter making his way across the street, buttoning his camera case as he walked to his car.

Fielding could hear voices from the dining room and when he turned, Claire was standing in the hallway.

"I thought I heard someone come in," she said, looking surprised to see him. She was wearing jeans and an old T-shirt advertising St. Hilda's 100th Homecoming Weekend. "You're awfully early."

"Yes. I just tidied up a few things and decided to call it a day. Too many distractions. I'll do a couple of hours' work here."

"Elena's here. And Dad," she said. "We had a late lunch." She looked as if she had been caught at something illicit. It was three thirty.

"I'll hang up my coat and just say hello. I don't want to be in the way."

"You won't be in the way," Claire said quickly and a little testily. They were still far apart, he thought. They hadn't found the words yet.

Standing by the hallway closet he wondered if this lunch had been some kind of strategy session. What are you going to do, Claire? Yet surely that kind of talk had been going on from the moment they knew. Maybe it was just a lunch. Period. They were still at the dining-room table when he made his entrance. Elena Burton, with her elbows on the table, was twirling a little white wine in her glass. She looked mischievous. Elena never dressed down, even for a casual lunch in a friend's home. An auburn-haired beauty in her Holt Renfrew pantsuit and silk blouse, her large gold earrings and high-heeled shoes, she looked to Fielding like a high-end courtesan, a source of countless erotic delights. She seemed to be smirking at him over the rim of her glass. The old urologist in his nifty tweed sports jacket and slacks was seated at the head of the table, and he had pulled his chair back. Fielding could see the black loafers with their little tassels. Over the years, the sight of the doctor's preppy shoes had always annoyed Fielding, though he didn't quite know why. Perhaps the youthful footwear symbolized the monstrous vanity of the man. He was nearly eighty, but the little moustache and silvery hair, fussed over weekly by costly hair stylists, made him look like a version of the old matinee idol Cesar Romero. According to Claire, her father was still pestered by widows in his lakefront condominium.

Dr. Moffat was frowning at him, but Elena got up and came around the table offering both cheeks European-style.

"Dan, we're all glad you're back home safe and sound." He could smell the subtly expensive perfume. In happier times she would flirt with him, though there was always a brittle irritation to it all. His mention of a book or magazine article she hadn't read or heard of could provoke sarcasm, a suggestion that the big-shot book editor was showing off. Elena was unconfident and unpredictable, and long ago he had learned to handle her warily. He had asked Claire, when they were first married, why her friendship with this volatile woman had lasted—they were so different in temperament. Claire said that, although Elena had many faults, she was loyal, good-hearted in her own way, and vastly entertaining. What more could one ask of a friend? And she was right. Elena was a good friend to her.

"Come," said Elena, "sit down and have something. There's not much left, I'm afraid. Claire made a lovely lunch for us, and I've been eating like a horse lately. Don't you think I've put on a pound or two, Doctor. Be honest now."

"I hadn't noticed," said Dr. Moffat gruffly. This all sounded familiar and out of habit Fielding and Claire glanced at one another. In the old days, they would have exchanged smiles at Elena's yakking and the old doctor's chronic irritability. Now they just looked quickly away, Fielding out the window to where Silas lay sleeping on the patio.

"Do you want a glass of wine or some coffee?" asked Claire.

"No, nothing for me, thanks," he said.

"Sit down, Dan, for goodness' sake," said Elena. "You're making me nervous just standing there."

There were three sandwiches left on the plate and he was tempted to reach for one, but decided against it. The circumstances seemed to demand a certain penitential air of him, and chewing a crabmeat sandwich in front of the three of them might suggest an inappropriate jauntiness.

Elena finished the wine in her glass. "You seem to be holding your own with the media. I'm sure it can't be easy."

"Actually, there was a guy from the *Sun* waiting for me in his car out on the street. I just got rid of him."

"They never leave you alone," said Claire. "The phone is always ringing. They bother Heather and her classmates at school. Some woman from the *Star* was around the school today asking questions. Heather phoned me about it." She looked aggrieved, and in her jeans and T-shirt, a little pallid, not at her best next to the resplendent Elena.

"The *Star*," said Elena, "likes these kinds of stories. Private schools. Addresses in the Annex. Rich people exposed."

"I'm not rich," said Fielding.

Elena smiled. "Well, you know what I mean. They think you are and that's good enough."

"When do you have to go back to England for this trial?" asked Dr. Moffat abruptly. To Fielding the old man always sounded as if the world was full of idiots who couldn't describe their symptoms in ten plain words.

"I don't know," Fielding said. "Maybe next spring."

"Damn it all," said Dr. Moffat. "I don't understand what you were doing when all this was taking place."

"Dad, please," said Claire. "I don't want to hear any of this right now."

Elena reached across the table and touched the doctor's sleeve. "Claire's right, Dr. Moffat. There'll be time enough to think about things."

They could now hear Heather at the front door calling out, "It's me."

"Good heavens," Elena said. "I should have gone ages ago." She got up and hugged Claire. "Thanks for the wonderful lunch, my dear. Can I give you a ride, Doctor?"

"I'll walk a bit," said Dr. Moffat, getting to his feet. "It's a fine afternoon now. I'll walk over to Spadina and take the subway."

By the patio door Silas was barking to get in. He had spotted Heather at the entrance to the dining room.

"Hi everyone," she said.

"Hello, pet," Elena said, hugging her. "How are things at school?"

Heather looked over at Fielding. "They're fine. Busy, busy, busy."

"How did the test go?" asked Claire.

"I think I did okay."

"You have to do better than okay, young lady," said the old doctor gravely. He was frowning again.

"I know, Grandpa," she said.

"Your mother tells me that you lost to Havergal yesterday," said Elena. "How could that happen? Why, we always beat them in the old days."

At the table, Fielding sat listening to Heather recount the details of yesterday's match, its closeness, the goal in the final minute, the keeper's negligence. He was grateful for these comforting details of ordinary existence. Biology tests and field hockey games were a welcome respite from the dark melodrama that had overtaken his life in these last few days. The others had moved towards the front door, the dog barking with excitement at the company in the hallway. With a half-eaten sandwich in his mouth, Fielding gathered up some dishes and took them into the kitchen, feeling almost at home again.

When Heather came into the kitchen, she said, "I need a hug."

"Me too," said Fielding, holding her. "Thanks for the phone message this morning. It cheered me up."

"Oh that." She appeared almost embarrassed now, as if her call had been foolish, a little girl's whim. "I'm glad you're home, Daddy." The dog had followed her in and settled himself on the floor. "Mom says you're going away again tomorrow. Up to that little town."

"Yes, Bayport."

"I thought the funeral was on Friday."

"It is," he said, "but I'm taking a friend of the family up. She lives in New York City and doesn't drive. She was very close to Denise." He added quickly, "To Miss Crowder. They worked together down in New York. Anyway, she wants to spend some time with Miss Crowder's family. I feel I have to do what I can to help. I'll be back Friday night."

"I'll bet the TV people will be up there." She was still clinging to him, talking against his chest.

"Oh, I'm sure you're right about that."

"Excuse me," said Claire and they stepped back out of her way. She was holding the rest of the dishes and nudging the dog with her foot. "Damn it, Silas, get out of the way." Scrabbling to his feet, the dog hurried off at once to the hallway.

"How many times have I told you, Heather, that I don't want him in the kitchen," Claire said, placing the saucers and plates and cups onto the racks of the dishwasher.

Heather looked chastened. "Sorry, Mom."

Fielding was picturing their dinner that evening. In her earnest and helpful way, Heather would try to fill in the gaps with talk of school and friends. But it would be heavy going, the air freighted with accusatory thoughts, recriminations, feelings of betrayal and guilt. In the tense silence, the three would listen to the scraping of knives and forks on plates, their chewing mouths and swallowing throats.

He was thinking that Claire felt wronged, but she was also humiliated. Having an unfaithful husband was one thing; having this fact broadcast on the evening news and read about in the morning papers was something else. She was a proud woman and this was terribly wounding. It would take time, and looking at her as she stacked the dishes in the machine he wondered if the air would ever entirely clear, or whether this past week had so disfigured their marriage that the middle of October would always be looked upon as a season to get through. An ugly anniversary like a bad car accident that you survive but never forget, something withheld perhaps and then produced to strengthen an argument years away. Would he still have to apologize when he was an old man? Would they still be together then? Or, for that matter, this time next year?

In a way, too, she was at a serious disadvantage. Denise's murder had overshadowed Claire's own sense of betrayal. She had been denied her full measure of outrage by the death of the "other woman." Complaining about her husband's unfaithfulness could be viewed by some as merely petty. After all, a young woman had lost her life. What was her husband's brief affair when placed beside that awful fact? Get over it, Claire. That was one way of looking at it, but he knew it wasn't Claire's way. She was twisting the dials on the dishwasher, her long back to him, and as she bent forward he could see the ridge of her spinal column through the old T-shirt. On another day he might have reached across and enclosed her, smelling her neck and hair, listening to her laugh as she told him to lay off. Now such a move would only look forced and embarrassing. She wasn't ready for anything like that and neither perhaps was he. Everything was still unsaid, unexplained, unforgiven. It was going to take words, and as yet there was no opening for words. Fielding looked across at his daughter who was pouring a glass of milk by the refrigerator. She seemed abstracted, a bit sulky.

"I have an idea," he said.

Claire turned to look at him, leaning against the dishwasher. Heather was watching them both over the rim of her glass. He had been thinking of the dinner ahead and how maybe tonight they could bypass the awkwardness, go out instead to a joint that served pizza and truck-stop spaghetti. A place where it was easy not to talk and still feel comfortable. It was mostly for younger people, but the lights and loud music, the clatter of others eating and talking and laughing might be diverting for the three of them.

"What about some pizza tonight? We could walk over to that place near Bloor and Spadina. Just a thought."

"Good thought, Daddy," said Heather. "Let's do it." She was now looking over at her mother.

"I just have a little work to do," he said. "We could go out, say about six thirty?"

He too looked across at Claire, who shrugged.

"If you like."

Three

Sandra Levine was talking about cigarettes and how much she had missed them over the past ten and a half months. In her handbag was a package of Winstons, and before the day was over, she was going to be smoking again. She told Fielding that it was a prospect that she was both thrilled by but also dreading. They were driving west on Highway 401 in Fielding's six-year-old Accord, leaving the airport and Toronto behind on a clear day. Waiting for her at the airport, he had spotted her at once among the other travellers filing through the doors to the Arrivals lobby. Sandra Levine was something of a presence in her slacks and red-and-black woollen poncho, with a wide-brimmed dark hat. As promised, she was carrying a copy of *Daisy Miller*. A stocky woman in her early fifties, she had given Fielding's hand a vigorous shake.

"Dan, it's good of you to meet me like this. Please call me Sandy."

They had talked about mutual acquaintances in New York publishing as they walked to his car. She was easy to talk to and gave him the lowdown on her twenty-five years in the business, her happy but childless marriage to Hiram Levine, who taught psychology at Columbia. She was amiable, funny, and shrewd, a woman comfortable in her own skin. Fielding could see how Denise would have been attracted to her.

"When I talked to Lucille on Monday," explained Sandy, "the first thing she said was 'Sandy, I'm smoking again.' As soon as she heard about Denise, she went out and bought a pack of cigarettes. And there she was on the phone telling me how badly she felt about letting Denise down. Last summer when Denise and I were visiting, we persuaded Lucille to give up cigarettes. Oh, I was so full of zeal then and Denise was after her mother to quit. 'Come on, Mom, it'll be good for you,' she kept saying. So we both worked on her all week, and by the end she decided to give them up after, I don't know how long, thirty-five or forty years. On the day we left, she told us she was smoking her last one. And do you know what? She had it beaten until last Sunday. On the phone she kept saying, 'And I promised Dee too. I promised her.' Loses her daughter like that and then feels bad because she broke a promise to her about smoking. When I told Hiram about this, he said people say all kinds of irrational things when they're in shock like that."

She was looking out the window. "These lousy habits of ours. Hiram is going to smell it on me. He's going to nag me to death. He warned me too. 'Buy some of that special gum before you go,' he said, 'because you're going to be tempted.' His words exactly. So what was the first thing I did when I got to La Guardia? I bought a pack of Winstons."

The highway was filled with trucks hurtling past them en route to Windsor and the American border. It was nine thirty on a Thursday morning, and a week ago, almost to the hour, he and Denise had finished their day at the Display Hall and were walking along the crowded streets back to the hotel past the enormous steel-and-glass buildings. He didn't like Frankfurt much. Never had. There was such a grim Teutonic earnestness to the place, a grey city of suits and Eurodollars. He liked it better at night with the lights on. But last Thursday walking back to the InterContinental, he was looking forward to dinner and another night in bed. He remembered how happy he felt, but he also recalled the slight unease surrounding everything, the speck in the eye at a picnic.

"So, how about you, Dan?" Sandy asked. "How have you been handling all this? It must have been a horrible shock for you."

Fielding took his time answering, for he had been thinking about it all week, and he was still unsure about his feelings. "I don't quite know how to explain it," he said. "They say that when you experience something like this, a horrendous episode in your life, it's just as though it isn't really happening. Everything is taking place in a kind of dream state. You hear that all the time. But I never really felt like that. To me, it was all very real. This is happening, I said to myself. Things like this happen to people every day. Why not us? And now here I am in the middle of it. Of course, you can't be analytical about anything at the time. It's just happening before you. You're shattered. You see everything in your life coming apart at the seams. You say to yourself, my life is never going to be the same again. And that's true. It won't be."

Sandy Levine was staring out the window at the brown

fields. "If you don't mind my asking," she said, "were you and Denise serious about one another? Had this thing between you been going on for some time?"

"Well, no," he said. "Not at all. In fact, I was surprised at how quickly it happened."

"She used to talk a lot about you. I think she had a bit of a crush on you. Do people nowadays still use the word *crush*? God, I sometimes feel so out of date." She looked across at him. "Anyway, I think she did. She was always mentioning you when we talked on the phone. When she joined your firm last June, she went on about this guy Dan Fielding. Denise was attracted to older men." Not always, thought Fielding, remembering the night he had asked her about the small tattoo on her shoulder blade, and she had told him about the young actor she met when she first arrived in New York.

"A mistake," she had said. "Both the guy and the tattoo. An idiotic mistake. He persuaded me to have it done. He had several in various places. I guess I thought it was cool at the time. A few months later he was gone from my life and good riddance. Someone told me he went out to California and got into porn movies. He certainly had the equipment for the job." And then she had laughed. She was sitting on the bed cross-legged in her Yankees T-shirt. "Why, Daniel, I believe I've shocked you. You're actually blushing."

"She was looking forward to going to Frankfurt with you," Sandy Levine said. "We talked on the phone the day before you left."

Fielding asked her what Denise was like when she first went to New York. It was as if he wanted to picture in his mind's eye a young woman with short dark hair walking along the streets and avenues, stopping to look in store windows, nervous but excited too by the blare and hectic energy of the big city.

"I remember the day six years ago when she came in for her interview. She'd come so highly recommended by her Toronto publisher, and I don't know why, but I was expecting this big powerful figure and then Denise came in. It was raining, and she was drenched, her hair soaked. She looked about twelve years old. But she was so eager and enthusiastic. You couldn't help liking her and being impressed at the same time. She listened carefully to everything you said. She was taking it all in. That's a rare quality in people. Knowing how to listen. I remember thinking that first day, this is one very smart young lady. And of course she was also sweet and charming. Everybody liked Denise. Well, that's probably not true. There were some who were jealous of her. That goes with being bright and pretty. But she worked very hard too. Hiram often had a late-afternoon class, and so I'd work until six thirty or seven and meet him for dinner somewhere and Denise would still be at her desk. I used to say, 'Okay, kid, we're all impressed, now why don't you go out and have some fun?' But you could see her confidence growing by the week. She was well read and a shrewd judge of books. And she could handle herself at literary parties. There was a kind of sexy French thing to her. Of course, Denise was part French. Her mother is French Canadian."

Sandy Levine was looking out her side window again. "She was a refreshing presence in our midst. That's perhaps the best way I can put it," she added, looking at Fielding. "We became very close. She'd spend a weekend with us now and then. Hiram was very fond of her too. He introduced her to some divorced colleagues. I didn't think much of his match-making, though Hiram's heart is always in the right place. Anyway, she went out with a few of these sad sacks, but nothing much came of it. For a while she was seeing a young novelist and then there was an actor in her life. That, I gather, was a total disaster. Then, after a few years, she got homesick. I could tell. And when she turned thirty, well . . . that was a big birthday for her. We went out to dinner and she got a little tight. Told me she was thinking of returning to Canada. To be closer to her mother. She was just waiting for the right opportunity to come along, and so when she heard about the job at your place, well, she was very, very keen. It seemed like just the thing she was looking for. I remember her coming back from Toronto so excited and happy. 'I think they liked me, Sandy,' she said. 'I had a good interview with the boss.' She was a little worried about you, though. She sensed that you weren't exactly overwhelmed. But she felt good about Seymour Hollis and as she said, 'He's the boss.'"

Denise was right, thought Fielding. He had not been as impressed as Sy Hollis or Linda McNulty. Denise Crowder, he felt, was a little too overconfident. There was also something vaguely condescending in her attitude. As if a little too much of New York had rubbed off on her. There were two other candidates, a woman Denise's age from a rival company and a man a few years older from a small press in British Columbia who had published several promising young writers. At the end of the interviews, Fielding was leaning towards the man from Vancouver; Denise he placed a strong second. That, of course, was not how Sy Hollis saw things, and Fielding knew it when they took Denise to lunch at Le Bistro on Bay Street. When Denise left for the ladies, Sy said,

"This is the one, Dan. Terrific enthusiasm and she knows her stuff. I think younger writers will love her. Linda thinks so too."

To be fair, they were probably right. Sy had good instincts about people. It was one of his strengths. And maybe the B.C. man had an impressive track record, but he was a little too intense. In his cords and Hush Puppies, his sensible high brow and specs, he carried about him a whiff of the West Coast ideologue. In any case, Fielding knew he could live with the decision, whatever Sy's motives. It could have been one of those days when a part of him no longer cared. A warning that maybe it was time to get out. A day for seeing himself on that balcony in Siena.

Fielding and Sandy were in Stratford now, and on the wide main street a busload of high school students was unloading, the girls talking excitedly in clusters on the sidewalk, the boys already horsing around in front of a store window, while two harried-looking teachers fussed about on the edge of things.

"They're probably going to a matinee after lunch," said Fielding. "You have to feel sorry for the old folks who will be in there with them." And there were plenty of older people on the streets, window shopping, enjoying the bright fall sunshine. Sandy mentioned a day in August when she and Denise had driven down from Bayport to see a performance of *All's Well That Ends Well*.

"I was totally knocked out," she said. "We don't get much Shakespeare in New York these days. At any rate, not *All's Well That Ends Well*."

At a village on Highway 8, they stopped for lunch at a restaurant on the main street. The locals glanced up at them shyly and then resumed talking as Fielding and Sandy made their way to a booth near the back. Roy Orbison was singing of missed chances in life and the air was full of cigarette smoke.

"I'm weakening, Dan," said Sandy. "Would it bother you if I had one?"

"Go ahead."

"Well, I know I shouldn't, but maybe Lucille will feel better if she sees me joining her. How's that for rationalizing a decision to resume a bad habit?"

"It's as good as any," said Fielding.

"God help me," she said, firing up a Winston. For a moment she looked dazed. "I'm dizzy as hell," she said. "Just like my first one about forty years ago. An unfiltered Lucky Strike. Those things were lethal."

The waitress, an older woman, set down two glasses of water. "What'll it be, folks?" They settled on the daily special—vegetable soup and chicken salad sandwiches on brown. Coffee.

Sandy was now used to her Winston and enjoying it.

"What about you, Dan? Did you ever smoke?"

"Yes, years ago when it seemed everybody smoked. But I was one of those persons who was never really dedicated to the habit. I could take it or leave it. I even smoked a pipe for a while. It's funny, but Denise once said to me . . ." He stopped. They had been in bed when she had said it, but there was no point in mentioning that.

"We were talking about how everybody used to smoke when she was a kid, her father and her mother, everybody else's parents. Or so it seemed. And she said, 'I'll bet you smoked a pipe too. I can just see you with a pipe. Pompous as hell.' And she was right. I was a terribly pompous young man when I started in publishing. Then I met a woman and she took that out of me."

"Your wife?" asked Sandy.

"No. It was a woman I worked with, and then she left publishing to become an agent. We never married, but I lived with her for about eight years. Then I met my wife."

"Any kids?"

"Yes, a daughter. She's fifteen."

"Nice."

This was a sombre mission, this visit to the little town where Denise grew up and where her grieving mother now awaited them. Yet sitting in this village restaurant with its frying meat and cigarette smells, with Roy Orbison on the local radio station, Fielding felt a brief and peculiar exhilaration. On this Thursday noon hour, it all seemed vivid and oddly worthwhile to be here among these people. Whole families, from babies in the arms of their teenaged mothers to skinny grandfathers and their stout wives. Going on about cancer scares and the closeness of lottery numbers, the idiocy of social workers and welfare functionaries, the unreasonableness of landlords, the awful unfairness of things in general.

An hour later, a few kilometres south of Bayport, they were passed by a pickup driven by a woman about Denise's age, blonde ponytail sticking out the back of her ball cap, an arm hanging out the open window. A country girl from the looks of her. Perhaps she had gone to the local collegiate with Denise and was now married to her high school sweetheart. Had two or three kids. Played softball on summer evenings and curled in the winter. Enjoyed a beer and an off-colour story now and again. Not a bad life and if it hadn't been for books, it might have been Denise's too.

He thought about her as a young girl, travelling these very roads on a Friday night with a boyfriend in his father's big heavy Pontiac, another couple necking in the back seat. The boys with their swagger and their hard-ons. The cigarette packs tucked into the rolled-up sleeves of their T-shirts. A dee-jay yakking on the radio. A case of beer in the trunk. She would have gone down these township roads past the woodlots and abandoned farms to the gravel pit where other cars already had their lights turned off and rock music blared from a ghetto blaster. Now and then headlights coming on and off to mark a score. Here, she allowed boys a certain latitude: shared a joint and returned their wet kisses, felt their weight upon her, but always careful about who gets to lay a hand on what. A smart girl who was already looking beyond those Friday nights. Who might even have preferred to be home reading, Fitzgerald or Hemingway, but too good-looking, too eager for experience to pass all this up, for this too was life and not to be missed. And always, stencilled on her brain, and never to be forgotten, the four words to freedom. *Just don't get pregnant.* And it really wasn't that long ago, thought Fielding. Say fifteen or sixteen years. Just about when Heather was born.

It had clouded over, a dark fall day now as they passed the gas stations and fast-food joints, the big warehouse stores on the edge of town. He and Sandy had not spoken for several minutes, both caught up, he guessed, in their memories of Denise. Finally Sandy asked, "Where are you staying?"

It was odd, but he hadn't thought of it until now.

"Well, I don't really know," he said. "I suppose I'll have to find a motel. I noticed a couple back there. They looked all right. I can't believe they're that busy this time of year. And it's early yet. I'll find something."

"I think," Sandy said, "I'll go the funeral home tonight, rather than this afternoon."

"Yes," he said, "I thought the same."

On the main street were the pizza restaurants and realtors' offices, the dollar stores and Quik Money outlets. Another little town whose business centre had been whacked by the shopping mall on its outskirts. Only the old and the poor and those without wheels now shopped downtown.

"I think," Sandy said, "we turn at the next light. I'm sorry, I can't remember the street, but their home is near the lake. A nice house. Denise's father bought it when he was still on the boats. He was an engineer or something and for a while before she had the children, Lucille was a cook. I don't know if you knew that. That's how she met her husband."

At the lights, Fielding turned onto a wide, pleasant street with trees and older yellow-brick houses. The road and sidewalks were strewn with leaves from the big oaks and maples.

"We're getting there," Sandy said. "This looks familiar. God, I'm so bad with directions. It's a couple of streets down now and then a right and a left. It's the last street before the lake." They passed a school and looked out at a young woman delivering mail. When he turned the final corner she said, "Yes, there it is. The house with the yellow siding on your right." Fielding turned into the driveway and parked in front of the attached garage. When they got out, he carried Sandy's suitcase to the front door, feeling strange, an intruder of sorts, a man who, after all, was partly to blame for this tragedy, yet who was now visiting the mourners. He could understand how many would see it that way.

Sandy rang the doorbell and a few moments later a large, broad-faced woman in slacks and a sweatshirt opened the door. She was somewhere in her fifties, and by the looks of her, a handful if crossed. She gave them a quizzical frown and then, spotting the suitcase, grinned at Sandy.

"You were here last summer with Denise. You're Sandy."

"That's right."

"I didn't recognize you at first."

"It could be the hat," said Sandy, taking off the sombrero and giving her short brown hair a little shake.

"I remember you now," said the woman. "Denise's friend from New York."

They could hear a voice from somewhere in the house. "Who is it, Del? Is it Sandy?"

The woman turned and shouted up the stairs, "Yes, it is, Lu. It's Sandy."

"Tell her I'll be right down."

Turning back to them, Del said, "Come in. Come in."

"Del," said Sandy, "this is Dan Fielding. Another friend of Denise's." The big woman gave him a guarded look as she shook his hand. She had heard of him all right. He could see that.

"Pleased to meet you," she said.

They followed her into the living room off the hallway. "Lucille's getting dressed," said Del. "She's going over to the funeral home in a few minutes. Ray's coming by to pick her up. He should be here any minute. Have a seat."

She had sunk into a chair near the sofa where Sandy and Fielding now sat. They could hear Lucille Crowder's footsteps overhead; she seemed to be hurrying from room to room. The house smelled of roast beef and cigarette smoke.

"You've come up from Toronto then," said Del. She had settled into the big chair, filling it entirely.

"Yes, we have," said Fielding.

"How was the traffic?"

"Very light," he said.

The woman had a hard time looking directly at him, though he could tell she wanted to. She chose instead a spot between him and Sandy and stared out the front window as she spoke.

"I suppose it would be now," she said. "The traffic in the summer up here from the south is something awful. I have a daughter who lives in Toronto, and now she just hates the drive up in the summer. It's getting so Jack won't do it. It's just too much of a hassle he says. He'd rather just stay at home. If Jeannie wants to come, he says, she can come on her own." She looked suddenly peevish as if recalling a family dispute on this very topic. They all listened to the floorboards creaking under the weight of Lucille Crowder's footsteps above them. In front of Fielding was the dining room with its table and a bowl of artificial flowers. Beyond that a window overlooked the backyard. Denise, he thought, might have done her homework at that table, feet curled around the legs of her chair.

Suddenly Del said, "Well, we're all just shocked by what happened." She stopped, as if wondering whether such an obvious statement was equal to the enormity of it all. "It's just so hard to believe," she continued. "Poor Denise. Why, I've known her for nearly twenty years. Bert and me moved in across the street twenty years ago. Denise was just a little kid then. Maybe ten or eleven. She used to play with my Jeannie. They were good friends there for a while, and then in high school they kind of drifted apart. Made different friends the way young people do. Jeannie was going to come up to the funeral tomorrow, but she had to go to the hospital for an operation on her knee. Isn't it always the way? But you have to go when they tell you, or you'll end up at the back of the line again. She's been on the list for months. It was just too bad the way it turned out. Jeannie was just sick when I phoned her and told her about Denise. And then she saw it on TV."

She lapsed again into silence and they heard footsteps on the stairway. A few moments later, Lucille Crowder came into the living room, holding a coat, which she threw across a chair. Here, thought Fielding, was Denise as she might have looked twenty-five years from now, a small woman with a good figure, dark hair streaked with grey. Still pretty. In the curve of the jaw, the swell of the cheek, the dark eyes, Lucille Crowder was simply and completely an older Denise. She was smiling tiredly but already Sandy had gotten up to embrace her, a broad, colourful figure in her black-and-red outfit, enclosing Lucille Crowder in her arms.

"I'm going over to see her in a few minutes, Sandy," said Lucille, pressing a balled-up tissue against her face. "My God," she said, "I'll have to go upstairs and fix these damned eyes again."

"No, you won't. You look fine, Lucille," said Sandy. Over Sandy's shoulder Lucille Crowder was looking at Fielding.

"You must be Dan."

He had been standing since she entered the room and he went towards her, and shook her hand.

"Denise thought the world of you, Dan," she said.

Del too had gotten up a little cumbrously from the chair and now made her way slowly into the kitchen. Lucille Crowder continued to dab at her nose with the tissue.

"Del's been just great. She's cooking supper for us. Have you people had anything to eat?"

"We ate along the way," said Sandy. "A little place down the road. We're not hungry."

"Those places along the road," said Lucille, laughing sharply, almost unpleasantly.

To Fielding she sounded exactly like Denise.

"You'll probably both need something for your stomachs later on. It's too bad. We could have made you a sandwich here. Del would have fixed something. She's looked after me all week." Lucille Crowder sat down on the edge of the big chair across from them. "Honest to God, I haven't done a thing. Just sat on that sofa and looked out the window and smoked. I'm such a mess. Sat here and stared out the window or watched the television. I couldn't tell you what I saw if you asked me."

Sandy reached across to pat her knee. "Lucille, for goodness' sake. You're entitled to feel like that."

"I'll tell you this much," said Lucille. "I'll sure be glad when I get through this week. Those newspaper people in Toronto have been such a nuisance. I know they're just doing their job, but my God they phone at all hours of the day and night. They pester you so."

Sandy had given her a cigarette and they both began to smoke, Lucille Crowder offering a bitter chuckle.

"Just look at us," she said. "All that high falutin' talk last summer. Right out there," she said, waving her cigarette at the dining-room window. "Remember, Sandy? We were standing by the barbecue? You and Dee telling me to get with the program. Isn't that how Dee put it? Get with the program, she said. And I did. Nine weeks almost to the day. And now you're back on them too. I hope to God it wasn't all this that got you on them again."

Lucille Crowder had the same straight black hair as her daughter, but she wore it longer and the hairdresser had over-done things, piled it up into something that was too youthful and didn't quite suit her. She was talking about a young woman from the local paper who had come to the house and asked for childhood and school pictures of Denise and of how she now regretted handing them over. They would be in tomorrow's paper and this now bothered her.

"They catch you when you're not thinking straight about these things," said Lucille.

From the kitchen they could hear the sizzling, and smell the roasting meat. It reminded Fielding of Sunday afternoons long ago in Leaside.

"Sandy, I'm going to put you in Ray's old room," said Lucille. She was leaning forward in the chair, her left hand clutching the tissue. If I photographed her at this moment, thought Fielding, I would surely entitle the picture *Woman at the End of Her Rope*. But how did you get through something like this? How would he and Claire deal with it if something ever happened to Heather?

Lucille caught his gaze and seemed abashed. "George Gladstone told me they got a really nice flower arrangement from your company, Dan. Thank you."

The incomparable Imogene Banks would have looked after that on Sy Hollis's orders.

"Dan has to have some place to stay tonight, Lucille," said Sandy. "Can you recommend a motel?"

Lucille was stabbing the ashtray with her cigarette. "Most people like the Bayport Inn. It's right near the water and pretty swanky for a little town like this. It's probably where the newspaper and TV people will stay, and if you don't care about that kind of thing, Dan, I can phone for you. I don't imagine they'll be too busy this time of year though sometimes there are hockey tournaments and the place fills up. But it's probably a little early in the year for that."

"Please don't go to any bother," he said. "I can look after things myself."

"You might," said Lucille, "be better off at the Moonbeam. It's not fancy, but it's out on the highway. Maybe you saw it coming in. You probably wouldn't be bothered out there. It's just an idea."

"It's a good idea," said Fielding. "I'll have a look."

"They don't have a restaurant, but they'll serve you breakfast. You don't have to worry about supper anyway. You'll eat here with us."

"That's not necessary," he said.

"Of course it is. You've come all the way up today. Drove Sandy up. We're expecting you."

She was firing up another cigarette, inhaling deeply. "We got plenty to eat. Ray and Kelly and Cala are going to join us. Then we can go over to the funeral home. It'll be busy tonight. Dee's school friends will be there. They're mostly working this afternoon."

Sandy Levine smiled at him. "Lucille is right, Dan. Please join us."

"Fine then," he said.

"We'll eat around five thirty," said Lucille.

In Lucille Crowder he could detect no rancour towards him, only this polite and cautious interest in a man her daughter had been involved with; they had obviously been lovers, but Lucille Crowder probably knew little more than that. She doubtless surmised that Denise had had many lovers in her short life and this fellow now sitting in her living room, this middle-aged stranger in his grey slacks and blue blazer, had been the last one. He imagined she was trying to put it all together because everything had changed so quickly. In a matter of minutes her life had gone into a tailspin and she was still falling, her sightlines skewed. Yet a common decency impelled her to offer hospitality, even to the man who in some way must share part of the responsibility for her daughter's death.

They could now hear the front door opening and Lucille got up at once, reaching for her coat.

"That will be Ray," she said. With the cigarette in her mouth, she pulled on her dark coat, and to Fielding it was an oddly touching gesture; he could almost see her doing this in another time, late for something, a little flustered.

"Ray doesn't like to be kept waiting," she said. "He's just like his dad."

Then Ray Crowder was at the entrance to the living room looking uncomfortable, handsome in the shirt and tie, the Dockers and black leather jacket. Denise's kid brother. The youngster who couldn't stay out of trouble.

Crowder was frowning and Fielding wondered how many women had mistaken that dark, intense look for seriousness instead of what it might just be, chronic sullenness, the impatient stare of a man used to being looked at. Ray Crowder gave off waves of unfriendliness, but there could be no dispute about his looks—tall, dark-haired, a lady killer who could pick and choose among those on offer.

"Ray," said Lucille, "you remember Sandy from last summer? She used to work with Dee in New York."

Crowder said nothing, merely nodded at Sandy.

"And this is Dee's friend, Dan Fielding."

Dee's friend. That was how he would be identified and talked about up here. At the funeral home that night and tomorrow at church, women would whisper behind their hands. "That's Dee's friend. That's the man who was with her in England."

Fielding, who had been standing nearby, now offered his hand to Ray Crowder, and for a horrible moment it looked as if Crowder would ignore it and Fielding would have to swallow the insult. But finally Crowder gave him a firm handshake and said to his mother, "We better get going. It's almost two o'clock."

Lucille was patting the pockets of her coat. "I know, Ray. I know, but I can't find my damn gloves."

"Never mind your gloves," he said. "We're gonna be late. People will be waiting for us."

Lucille was already hurrying from the room. "I think I left them on the hallway table. Here they are," she cried a moment later. When they joined her, she was putting the gloves on. Del had come from the kitchen to see them off. She was standing in the hallway smelling of roast beef and wiping her hands on a dishtowel.

"Make yourselves at home, okay?" said Lucille. "There's beer and pop in the fridge if you're thirsty. Del will show you where. Sandy, I put towels on the bed."

"Thanks, Lucille."

"We'll be back around five."

"May I bring some wine for dinner?'" asked Fielding.

Lucille Crowder gave him an odd look, not exactly unfriendly but puzzled, and he wondered if he had breached some rule of household etiquette.

"Some wine would be nice," she said.

"Kelly is bringing the wine," said Ray Crowder. There was an intonation in his voice, a sarcastic colouring that reminded Fielding of Denise.

Fielding could sense Ray Crowder's dislike. Understandable. Here was the man who had taken his sister to some place in England where she was murdered. He didn't look after her the way a man was supposed to look after a woman in a foreign country. An old, soft-looking guy from the city. What was Denise thinking of? Maybe something like that was going through Ray Crowder's mind. Lucille followed her son out the door calling back to them, "See you later."

They watched her step up and into a red Dodge Ram with dark windows, a brutal-looking machine nudging the Honda. Crowder backed out swiftly and then gunned the truck down the street.

Fielding and the two women stood in the hallway without speaking until Sandy said, "Ray's a good-looking guy, isn't he?"

"All the girls are crazy about Ray," said Del. "Always have been. When he played hockey as a kid, the girls used to go to the rink just to watch him take his helmet off. He was pretty wild as a youngster. Goes out with a nice girl now though. Kelly got herself into a bad marriage when she was younger, but she's straightened her life out. Has a cute little girl. You'll see them tonight when they come for supper. I don't know if Ray's gonna marry her, but I wish he would. They make such a nice-looking couple. Ray looks like his father. Cliff Crowder was the best-looking man in Bayport. When he came home for the winter, we all envied Lucille. I don't mind saying that now, and I'd say it to her face if she was here. We all envied her.

Poor Cliff. He was such a big strapping fellow, but at the end I don't think the man weighed a hundred pounds. That cancer can turn you into a pitiful sight." Del stopped as if to acknowledge that there was nothing more to be said about the gruesome finality of cancer. "Well, I better get the vegetables peeled," she said, and turned for the kitchen.

"Can I help?" asked Sandy, though she didn't look to Fielding like the type of woman who would be entirely at home in the kitchen.

"Not at all. I can manage," said Del without looking around.

It felt strange to be there in Lucille Crowder's living room, standing by the front window with Sandy Levine, with a neighbour woman in the kitchen. They could hear Del at work with her pots and pans. These were people he didn't even know yesterday, and now they were all a part of something larger, strangers orbiting the enormous fact of Denise's sudden absence from the world. In England, he had been distracted by the police investigation, by the unfamiliar air of another country; he had moved through it on adrenalin and nerves. Now in this small Ontario town nearly a week later, his mind was clear enough but he felt peculiarly disoriented.

"I better get on my way," he said. "Look for a place to sleep tonight. I think I'll try that Moonbeam Motel."

"I noticed it on the way in," Sandy said. "It looked a little down-at-the-heels to me, but I take Lucille's point about the media. You're not likely to find any reporters out there, Dan."

Fielding was looking out the window at the street, but he could feel Sandy Levine's eyes upon him.

"I'll bet they've been after you," she said.

"Yes," he admitted. "And I haven't said anything to them,

which may have been a mistake." He walked to the hallway and took his raincoat from the closet. "I'll see you about five thirty," he said.

"Fine, Dan," she said. She was lighting a cigarette. "Good luck with the Moonbeam."

As he closed the front door he could hear the phone ringing. It was the middle of the afternoon, a quiet time with the children in school, and housewives watching soaps; a time for retired men to rake their lawns, and as he drove away, he saw along the street clear plastic bags filled with leaves. On his way in, he hadn't noticed them.

In Room 17 of the Moonbeam Motel, Fielding lay on the bed reading about the forthcoming shortage of water. According to Tom Lundgren, unless the developed world changed its consumption patterns, the shortage would be inevitable, probably within thirty years. Not Fielding's problem exactly, but certainly Heather's and billions of others'. A shortage of water throughout the world in thirty years! Even in Canada, if you could believe the professor with his tables and graphs, his pie charts and formidable sentences. Lundgren was no crank, and it all looked convincing enough to Fielding, though he had only reached page 98. There were 250 more pages. The manuscript was looking worn, its edges nicked from removing the rubber bands that held the pages together. He had always liked the heft and feel of a manuscript, the black words on white paper, a writer's thoughts transformed into substance. Now called *hard copy*. He knew the time was not far off

when all this would be obsolete, though he would likely be out
of it by then. Once more he wrapped the rubber bands around
A History of Water. It could be an important book, he thought.
Something worth doing. Where else were people going to get
this kind of detailed argument if not in a book? Certainly not
from television. Who could remember anything from television a day later? An hour later?

Room 17 was at the back of the motel overlooking the stub-
ble of a cornfield. When he checked in, the lone guest at the
time, he had asked for a quiet room, and so now he could hear,
but only faintly, the cars passing and the trucks gearing down
along the highway on the other side. His clothes were hanging
on racks near the door of this bare room with its bed and chair,
a television set on a dresser, a shower and toilet. It was enough
and its simple functionality suited him; he was far enough
away from the splashing fountain, the elevator music and bar
chatter he imagined were part of the Bayport Inn. The Moonbeam, he thought, was an ideal place for people in hiding.
There was something forlorn and illicit about it all, a room
near the highway on the edge of a town where a man alone
might watch a porn movie or write a suicide note. Or perhaps
both.

Years ago, mad Jack Balsam had told him how he lived in
places like this for several weeks. He was then fleeing the
wrath of one of his wives and seemingly had disappeared off
the face of the earth. Acquaintances wondered if he had
jumped into Lake Ontario. It turned out he was driving across
the country in a rented car, and he later claimed it was one of
the happiest periods in his troubled life. Eating in roadside
diners and chatting up the waitresses. "Banging" a few of

them, to use Balsam's 1940s lingo. Staying in places like the Moonbeam. Watching the chambermaid change his sheets in the morning. Lonely women, he said. Trying to make a dollar and keep it from the brute back at the trailer park. They were always grateful for a little attention.

"Some of the best tail in my life, Dan." Of course, Balsam was a habitual liar, and he could have invented most of it.

Fielding looked out the window at the cornfield and the darkening afternoon. It was nearly four o'clock and time to touch home base. But when he rang through, all he got was Claire's recorded voice. *You have reached the Fieldings, but none of us can come to the phone at the moment. Please leave a message at the tone, and one of us will get back to you as soon as possible.* He gave her the motel's goofy name and phone number, mentioned that he was going to the Crowders' for dinner and would call later. "Hope all is well and love to you both," he added, trying not to imagine the sardonic look crossing Claire's face at the word *love*.

On the dresser by the telephone were a bottle of Italian red wine and a pint of Scotch from which he had taken one drink. He now helped himself to another small one and undressed for a shower. His head was filled with Lundgren's graphs and statistics; the data was already a bit overwhelming and he was not a third of the way through. Some of it would have to be toned down. Academics fought for every syllable and integer of detail, yet they also wanted popular attention. There would be a skirmish or two over that. He should have been taking notes, but that could wait for the second reading. He didn't know Tom Lundgren well, had met him only twice, but knew he had a family, teenagers. In fact, a boy and girl Heather's age. Stepping into the shower, he wondered how the man, harbouring these dire predictions and knowing full well that most of us don't change our habits until it's too late, could bear to look at his children.

Ray Crowder's truck was in the driveway and behind it was a big sedan from another time, a heavy, old Buick from the looks of it. Fielding could see figures moving in the front room behind the partly closed drapes. Every light in the house seemed to be on. Clutching the wine, he got out of the car and walked across the street to the Crowder home and rang the doorbell. It was a damp evening and someone in the neighbourhood had his fireplace working. The mild, smokey air was pleasing. Through the window in the door, Fielding could see a woman in a skirt and blouse coming along the hallway from the kitchen. When she opened the door, Fielding remembered Denise's take on her brother's latest girlfriend. "Former exotic dancer with big hair." And even in the chaste blouse and skirt, this was an alluring young woman and she did have a head of abundant reddish-brown hair that fell about her shoulders. She stood by the open door taking his measure.

"You must be Mr. Fielding?"

"Yes, please call me Dan."

"Kelly Swarbrick," she said. "I'm Ray's friend."

She held the door open to let him pass, and he could smell her perfume, a scent from younger days when he had known a girl who wore this very fragrance. Pam Scott. Christ, that was thirty-seven years ago, his first year at university. Pam Scott. A big, horsey girl who had asked him to help her write an essay on *The Waste Land*. He went to her house somewhere in

Rosedale, and she met him at the door in plaid slacks and a man's white shirt. Her parents, she said, were out for the evening, and so they worked in her bedroom trying to make sense of Eliot's poem. Fielding finally concocted an ingenious argument for her essay and Pam Scott was so pleased that before long they had clambered into her bed. She had reeked of this perfume, and on his way home, Fielding could smell it as he walked along the quiet dark streets, repeating her name again and again until it sounded like nothing but a ball ricocheting around a squash court. Pam Scott. Pam Scott. Pam Scott.

Lucille Crowder was sitting on the sofa next to Sandy, and Del was still in the kitchen. He could hear her talking to someone. The dining-room table was set for dinner.

"Can I get you a drink?" asked Kelly. "A beer or some wine?"

"Maybe just a glass of wine," he said.

"Sure."

He handed her the bottle of wine and she took it into the kitchen. Sandy Levine was smiling at him, looking solid and dependable in a dark business suit and cream-coloured blouse. A girl of about eight was sitting in the chair looking at him with solemn curiosity.

"Hello again," said Lucille Crowder. "This is Cala, Kelly's daughter. Cala, this is Mr. Fielding. He was a friend of Dee's." The little girl continued to look at him, but said nothing. Like her mother she was a beauty with long reddish-golden hair and she was dressed for the occasion in a black velveteen dress and white leotards, patent leather shoes. A ribbon in her hair.

"How is the Moonbeam, Dan?" whispered Sandy.

"It will do just fine," he said. He could hear Ray Crowder's voice from the kitchen. He had been down in the basement getting something for Del, and now he walked into the dining room unscrewing the top of a jar. His mother was watching him.

"Oh, put those pickles in a dish, Ray, for goodness' sake," she said with her small, sharp laugh. "Don't leave the jar on the table like that." Crowder did as he was told, but he was still wearing his customary scowl.

Kelly Swarbrick returned with Fielding's wine. "Here you go," she said. "It's stuff we already opened. Hope you don't mind."

"Not at all," he said. "This is fine." Cala asked her mother if she was going to eat with everyone else.

"Of course you are. You didn't think we'd leave you out of things, did you?"

The little girl looked to be on the edge of a pout. "Why can't I just eat in the basement and watch TV?"

"Not tonight, honey," said her mother.

Ray had gone into the kitchen and Lucille began to talk about the visitors to the funeral home that afternoon. There were more than she'd expected, people in town she scarcely knew who remembered Denise and wanted Lucille to know how sorry they were for what happened. Sandy asked gentle questions about them. Who were they and what did they do? This, thought Fielding, was how people dealt with loss. Friends prepared meals and poured drinks. Filled in the silences when conversation faltered. Answered telephones and offered explanations to strangers. Life, as people were fond of saying, had to go on, even though at the moment it must seem to Lucille Crowder furiously unbearable.

"Okay, everybody. Come and get it," said Del. She was putting an enormous platter of roast beef on the table, while Ray Crowder carried in bowls of potatoes and green beans. There was a cabbage salad. Wineglasses were filled. Ray had a beer by his plate.

"Oh, Del," said Lucille, sitting down. "This all looks so good. You've gone to so much trouble. I wish I had a better appetite."

"Eat what you can, Lu," Del said briskly. "Don't worry about it." She was pulling the drapes across the dining-room window, closing out the trees and the lake beyond.

Lucille talked about her two sisters and their husbands who were driving from Montreal and would be arriving later in the evening. She had booked rooms for them at the inn. A brother now lived in Australia and could only send a telegram of condolence. Another brother had died years ago in a traffic accident. An old family friend, "a man Cliff sailed with for years," was also coming, but not until tomorrow. "Dear old Bonneverre," said Lucille. "I haven't seen him since Cliff's funeral." Again it was Sandy who elicited all this with her questions. Others ate and listened, except for the little girl who stirred the food around her plate, an elbow on the table and a fist on her cheek. The novelty of wearing her best dress on a weeknight was no longer the pleasure she had supposed it would be. She now looked determined to be cross about everything.

"Eat your dinner, hon," said her mother softly.

"I'm not hungry," said Cala.

Kelly looked across the table at Ray Crowder, but he was eating quickly, and seemed abstracted, sending out his message of indifference. *She's your kid. You handle it.* Lucille tried quiet encouragement, leaning into her and whispering. But the child was in a funk and could not be persuaded. After a few minutes, Kelly took her downstairs. Soon they could hear the squawk and gabble of cartoon characters. When she came back into the room, she looked flushed and apologetic.

"She's upset and asked if she had to go to the funeral home," Kelly said, sitting down. "She's worried about all that. Cala's never seen anyone . . ."

Lucille's hand was on her arm. "Kelly, it's all right. She doesn't have to go if she doesn't want to. You take her home after supper. She can come to the church tomorrow."

"I think she can handle the church," said Kelly, drinking some wine. "But tonight . . . it could be a shock at her age."

"It could be," said Del. "After Bill's funeral my grand-daughter had these awful dreams. Seeing her grandfather like that. Of course, she was a little younger than Cala at the time."

It was probably true, thought Fielding. He doubted whether Heather had ever seen a corpse. Claire's mother had been dead for thirty years and his own parents had died before he was married. Death surrounded kids nowadays in the movies and on television, but it was all just a big cartoon. It never really happened. The real thing, on the other hand— the person you once knew who is now lying in a box and won't be getting up anymore—that was another matter altogether.

There were apple and lemon pies and coffee, and afterwards the women began to clear the soiled dishes, carrying them into the kitchen. Fielding and Ray Crowder sat amid the debris of the meal without anything to say to one another. Then Crowder's cell phone began to beep and he got up and stood by the draped windows, listening to his caller. In the kitchen, Lucille was being mildly scolded.

"Lu, you'll be on your feet over there for two solid hours tonight," said Del. A drink or two had stirred the bossiness within her. "Go into the living room and relax. Take her in, Sandy. Kelly and I can do these things up."

Fielding escaped, climbing the stairs to the bathroom, where he took a long piss. By the hall light, he could see into the bedroom that overlooked the back lawn and the trees and lake. Here Lucille Crowder now slept alone. The two smaller rooms, one on each side of the hallway, had obviously been Denise's and her brother's. He could see Sandy Levine's suitcase at the foot of a bed. When he walked into the other room, he turned on the light and was startled by the books. Two entire walls had bookcases and they were filled. Denise seemed to have kept every book she read while growing up, and one could almost track her early progress through literature from childhood favourites like Nancy Drew and Judy Blume, to the required texts of high school. *The Chocolate Wars*, *A Separate Peace*, *The Catcher in the Rye*. And there were scores of books she must have sought out for herself. *The Good Soldier. To the Lighthouse. Portnoy's Complaint. Pictures from an Institution.* Where did she find such books? An entire shelf looked to have everything Henry James had ever written.

Taking down a copy of *To Kill a Mockingbird*, he stared at the large, round letters. *Denise Crowder. Bayport C.V.I. Grade 9. 1983–84.* At the end of each chapter were questions, probably taken off the blackboard for homework. *How are Scout and Jem different in their attitudes towards Atticus in this chapter? How does it affect their behaviour? Give examples.* Fielding could see her reading her careful responses aloud in class, her erotic gravity attracting the attention of even the dullest boy, sparing her the isolation of the plain Jane who likes to read.

There were also family pictures on the bookshelves and dresser. In one, Cliff Crowder, a big man with surly good looks, is standing in the backyard with Denise. She is thirteen or fourteen and the picture may well have been taken just about the time she was answering questions on Harper Lee's novel. The trees behind the two figures are smaller and leafless and there is snow on the ground. Denise is wearing a parka and toque, and she still looks cold though she is grinning at the camera. In her high school graduation photo, she is in the middle of the second row, primly serious in her gown. This is the picture that mothers will show their teenaged daughters in the years ahead, he thought.

"And that's the girl who was murdered in England. Denise Crowder. She went there with some man though he didn't kill her. I think she was abducted from a car or something."

And their daughters will look closer at the girl in the middle of the second row, hoping perhaps to divine in her face some warning, a hint of the calamitous end that awaited her.

From down the hallway came the sound of the toilet flushing and he wondered if he should leave Denise's bedroom. Yet he was moved by these photographs. Whether he liked it or not, he had now become a part of Denise Crowder's life, and these images of her childhood and youth seemed valuable and worth studying. He could hear footsteps in the hallway.

"Is that you, Dan? We wondered where you got to," said Lucille.

"I was just looking at these books and pictures," he said as she stood in the doorway.

"Yes," she said, "aren't these books something? I kept them after she went off to university. She bought them all herself, you know. Worked at the Dairy Queen on Lake Street on weekends and in the summers. Spent all her money on books. She'd go down to London and buy them there. She couldn't get those kinds of books up here. After she was out working, when she'd come home on weekends she'd say, 'Oh Mom, why don't you get rid of some of these? I'll take the ones worth keeping and you can have a garage sale or something. I'll never look at most of them again.' But you know what? I don't think she meant it. I think she kind of liked them here when she came back to visit. As she got older she never mentioned getting rid of them again."

Lucille had come into the room and was looking at the shelves. "As a little girl, Dee loved her books. I used to read to her every night, but she was reading by herself before she went to school. She knew her alphabet. She worked out the letters and put them together into words."

As he stood next to her, Fielding wondered if she was trying to gather strength for the evening ahead at the funeral home.

"I read too, Dan," she said. "Mostly mystery stories. I always liked them better than the romance things, which I always thought were foolish. And after Dee was working in publishing she would bring home books by Alice Munro or Carol Shields. I could read those and I enjoyed them. I understood the kind of people who were in those books. Cliff was a reader too, but mostly he liked history. He enjoyed books about war and boats, shipwrecks, that kind of thing."

She sat on the edge of the bed, and Fielding sat down beside her; he could see only half of Lucille's face in the dresser mirror, her piled-up hair.

"Cliff was an engineer on the *Tilden*," she said. "That's how we met. I got a job as a cook on that boat. A girlfriend of mine

worked on the *Tilden* and this other girl quit so they needed
someone. They were docked in Montreal then, unloading
grain, and this other girl had walked out on them. So my girlfriend asked me if I wanted the job. I didn't think so even
though I was out of work at the time. I'd been a waitress. It
was the year of Expo 67 and I was going to go down to the
park and try to get a job there. Better money, you see. But my
girlfriend persuaded me to go on the boat and have a look
around, so I did. We were in the galley, and this man came in
to make himself a cup of coffee. And I had never felt anything
like it before. I guess you could say it was love at first sight. So
help me God, I felt weak in the knees. Like some girl in a story-
book. This guy just looked over at me and that was it. Never
said a word at the time. After he left, I said to Annette, 'My
God, who is that? Do they all look like him?' She laughed at
that. 'No, they don't all look like him,' she said. 'Cliff's the second engineer. Married, but not very happy.'

"You know, I was only twenty-two years old, Dan, but I
remember thinking, I would like an adventure with a handsome guy like that and if his marriage is not good, then who
knows what can happen. It was unlike me, a Catholic girl with
a good upbringing to think like that, but I did. And I was not
bad-looking, if I say so myself." She gave another of her sharp,
angry laughs. "Not that I like to brag, but imagine! Lucille
Plante, a good Catholic girl with a strict upbringing deciding
to have an adventure like that. So I took the job and got to know
the man who would become my husband. It all seemed settled
in my head. I had met this big, handsome, English guy and I
was going to have an adventure with him. And, you know it all
worked out. Not right away, of course. His wife ran around.
She was . . ." Fielding watched her in the mirror.

"Strange . . . one of those flower children. Like Trudeau's wife. Cliff had a hard time with her. She ran away to the States with some hippies and he couldn't find her. It took almost two years before he got a divorce and we could get married. And that was a pain in the neck too because the Church would not marry us since Cliff was a divorced man." Lucille shrugged. "Today, I suppose you would just go away and live your life. But we wanted to get married and we did. I had to leave the Church. My parents were heartbroken. You know, I don't think my father every really forgave me. They never even came to the wedding.

"When we had the kids, they started to get used to the idea, but I don't think my father ever really liked Cliff. I think he believed that Cliff had stolen me from the Church. They would visit us for a week every winter and my father always made a big deal out of going to Mass on Sunday. I can still see him standing at the front door, all dressed up, pulling on his gloves and galoshes. And when he came back, the look we got! You'd have thought he was staying with heathens. I felt bad too. I felt the children were missing out on something. Once in a while, I would go to the Anglican Church here in town, but somehow it wasn't the same. My mother was okay about all this, but my father . . . he was always asking on his visits about the children's religious training. My father was very fond of Dee and he worried about her *salutiste*. You would say in English, I suppose, her salvation. My mother always said he should have been a priest, not a bus driver. And you know it hurt me to go like that between my father and my husband, because of course I loved them both. But you have to choose and I chose Cliff and I have never been sorry about that.

"We got married in Owen Sound. That was his hometown. In a United Church there. They didn't seem to mind a Catholic girl marrying a divorced man back in 1969."

Lucille stopped as if she had put a good deal of thought into what she was about to say.

"You know, I miss the old religion, Dan. You hear now about the priests and how bad some of them were with the kids. All that stuff. But still, I wish I had the old religion with me now. Right here inside me." She tapped her knuckles against her chest with surprising force. "At times like this I wish I could believe the way I used to. At my Grandfather Plante's funeral, I remember saying to my grandmother, 'Oh, Grandmaman, I am sorry,' And she said to me, 'Don't worry, little one. In time I will see your *grandpère* again in heaven and long, long after that, you and your brothers and sisters and mother and dad too, you will join us.' Of course I was just a girl then. Maybe nine or ten."

She began to weep quietly and Fielding put his arm around her shoulder. She leaned against him and whispered, "This is very hard, you know."

"I know," he said.

"For you too. You've been through a lot."

Fielding was silent and Lucille straightened herself, taking out a Kleenex.

"Well, enough," she said. "I want to show you a picture of Dee. My favourite."

She was blowing her nose as she went to the dresser and pulled out a small framed photograph from one of the drawers. Sitting down again next to him, she put on her glasses and this made her look older, a bit severe. He was reminded of Denise reading her manuscript on the plane.

"Look at this," she said, with another of her sharp little laughs. "My God, I should throw it out. It makes me so sad when I look at it, and yet I keep going back and back. This morning I must have spent an hour staring at the damn thing. There you are. You can see the mischief in her. That day her father was so mad at her. Dee wouldn't behave. She was doing all this fooling around while Cliff tried to take our picture. He had this new camera he was so proud of. The pictures came out as soon as you took them. Oh, he thought that camera was something. And Dee was just making the fool all the time. There is a word in English, I think."

"Mugging," he said.

"Yes. Mugging. That's the word. Look at her."

They both looked at the framed picture from the dresser drawer. Had Denise put it there one day, he wondered, because she no longer wished to see herself as a ten-year-old show-off? But that didn't seem like Denise; she would have been the first to admit that she liked attention. Maybe she just got tired of it and decided it was time to give another picture shelf space. It was odd to be sitting in her bedroom thinking of a day in her past when she decided to replace this photograph with another. The picture they were looking at had been taken on a freighter somewhere on the Great Lakes. A summer day and Lucille was standing on the deck between her two children. A small Ray Crowder looked quizzically at the camera, but Denise was laughing, making a face and standing on one leg like a stork. The other leg was neatly tucked behind her. Yes, she was mugging and probably irritating her father with his newfangled camera.

"Cliff was chief engineer when this was taken," said Lucille, "so we got to spend a couple of weeks every summer on the boat. Dee was ten then and her brother was eight. Twenty-two years ago last July. I should throw the damn thing out," she said, getting up and returning the photograph to the drawer. "You know, Dan, my two sisters want me to move back to Montreal and get an apartment near them, and sometimes at two o'clock in the morning it looks good. But then I think this. My husband is buried in the cemetery here and Dee . . . she will be in the ground near him tomorrow. Me too one day. How can I leave that? And then Ray is here with Kelly and Cala. Maybe Ray will get married. Who knows?"

She sat down again beside him. "Nobody knows. My God, a week ago Del and I were on our way to the Legion." She looked at her watch. "Almost to the hour. Thursdays are our euchre nights. A couple of widows going out to play some cards. Just a week ago. So who knows what can happen in a week, eh?" She had taken out a cigarette and lighter. "I read once in this pamphlet that George Gladstone gave me when Cliff died. This pamphlet said that you should never make any big decisions for six months." She shrugged and lit her cigarette, inhaling deeply, talking through the smoke. "I shouldn't be smoking in her room. I don't know what I'm thinking of."

They sat for a moment in silence and then, getting up, Lucille said, "We better go now or Ray will have a conniption fit. That's what his father used to call it when Ray lost his temper. 'He is having a conniption fit,' Cliff would say. 'Let's go now.'"

The others were waiting at the bottom of the stairs, Ray Crowder looking up at them as they descended, as if wondering what they could have been talking about. Kelly was kneeling, helping Cala with the zipper on her jacket, which seemed to be stuck, and Sandy in a smart, dark coat was smiling up at them.

"Lucille," said Kelly, looking up briefly as she worked on the child's coat. "I'm going to take Cala home. I've phoned Tracy and she's going to look after her, so I'll see you guys at the funeral home. Okay?"

"That's fine, Kelly," said Lucille. "Where's Del?"

"She's gone home to get dressed," said Sandy. "She'll make her own way over to the funeral home."

"That's good." They all filed through the front door and across the lawn to the truck and cars.

In the car Sandy said, "I'm not really looking forward to this, Dan. I've always had a problem with dead people. And Denise . . . Jesus, she's so young." She was staring out the window at the lighted houses. Halloween decorations were already up on some of the front porches and lawns. Fielding watched the truck's brake lights blazing two blocks ahead as Ray Crowder stopped and then turned right.

Sandy was looking over at him. "I guess you had to identify the body over in England."

"Yes," he said. "They phoned me on Sunday morning, and I had to go up to Exeter."

"That must have been awful for you."

He wouldn't easily forget that Sunday morning and the walk along the green-tiled corridor with Kennedy. The antiseptic smell and the mark on her cheek. It *had* been awful, but he said nothing more about it and they drove along in silence.

A few minutes later they saw the truck in the parking lot beside a large brick house near the main street. On the lawn was an illuminated sign, white with blue lettering. *George Gladstone & Sons. Funeral Directors.* Several people were going up the front walk. The house, he thought, was probably once the home of some prominent family that had made its fortune in shipping or lumber. He and Sandy got out of the car and followed the others up the steps to the tall front doors that opened onto a dark hallway. There a stout young woman with a pleasant face was directing the visitors. There were three viewing rooms and this evening two were occupied. The young woman smiled at Fielding and Sandy, directing them to Room 1. Organ music was playing discreetly in the background and Fielding recognized an old reliable, Handel's *Largo*. They had played it at his own father's funeral.

At the entrance to the room they signed the visitors' book. In the room, a couple of dozen people had already gathered and were talking in little groups. Fielding watched a woman hugging Lucille, who was standing with Ray near a table covered with flowers and cards. Fielding and Sandy were strangers, and so they were glanced at as they entered. But people had seen him on television; he could tell from the way they looked at him. The line was moving slowly past the coffin and they waited. Then a couple in front of them finished looking and stepped aside, the man still clasping his hands behind his back. Fielding and Sandy moved forward and stood in front of the half-opened casket staring down at Denise. Fielding thought he heard a small gasp from Sandy. Someone, perhaps the stout young woman with the pleasant face, had drained the blood from the body and filled it with formaldehyde, applied cosmetics and combed the dry hair. The bruising around the throat and the mark on her cheek were gone. Sandy said nothing, but she was holding tightly onto his arm. Fielding could hear the laboured breathing of an old man who was standing behind them awaiting his turn. And so they moved off to the side.

On the table holding the flowers was Denise's university graduation photograph with its customary air of forced earnestness. Not like her at all, he thought. Not one bit and he felt an obscure irritation with the photographer. Lucille was introducing them to neighbours and acquaintances: the mechanic who serviced her car, a woman from down her street, a couple from her euchre club who travelled with her on outings to the casino at Point Edward. They eyed him carefully, neither friendly nor hostile; they were leery of him though and he could understand that. For Sandy the hard part was now over and talking to these people about Denise would not be so difficult. Fielding watched her move easily amid the comforting murmur of the room.

Standing next to Fielding was a small, elderly woman who, like him, seemed not quite at ease there. He found himself looking down at the head of tightly permed white hair, the beaky profile. A faint sweetness in the air around her. An old sachet perhaps, from a dress taken off a wooden hanger. She looked up at him and he bent forward to hear.

"My name is Florence Robertson. Who are you?"

"Dan Fielding," he said.

She had tilted her head back to appraise him, the light glinting off her glasses. His name obviously didn't register with Florence Robertson.

"I was a friend of Denise's," he said. "We worked together in publishing in Toronto."

"Is that so?" said the old woman.

Apparently he had happened upon the one person in the room who had not read about him in the newspapers, or seen his baffled face peering out the taxi window on television. But maybe she lived alone in one of the large brick houses nearby, a house she'd lived in all her life. The last of a vanishing breed, the solitary virgin. Reading her library novel or working on her crossword puzzles. Still gamely driving her twenty-year-old Chrysler to church every Sunday. Listening to CBC Radio and scoffing at the trash on television. She could easily have missed his connection to Denise Crowder.

"Yes," she said. "I heard that Denise went into the book business. When I taught her, I thought she might one day become an author."

She looked too old to have taught Denise, but he was anxious to hear her story; she was someone to talk to in this roomful of strangers.

"What grades did you teach her, Miss Robertson?"

"I taught her in her last two years at the collegiate, when I was head of the English Department. As it happened, they were also my last two years. I retired the year Denise graduated."

"Was she a good student?" he asked.

Florence Robertson was again directing her reproachful gaze around the room. This rudeness, Fielding decided, was not intentional, but merely a part of her disposition. Nor had she lost the thread of the conversation.

"Denise," she said, "was an excellent student. A great reader. Well ahead of the others. And she wrote very fine essays and book reports. However, she was also . . ." Florence Robertson pursed her thin lips in search of the exact word to describe Denise Crowder's shortcoming. At last she said, "Denise was wilful. She could not be moved on certain opinions she held in the classroom. We had our battles, Denise and I." Having summed up Denise's major character flaw, the old woman stepped back as if to guess at Fielding's. She appeared to have no curiosity about his connection with her former student whose life after high school seemed to hold no interest for her. This starchy and solipsistic old woman had known Denise at a precise time in her life, and that had been enough to bring her out for this evening. When Fielding looked her way again, she was inspecting the cards of sympathy on the table.

The room was now warm and crowded, and he eased his way towards the entrance where people were lined up. Surely, thought Fielding, there were many here out of nothing more than lurid curiosity; someone from their town had been murdered and murder has a glamour all its own. They wanted to look at her. But he felt restless, smothered by the press of bodies around him. He longed for the drab isolation of the Moonbeam Motel with its window overlooking the cornfield and the shower with its stained walls. He wanted to phone Claire and explain what had happened between him and Denise in Frankfurt and England. Wanted to tell her how these things came to pass and how sorry he was and could they not talk about it when he got home? Making his way through the people, he felt a kind of panic bearing down upon him. Wondered why he had come up to this town a day early when he could have waited until tomorrow and arrived with the others. Yet how eager he had been to get out of Toronto this morning. How exhilarated he had felt in that restaurant only hours ago.

He made it to the hallway where the lineup extended to the front door, and leaning against the wall he closed his eyes.

"Are you all right, sir? Would you like a glass of water?" He opened his eyes and saw the people in the line staring at him. The young woman in the black dress and dark stockings said, "Why don't you come along to the office and sit down for a while?"

"Yes, thank you. I'd like that," he said, walking along beside her past the front door towards the office. He was sweating a little, but there was no pain in his chest or arms. Probably his blood pressure had spiked again in that crowded room. On a chair in the office he tried some deep breathing and that seemed to calm him. The young woman's name was Sharon. He noticed the name tag on her dress as she handed him a glass of water.

"Feeling better now?"

"Yes, thanks," he said, looking up at the round, amiable face. She looked like a big farm girl who had found her place in the world by helping others bury their dead. A useful trade and not for the faint of heart. He drank the water greedily.

"If you'd like to stay here for a few minutes, that's fine," she said, "but I have to go back out. There's quite a crowd tonight."

"Yes, of course," he said. "Go ahead, please. I was just a little woozy for a few minutes. I'm fine now."

"Are you sure? Would you like me to tell anyone in particular where you are?"

"No, I'm fine. I'll be out in a few minutes."

"Okay, then. Take your time, sir," she said, lightly touching his shoulder as she left and closing the door behind her.

The office was sedate, old-fashioned except for the computer at a table to the side of the desk. There were pictures along a wall of the Gladstone generations, men in dark suits standing beside hearses, big boxy cars giving way to more streamlined models as the figures in the photographs aged over the years. Across from him was the desk and chair where George Gladstone likely sat while calling him last Sunday. Fielding waited a few more minutes and then left. There was no longer a lineup at the door, and Ray Crowder was standing by the entrance to the viewing room, talking to a man who was leaving. As Fielding approached, Crowder nodded to him.

"Do you want to go out for a drink after this?" he said. Fielding looked into the room, which was still crowded. The offer of a drink was there, delivered in Crowder's tight-lipped, sardonic manner. Take it or leave it and Fielding was inclined to leave it. Why would he want a drink with this sullen young man who obviously didn't like him? Yet he felt an obligation to Denise, to her family in whatever guise they appeared. He hoped the invitation included others, maybe Kelly and Sandy, and he said, "Sure."

"A friend of mine would like to meet you," Ray said. "He used to go out with Denise."

Fielding was sorry now he had accepted. He was not interested in meeting one of Denise's old boyfriends. Why would he be? What could they possibly have in common?

Ray was now talking to a couple. The woman was signing the guest book.

"Hey, thanks for coming, Brent. Sheila."

"No problem, Ray," said the man. "You take care now."

Crowder turned to Fielding. "We should be out of here in about twenty minutes. You can follow me."

"What about Sandy?" Fielding asked.

"Kelly will take her back with Mom. Don't worry about it." And he was gone, working his way through the still-crowded room.

Walking down the hallway in search of a toilet, Fielding passed the open door to Room 3; glimpsed the pale, bald head of the corpse on display. A half-dozen people had gathered around the widow who was seated nearby; they were talking quietly among themselves. A young man came along the hallway and smiled at Fielding.

"Are you looking for the washroom, sir?" he asked. On his lapel was the name George.

"Yes."

"Just down the hall on your left."

"I'm with the Crowder family," said Fielding. "My name is Dan Fielding. Did I speak with you on the phone from England? I was with Miss Crowder."

The young man smiled. "You spoke to my dad, Mr. Fielding. George the Third they call me around here."

Fielding could remember the calm, Canadian voice travelling under the Atlantic Ocean towards him last Sunday. It had helped.

"Your father knew exactly what to do. It relieved my mind. I would like to have thanked him."

"Well, Dad's on a call tonight with my brother, Geoff. They're out in the township, so they'll be a while. But I'll tell him what you said, Mr. Fielding. He'll appreciate your comments."

In the parking lot he stood with Sandy and Lucille. They were having a cigarette while they waited for Kelly and Ray, who were talking near the front door of the funeral home. In the shallow light of the parking lot, Lucille's face looked drawn.

"How is it going, Lucille?" Fielding asked.

"My feet are tired," she said without looking at him. She sounded out of sorts. "I don't know what's happened to my sisters," she said. "I hope to God they haven't been in an accident. They should have been here by now. They'll want to see Denise."

It was the first time she had used her daughter's full name. A sign perhaps of irritation at how matters were unfolding, but maybe a glimpse too of the long slog ahead when everyone has left, and she faces the winter afternoons alone, wondering what to do about the books and pictures, the summer clothes hanging in the closet. Afternoons when she's likely to ask herself whether it isn't a bit pointless to stop smoking. He watched Kelly and Ray walking towards them across the lawn; Ray was on his cell phone and Kelly was holding onto his other arm as she picked her way carefully across the damp grass in her high heels.

Lucille said, "Dan, you make sure that Ray doesn't get into the liquor tonight. Just beer is all he should be drinking."

"I'll do my best, Lucille," he said, wondering how in the world he could be expected to stop Ray Crowder from drinking whatever he felt like drinking tonight.

"Sorry to keep you guys waiting," said Kelly. She had put a scarf on her head and was working the key into the lock of her car. Crowder, still talking on the cell phone, had gone off to lean against his truck. Fielding watched the women getting into the car; he was trying to figure out the possible contours of the next hour or two with Ray Crowder. In the back seat of the Buick, Lucille, a small huddled figure, rolled down her window and called out, "You be careful in that truck tonight, Ray."

As he bent into his phone to listen, Crowder absently waved to his mother.

The big car moved slowly out of the parking lot, with Kelly braking cautiously as she approached the entrance to the street. In the moist night air the windshields were coated with mist and Fielding's hair felt wet. Crowder had put his cell phone away and was opening the door of his truck with one hand, loosening his tie with the other.

"Lyle is just leaving the arena," he said. "He'll meet us out there. You follow me, okay?"

"Okay," said Fielding, getting into the Honda. Presumably Lyle was Denise's old boyfriend, and he was leaving an arena, which meant that he must play hockey, or coach it or watch it or do something with it. In the lacunal code of small-town communication, the visitor was expected to fill in the blank spaces himself. And so again he was following the brake lights of the red pickup through a town that now looked mostly deserted, the main street a dead zone with only a pizza joint and a Chinese restaurant still open. Farther out on Lake Street, though, the gas stations and fast-food places were all in lights, and he followed the truck into a wide lot next to a roadhouse. When he turned off the ignition, Fielding could already hear the deep, thudding notes of a bass guitar. With his hands in his pockets, Crowder stood waiting for him by the entrance.

Blackie's was a large, plain room with exposed beams and a bar running along one side. There were dozens of tables and a few couples dancing to the piped-in rockabilly. Waitresses carried trays of beer among the patrons who were in their twenties or thirties, the men in jeans and shirts and caps, the young women in low-slung denims and T-shirts. A lot of flesh and tattoos on display and, in the air, a cheerful raunchiness laced with menace. A meat market, thought Fielding. Beer and tits and testosterone. It probably wouldn't take much to start a fight in the place. Crowder led the way through the crowd towards a table and a beefy-looking man

in a hockey jacket. He was combing fingers through his thick
blond hair, as if he'd just arrived. On the table was a tractor
cap, a pitcher of beer and three glasses. The bar was smokey
and hot and Fielding draped his raincoat over the back of a
chair feeling absurdly overdressed. The blond-haired man
was watching him, waiting perhaps to be introduced.
Fielding stuck out his hand.

"Dan Fielding."

The man looked at him blankly and shook his hand. "Lyle
Parsons. How are you doing?"

"I'm all right, thanks," said Fielding.

"He was with Denise in England," said Crowder, sitting
down and filling the glasses with beer.

Parsons nodded. "A terrible thing."

"Yes," said Fielding.

They drank their beer and all three looked across at the
television above the bar. A hockey game, the tiny figures
swirling across the ice, the referees in striped jerseys following the play. A woman was singing of heartbreak. There was
a clumsy silence among the three of them and Fielding was
glad when Crowder asked Parsons how his team looked this
year.

Parsons' fleshy, handsome face brightened. "They're going
to be okay. I got three or four really strong defencemen and
the Thompson boy is back in goal for another year. We'll be
all right behind the blue line. The forwards . . ." He shrugged.
"We're a little thin upfront. We may have trouble scoring. But
nobody is going to get too many on us either."

Crowder looked across at Fielding. "Lyle coaches a ban-
tam team. We used to play hockey together. He's with the
OPP now."

Had Crowder brought him to this place to show him Denise's old flame, now a policeman and solid citizen who spends his Thursday nights coaching kids' hockey? Did he want Fielding to look at the man Denise could have married if she hadn't had such big-shot ideas about herself? And where had those big-shot ideas led her anyway? To guys like the dork sitting beside him in his grey flannels and blazer, his polished brogues and the fruity green raincoat with the fancy shoulder straps. A guy she went off to Europe with and we all know what happened over there. Something like that was probably going through his mind, thought Fielding, as he listened to the two men talking about the road construction that was underway just north of town. From their conversation, Fielding deduced that Ray Crowder earned his living driving a truck that was currently hauling gravel. He also learned that Kelly Swarbrick worked at the new call centre on the outskirts of town. From time to time Fielding stole a glance at Lyle Parsons. Maybe he was somewhere in that high school picture on Denise's bookshelf, one of the taller guys in the back row. And what if she had married him? Gone off to university and returned as a schoolteacher. Settled down with this man and had a couple of kids. They would be seven or eight now, and she would be home reading her novel while Lyle coached at the arena or worked a night shift, chatting up the folks at the 24-Hour Coffee House on the highway. Yet it was hard to fit the Denise Crowder he had known into this picture.

A young man, slightly drunk, had come over to the table, and leaning down put an arm around Crowder's shoulders. "I'm sorry to hear about your sister, man."

"Thanks," said Crowder quietly, without moving.

The man straightened up. "You take care, Crowder, okay?"

"Yeah, sure," he said, watching the man move away through the crowd. "Dumb prick," he muttered.

"You got that right, Ray," said Lyle Parsons as they watched the man's mild stagger. He disappeared down a corridor towards the toilets and Fielding was left to imagine that there had been something going on between him and Crowder, some bad blood and now, with Denise's death, a truce of sorts had been declared. He wondered how many fragile arrangements like this were part of life in a town like Bayport.

"Hey, we need some more beer," said Crowder, waggling the empty pitcher. Lyle Parsons already had his arm in the air. "How about a bite to eat too? I was thinking of some wings."

Crowder was slouched in a kind of captain's chair. There was one to each table.

"Sure," he said. "I could eat a few."

When Parsons looked his way, Fielding said, "Why not?" He was conscious of quickly adopting the laconic style of local discourse. This verbal colouring was a habit he could seldom resist when travelling. Returning once from an editors' conference at Southern Methodist University (*The Perils of Publishing Fiction*), he noticed Claire looking at him with a puzzled expression, asking finally, "Why are you talking like that?" And he realized that without thinking about it he was drawling like a Texan.

The waitress in jeans and a black T-shirt placed another pitcher of beer on the table and took an order for thirty wings, medium heat. Parsons filled the glasses.

"What time is the funeral tomorrow, Ray?"

"Two o'clock."

"St. John's?"

"Yes."

Lyle Parsons looked down at his big hands encircling the glass. "It'll be a circus, I bet. The TV people are already in town. They're staying at the inn. Cooney told me he saw their truck this afternoon."

Crowder was looking up at the game on the television screen above the bar. "You got that right. It'll be a circus. They don't fucking well need to try talking to me. I'm not interested in saying anything to them. They better leave Mom alone too."

"Don't blame you there," said Parsons. "They can get really pushy. I've seen it after bad accidents. You remember that one up on Northport Road last spring when those four Indian kids got killed? The TV people were all over those funerals like a bad smell. They were interviewing everyone's grandmother. People were crying. Pulling their hair out. That was a circus." He looked across at Fielding. "I suppose you know all about that. They were after you down in Toronto."

"Yes, they were there all right."

"I saw you on TV when you were out at the airport. You looked a little spooked."

"Spooked is a good word," said Fielding, and Parsons gave him a funny look, as if his word were being ridiculed; in fact, Fielding thought *spooked* was as good a term as any to describe his appearance on the box.

"So," said Parsons, finishing his beer, "how long have you known Denise?"

"Since the summer," said Fielding. "She came to work for us in June. Actually, she came up for the interviews in May."

"So you were, like, her boss?"

"Not exactly her boss. I did interview her for the job along with several other people in the company."

"But you were over her in the company, right? She was junior to you."

"We pretty well treated one another as equals. But I was senior editor, yes. I had been there longer, obviously."

He could see where Parsons wanted to take this. He saw Fielding as the older man with power over a younger employee; he had persuaded her to accompany him to Europe and then had taken her to a resort town on the south coast of England for the weekend. In other words, he was a man who had abused his position of power in the workplace, blah, blah, blah. But then Parsons was a cop and a cop's mentality was to look for someone to blame. Still, Fielding resented the big hick's presumption. What did he know about it anyway? If he wanted to believe his myth about the evil master and the helpless maid, he wouldn't be alone; most people were probably construing the narrative in the same way. He didn't feel like defending himself and was grateful when the waitress brought their food.

All three of them looked at the enormous platter of barbecued chicken wings with the bowl of blue cheese sauce and the celery sticks.

"We better get another pitcher," said Crowder, and the waitress smiled at him. He was a sympathetic figure to all the women in Blackie's tonight, thought Fielding. Not only the brooding good looks but also the tragic loss of his sister would appeal to them. There wasn't a woman in the room who wouldn't take him home and comfort him in any way she could.

"Okay," said Lyle Parsons, "but that's it, I think. Drinking and driving, gentlemen." He laughed grimly.

The three ate wordlessly, looking up now and then at the hockey game. They wiped their mouths with napkins and drank more beer, though Fielding already had had enough. Parsons was now paying attention to the task at hand. A big man with food in front of him. The waitress came by again.

"Everything okay, guys?"

Parsons looked up, pausing to admire her chest. "How about some more napkins, Heidi?"

"No problem."

A few moments later Ray Crowder said, "Where exactly were you when my sister was murdered by that English bastard?" He was holding a piece of chicken, looking at it as if maybe he wanted to throw it at someone, most likely me, thought Fielding. So here it was at last. The reason why he was in Blackie's with Ray Crowder and Lyle Parsons. They wanted details.

"I was in the car," said Fielding. "We'd both been sleeping and then Denise woke up." He hesitated. "She had to go. Had to urinate. It was dark. Nobody was around, or so we thought. So she got out of the car and I went back to sleep. I was barely awake when she got out of the car."

Both men were now staring at him, trying, he supposed, to imagine the scene.

"Where was all this happening?" asked Parsons.

"We had stopped in the afternoon," said Fielding. "At a lookout, a scenic spot off the road. There were steps down to the beach, so we took a walk and then it began to rain and we came back to the car." He wasn't going to tell them about seeing Woodley on the beach. Things were precarious enough.

"Why would you be sleeping in the car?" asked Parsons. He looked serious now, even a little unfriendly. These were the same questions the cops had asked him in England, and they would be asked again at the trial.

"We were both tired," he said. "Neither of us had slept well all week. And we'd had a couple of drinks there in the car. It was raining hard." He stopped. There was no way to put a good face on what had transpired in that car park last Saturday. Parsons and Crowder had stopped eating; perhaps it had struck them both as singularly obscene to be eating barbecued chicken while listening to this man tell his sordid tale. Nor was it difficult to figure out that sex was at the heart of everything that had happened. He had seen it in their faces when he was trying to explain why he and Denise were asleep in the car. But neither of these men was prepared to go down that road. Ray Crowder did not want to hear about him having sex with Denise in the car, and neither did the old boyfriend.

Crowder was staring again at the television screen. "So she got out of the car to take a piss, and that's the last you saw of her alive?"

"Yes," said Fielding. "It was dark and I didn't imagine for a moment that there was anyone else around."

Ray Crowder continued to look up at the television. He seemed to be waiting for more information. Finally he asked, "Well, when the fuck did you think something was wrong?"

"When I woke up," said Fielding. "That was maybe an hour later. Maybe an hour and a half. I can't really be sure because I don't know exactly what time it was when Denise left the car. But it was nearly seven thirty when I woke up."

"And what did you do then?" asked Parsons.

"Naturally, I wondered where she was. So I got out of the car and looked around the parking area. At first I thought she might have lost her way in the dark. Stumbled down the cliff-side maybe, but that seemed unlikely. I just had no idea."

That, of course, was not true. He was dissembling. He did have an idea about what might have happened to her, and it had filled him with horror and panic. He could very well remember thinking about the man on the beach, that minatory face and frenzied stride, the oddness of him. But the version of the story recounted here in this noisy, fourth-rate saloon, sitting next to Denise's brother and Lyle Parsons, would not include his knowledge of Woodley's presence on the beach. He would not tell them how, as he wandered around that god-forsaken car park in the rain last Saturday night, he already had an inkling of what might have happened. He realized that this was not a sterling moment in his life, but it was the way it had to be for now.

"Then I went back to the car and phoned the police."

"Jesus," Crowder muttered.

"He must have been waiting out there in the dark," Fielding said. "You wouldn't have expected a man to be out there waiting in that downpour."

"And so he grabbed her," said Crowder quietly.

"Yes. Apparently he had a van somewhere, but I couldn't see anything."

Crowder looked at him briefly. "No, you were sleeping."

"Easy, Ray," said Parsons.

"Yes," said Fielding. "I was sleeping."

Crowder pushed himself forward, overturning an empty glass, which Parsons adroitly caught before it rolled off the table. Crowder was leaning in on his elbows, his face mere inches from Fielding's.

"You should have taken better care of her, Mister. Out there in the middle of fucking nowhere in the rain. With a fucking lunatic walking around."

"Come on now, Ray," Parsons said. "The man didn't know the guy was out there."

Crowder had slumped back in his chair and was staring again at the television screen. He looked so disgusted with everything that Fielding felt sorry for him. One of the teams had scored a goal and there was cheering at the bar. With the others, Fielding watched the endless replays of the goal.

For Lyle Parsons, the worst of the narrative seemed to be over. He dabbed a chicken wing in the blue cheese sauce. "So they picked up this guy the next morning?"

"Actually," said Fielding, "Woodley's brother-in-law brought him in. Woodley had been living with his sister and brother-in-law, who has a plastering business or something. They were away for the day and when they got back and Woodley wasn't there, they got worried. Then the brother-in-law noticed that his van was gone and Woodley didn't even have a driver's licence."

"Why didn't he call the police?" asked Parsons.

"I don't know the answer to that. Maybe he thought there was no point in involving the police then. So they sat up waiting for him and when he showed up about two o'clock in the morning, the brother-in-law suspected something and I guess he finally got out of him what happened and took him to the police. They phoned me at the hotel later that morning."

Parsons was leaning in on his elbows. He now seemed professionally interested. "And the guy had been in prison before?"

"Yes. The police told me he'd served eight years for an attempted rape or sexual assault. The victim was the daughter of a woman he was living with then. I'm not clear about the

details, only that he served all his time. He was released last
Christmas."

Crowder snorted in disgust. "These guys get out. It's a
fucking joke, isn't it? He gets out and what? seven, eight
months later, he does it again. The fucking cops don't do anything about it."

Parsons looked across at him. "I know where you're coming from, Ray, but don't blame the police. The man served his
time."

"They should keep an eye on guys like that," said Crowder.
"They should keep them under surveillance or something.
You can't have them walking around the fucking streets like
that."

"We can't keep an eye on everybody, Ray. You know that.
If the man had been out on parole, then yes, I could see it. A
man on parole. We keep an eye on him. But this man had
served his sentence." Parsons shook his big head in wonder-
ment. "It was just bad luck. But if you ask me, Mister, I don't
think you had any business taking a young woman out to that
place and drinking in a car like that. My God, what were you
thinking of?"

"He wasn't thinking," said Crowder, still looking at the TV.
"He was sleeping."

It was surely time to leave, thought Fielding. He didn't
really have to sit in this joint and be scolded by these two guys,
though he couldn't blame Ray Crowder for feeling the way he
did. This afternoon Ray had looked into a coffin and seen the
painted shell of what used to be his sister. Tomorrow he would
watch that coffin being lowered into the ground. Maybe like
Laertes he would try to throttle Fielding at the graveside. And

all this misery, spreading like a dark stain across the ocean to this roadhouse in Ontario, had been caused by one man who was now sleeping in his cell somewhere in England, dreaming perhaps of other young women in deserted car parks or alone on Sunday walks in country lanes. In a few hours, he would awaken to his porridge and tea, his hour in the exercise yard, the visit from the Salvation Army man who might read a passage from the Bible, which George Allan Woodley might attend to or not. Who could possibly fathom the mind of a man who inhabits his own world and ministers solely to his own urges? All that can be known for certain, thought Fielding, is that such men spoil the lives of others.

Over the noise of the roadhouse, he was trying to listen to Lyle Parsons, who was talking about Denise and high school days in Bayport. How he had lived on a farm on the tenth line and was bussed into town for high school. How he had admired Denise Crowder from afar, but didn't work up the courage to ask her out until Grade 12. How surprised he was when she said okay. Listening to all this, Fielding could see Denise as a sexy little seventeen-year-old, joking with this big blond farm boy by a drinking fountain on some long-ago Friday noon hour.

"She was one smart girl," said Parsons. "Always reading, but she was fun too. A good sport. A lot of those girls who were smart were often stuck-up. Do you remember Leah Seward, Ray? And Bernice Coleman? God, they were stuck-up."

"They wouldn't say shit if their mouths were full of it," said Crowder.

"You got that right," Parsons said. "But Denise just fit in anywhere. She'd go to parties. Take a drink."

Of course she would, thought Fielding. But not because

she was a "good sport," which was how Lyle Parsons wanted to remember her. She went because she was curious—not only about what was in books, but also about what went on at parties. What a boy's hard-on felt like in her hand in the back seat of a car. What a second slug of Captain Morgan's and Coke did to her head.

"She was careful though," said Parsons. "I never saw her drunk. She'd have a couple and that was it. Your mother can be proud of the way she raised that girl."

"She was a good kid," said Ray Crowder, who now looked bored. He seemed to have exhausted his rage and gave the impression of wanting to be left alone.

When his cell phone rang, he slumped backwards in the captain's chair and listened, muttering a reply from time to time. His caller had to be Kelly Swarbrick, thought Fielding, for only she could tease a grin from this unhappy young man. She wanted him home and in her bed and when he finished listening, Crowder seemed in better spirits.

"Women," he said to Parsons, "always think you're going to get wasted and run your truck into a tree. Christ Almighty, I got thirty thousand dollars sitting out in that parking lot."

"Well," said Parsons, "you have to admit that some do just that, Ray. I've seen enough of them wrapped around trees and other things too."

"Well, not me, Constable," said Crowder, leaning forward. "Want to try that Breathalyzer thing on me?"

Parsons gave him a sour smile. The word *constable* seemed to rankle him; maybe by now he should have been further up the ladder. But Crowder was enjoying himself. Mockery suited him. Humour and sarcasm were one and the same.

"We'll all be just a little careful tonight, and everything

should be just fine. You didn't drink much," said Parsons, turning to Fielding. "You should be okay."

"I'm not much of a beer drinker," Fielding said.

"Well, we could have ordered something fancier for you," said Crowder.

"I think I'll be on my way," Fielding said, getting up and reaching for his coat.

"You staying at the inn?" asked Parsons.

"No, I'm at the motel just down the road."

Crowder grimaced. "The Moonbeam? Jesus, it's a dump. You better check the sheets."

"Well, it's not far at least," said Parsons.

"How much do I owe you?" asked Fielding.

The big man waved his hand lazily over the table. "Never mind that."

"You're our guest," said Crowder slowly.

Fielding shrugged. "Well, I guess I'll see you tomorrow at the church."

"I guess," Crowder said, looking up again at the hockey game.

It was a relief to be outside, inhaling the damp mild air, and to know that he would never again have to set foot in Blackie's. They had wanted some idea of what happened in England, and he had tried to give them that. It was enough and he was glad to get in the car and drive on to the motel. There were only three other cars parked in front of the units. As he passed the office, Fielding saw a woman sitting in a chair at the front desk watching the news. Images of a city somewhere in the

Middle East. A crowd of angry, dark-haired men in shirt sleeves carrying a coffin through the streets. Punching the air with their fists.

The little red button was blinking on the phone, just as it had in the hotel in Glynmouth, and when he picked it up, he heard Claire's voice asking him to call home. She sounded irritable and Fielding hesitated, wondering if he should pour himself a nightcap before talking to her. But he thought better of it and when she answered, he said, "Hi. It's me."

"Yes, hi. Where have you been all night?"

"I was at the funeral home until nine and then I went out with Denise's brother and an old boyfriend of hers. They wanted to grill me. Took me to this bar on the highway. I don't know why I went. I suppose I felt I owed something to her brother. He was furious with me, of course."

"Sounds like fun."

"Yes. Well, I survived."

Claire paused. "Heather's had a really bad day."

"What's the matter?" he asked. "What's happened?" He could feel the tension gripping him, the adrenalin doing its work.

"She's become the subject of e-mail chat lines and some of it, I gather, is pretty ugly. I think you can imagine what fifteen-year-old girls can come up with. You, of course, are cast as the stud father. There's a lot of talk about your dead girlfriend. Questions like, 'Will Heather be going to the funeral of her father's girlfriend?' Allison Harvey showed her some of this stuff today. That's what your friends are for, right? To show you how many people out there are happy that you're miserable."

"There's a word for it," he said.

"I know the fucking word, Dan. Don't patronize me. Anyway, she's heard about this stuff that's out there. And from other schools too. Girls she's played against."

"Little bastards."

"You can call them whatever you want. It doesn't change anything. Today, it just got to her and she came home early in tears. She couldn't face practice and you know how she hates to miss her practices. I'm thinking of keeping her home for a few days. I wanted to earlier in the week, but she insisted on going. Said she wasn't going to hide from anybody. And she wanted to be ready to play on Saturday. It's a big game. But she hasn't been eating or sleeping properly all week. Surely you noticed those dark rings under her eyes. And today she just couldn't take any more. Came home early and flopped on the bed. Thinks her life is ruined, of course."

"Jesus. Can I talk to her?"

"An hour ago maybe, though I don't think she really wants to talk to anybody. In any case, she's finally fallen asleep and I'm not going to wake her up. She's still in her uniform. I just threw a blanket over her. All this stuff is still on television. Jesus, they had it on again tonight. Pictures of the town, the church, the high school she went to."

"You shouldn't watch it."

"I'll watch what I feel like watching. Don't tell me what to watch."

"We have to take this a day at a time, Claire. Sorry for the cliché."

When she didn't answer, he said, "I'm sorry about everything."

"Yes," she said. "I believe you *are* sorry." Her voice sounded tired, as if she had thought long and hard about everything, and was now discouraged with how her life had turned out. "But it still happened, didn't it?" she said. "Nothing can change that. Heather is going to have to deal with it. So am I. So are you. In a way, it doesn't change anything to say you're sorry. It helps, but it doesn't change anything. We all have to work through this, but it's still going to be there. Once something's happened, it's happened. There it is. A part of your life. It can't be erased."

"What exactly are you saying, Claire?"

"I'm saying that we can't change what happened. It will always be there. Your weekend fling. Denise Crowder's death. Heather's memory of those hateful e-mails. The way friends of ours will always think of us in a certain way. 'Remember all the trouble they had when that girl Dan was seeing was murdered in England.' All that will be there forever and nothing can change it because it happened."

He could imagine her thinking this through all week as she watched the news, or lay awake in bed; it was now consuming a part of every waking hour, and it was there again the next morning, the first thing to confront her. A different species of grief from Lucille Crowder's, certainly, but grief nonetheless, grief for this fissure in her marriage and for her daughter's unhappiness.

"Are you still there?" she asked.

"Yes, of course."

"Do you understand what I'm saying, Dan?"

"I do, yes."

And perhaps they both realized that enough had been said for the moment, that pursuing this line of thought any further could now be dangerous.

"What time is the funeral?" she asked.

"Two o'clock."

"When will you be coming home?"

"I'll try to get back as soon as I can. Probably early evening. It's about a three-hour drive from here." He stopped. There didn't seem to be anything more to say. "I hope Heather's all right tomorrow."

"She needs a good night's sleep."

"Yes."

There followed a brittle moment of silence before Claire said, "Goodnight, then."

"Goodnight," he said.

Fielding hung up the phone and undressed for bed, thinking of a day in his life not long ago. A Sunday morning in September and he was going down to breakfast, listening on the stairway to Claire and Heather in the kitchen. They were laughing and talking about the game the day before, a game St. Hilda's had won and in which Heather had played well. This joking in the kitchen was a rare truce between mother and daughter after a difficult beginning to the school year. Fielding had promised himself that he would read no manuscripts that day—the morning was reserved for the *New York Times Book Review*, and later they were having dinner at the Burtons'. Heather was going to a friend's in the afternoon and Fielding hoped for a daytime hour or two in bed with his wife. When he reached the bottom of the stairs, he noticed the sunlight streaming through the French doors across the dining-room floor and over the dog who was sleeping. September was Fielding's favourite month and he enjoyed especially the light as it fell through leafy trees, a subtle and airy light peculiar to the season and the waning strength of the sun. On the radio was sacred music from centuries ago, Monteverdi perhaps.

Fielding could smell French toast and hear his wife and daughter talking about the game, and as he walked to the kitchen he was thinking, "This is a good moment in my life. I am happy. Try to remember this."

Lying in bed now in the Moonbeam Motel, he tried to summon forth every detail of those few moments on that September morning and, as he remembered, he could hear the rain starting, a sudden downpour that was soon drumming on the roof and splashing from a drainpipe into puddles beneath the window. He wanted the rain to last all night and into tomorrow. A pathetic fallacy if you wanted to call it that, but it seemed only fitting to bury a young woman on a day when the sky was dark and sodden.

On his way into town, Fielding's head was still jammed with unfamiliar and ominous information: over the past fifty years the glaciers on Western Canada's mountains had shrunk to the size they were ten thousand years ago; all the world's major rivers were polluted, many with severely diminished water levels; the increase in the consumption of bottled water was drying up streams and aquifers; every day North Americans used four times more water than Europeans and fifteen times more than people in Asia and Africa. All morning he had been reading *A History of Water*, sitting on the bed in the motel room, his back supported by pillows, making notes, using the top of the manuscript box as a kind of writing board. Twice he had been interrupted by a woman with lank, pale hair and a tattoo on her ankle who was carrying sheets and wanted to make up the room. Each time he sent her away. He had rented the place until one o'clock, and he was caught up at last in Tom Lundgren's grim scenario of a future in which border wars could erupt over the ownership of water; its price might one day rival that of oil or natural gas, electricity.

Fielding had scarcely noticed the passing hours and now, after hurriedly eating a sandwich at a restaurant on the highway, he was running late. It was nearly two o'clock and he was looking for Metcalfe Street and St. John's Anglican Church, his mind still ranging over the professor's forecast of possible social and political chaos unless we change our profligate ways. It would be Heather's world, he thought, and even if Lundgren's view was too pessimistic, it was becoming clear that the new century was going to be very different from the last one. And he had to wonder if an individual life would matter as much in a world where people might kill one another over water. Would a single death like Denise Crowder's be dutifully attended to with sorrowful ceremony? Or would the end of life be something like the plague years of the Middle Ages when the dead were cast into pits and the mourners stayed home?

The rain from the night was long gone, swept away by a wind off the lake that had cleared the air and left another gusty, bright day. When he reached the side streets of the town, he could see his error in arriving so late; cars lined both sides of the street near the church, and he had to park several blocks away. It was just past two when he rounded the corner onto Metcalfe Street, panting a little after his run from the car. A crowd had gathered behind the police tape in front of the church, a subdued band of the idle and the curious, brought out on this windy fall day by their own *schadenfreude* and the TV cameras: housewives and pensioners, men in baseball caps and windbreakers, teenaged girls taking the afternoon off school. On the church lawn were clusters of flowers wrapped in plastic cones, remembrances from strangers who had been moved to pity by a young woman's death.

Shouldering his way through the crowd, Fielding identified himself to the policeman and was allowed through. He could hear the whispered comments from behind him.

"That's the man she was with."

Stone steps with iron railings led up to the church and Fielding climbed, grateful that the service had not yet started. But surely it was about to, for the rear door of the hearse in the parking lot at the side of the church was already open. Fielding could see Ray Crowder and Lyle Parsons standing in their dark suits with other men. Two young women from the choir had come out a side door in their white gowns and were watching a cameraman film the crowd on the street. When he stepped into the church, Fielding was approached by the young woman from the funeral home with her round, innocent face. What was her name? Sharon? Yes.

"The church is full, sir," she said. "But we have a seat for you. Mrs. Crowder asked me to keep an eye out for you."

"Thanks. I'm sorry I'm late."

Above their whispering he could hear the "Nimrod" theme from Elgar's *Enigma Variations* played with surprising vigour and skill.

"We've put you with your friends from Toronto," Sharon whispered.

"Fine."

An elderly man escorted him to his seat halfway to the altar. He was mortified at being so late, inviting all the looks that accompanied him as he slid in beside Linda McNulty, who squeezed his arm without saying anything. When he glanced down the row, he saw Loren Schultz and Sy Hollis, Martha Young and Imogene Banks. In the first pew were Sandy Levine, and Lucille Crowder under a wide black hat; there were two older women next to her, the sisters, Fielding imagined, and an old man in a brown suit, and Kelly Swarbrick and her daughter. When the music stopped, he could hear the rustling sound of the choir assembling for the procession. Then he heard a woman's voice. She had an English accent that reminded him of Fiona Anderson.

I am the resurrection and the life, saith the Lord: he that believeth in me, though he were dead, yet shall he live: and whosoever liveth and believeth in me shall never die.

Moments later they were bearing the shrouded coffin past him in silence, Ray Crowder freshly barbered and Lyle Parsons and four other men, followed by the choir and the priest, a middle-aged woman. In its solemnity and ritual the service was calming, and as Fielding listened to the English woman reading the *Collects*, he thought of the numberless dead who had lain in caskets throughout the centuries while these very words were spoken above them. When the choir began to sing "Softly and Tenderly, Jesus Is Calling," he remembered a summer evening more than forty years ago when he was thirteen; a summer of loose ends with friends away at camp and high school ahead in September. He was tall for his age, but ungainly and nearsighted; soon he would need glasses and he dreaded the thought of wearing them at a new school. How lonely and lost he had felt on those early, light-filled summer evenings, wandering the streets of Toronto, thinking of the empty weeks ahead and high school.

One evening, he got into a fight with a rough-looking boy. He was crossing an unfamiliar schoolyard when the boy and his two smaller friends surrounded him and pushed him to the ground. To his surprise, he got up quickly and fought back, emboldened perhaps by the only weapons left to the bullied and miserable, his own fear and rage. Within minutes he had to be pulled off the boy by two men passing on the sidewalk. He could still remember one of them saying, "Hey, let go, buddy, you're going to choke him to death."

He escaped with his narrow victory, but felt chastened too; when he left the schoolyard, the boy was white-faced and coughing. What if the police came after him? He had sought refuge in the open doors of a church hall where he could hear a choir singing.

It was some kind of Youth for Christ rally in a Sunday school auditorium, and he had followed others into the hall with its old-cupboard smell and its wainscotting and folding metal chairs. There were men in shirt sleeves and women in flowered dresses and boys and girls his age and older teenagers too. The preacher was an American and he talked about godless Communism and the hydrogen bomb, the approaching conflagration, and the love that Jesus had for each and every one of them. He was a stolid-looking man with a dark, receding hairline and a five o'clock shadow. He had taken off his jacket and when he raised his arms to call upon the young to come forth, people could see the sweat marks. A woman in the choir began to sing, "Softly and Tenderly, Jesus Is Calling," and the rest joined in. The American preacher implored them to come forward and embrace their Saviour, and soon people were shifting sideways in their chairs to let others pass. From various parts of the hall, young people stood up and prepared to be saved.

In front of Fielding was a girl about his age in a dirndl skirt and a white blouse. She was with her parents and they looked poor. He had been watching her when she sat farther down the row, but to make room for others she and her parents had moved to seats in front of him. Before they moved, however, Fielding had seen something harsh and unlovely and powerful in the girl's listless gaze. When she was seated in front of him, he could see her bra strap through the blouse and everything was at once unsettling and wonderful: his fight with the rough-looking boy, the long evening light in the auditorium windows, the preacher's words of healing and redemption, the swell of the girl's cheek. When she got up to make her way past the others, she reached behind to pluck the skirt from between her buttocks and a moment later Fielding too arose and followed her up the aisle.

That summer evening was the beginning of his brief and passionate love affair with Jesus. He never saw the girl again, but he didn't care. Actually nothing mattered and that was the joy of it—not the absence of friends, nor the prospect of high school, nor his mother's mocking asides as he read his Testament on the front porch in the afternoons. He was intensely happy in the knowledge that if he lived a good life and prayed to Jesus for guidance, he would one day have eternal life. He even joined a Bible study group and after meetings walked a shy girl home now and then. When high school began, he was seen as an outsider, an oddball, but he was left alone, and sometimes, in the middle of a class, or walking down the hall, he would feel a surge of elation in knowing that none of this was important. Yet with the passing months, the intensity of his feelings became diluted with the realization that it was hard to lead a good life, difficult to be free of sin every day, almost impossible to look at a pretty girl without lustful dreaming.

One afternoon he heard his parents talking about him in the kitchen. With his customary reasonableness, his father was defending him.

"He has to work these things out for himself, Jean."

But his mother sounded adamant; she was restless and in a hurry, on her way out the door to the hospital to work an evening shift.

"Well, if he doesn't get off this religious nonsense, he's going to lose his year. You saw his last report card."

A few weeks later, he had his eyes examined and was fitted with glasses. The world was suddenly a larger, clearer space and he could now see the numbers and words on the blackboard. He fell in love with a girl who, when he now thought about it, was very like Denise, sexy and smart and adventurous, but far too sophisticated for him. She went out with boys in older grades. It was all so long ago, he thought, listening again to the words of the priest.

The service was nearly over and she had come down to the coffin and was sprinkling sand over it.

Almighty God with whom do live the spirits of them that depart hence in the Lord, and with whom the souls of the faithful are in joy and felicity: We praise and magnify Thy Holy Name for all thy servants who have finished their course and kept their faith; and in committing our sister Denise to thy gracious keeping, we

pray that we with her, and with all those who are departed in the
true faith of Thy Holy Name, may have our perfect consumma-
tion and bliss, both in body and soul, in the eternal and everlast-
ing glory;
   through Jesus Christ our Lord.
   Amen

The six men grasped the handles of the coffin and carried it down the aisle, looking stony-faced and straight ahead. The priest followed and then Lucille and Sandy, arm in arm, and the sisters and Kelly Swarbrick and the little girl in her black velveteen dress and white leotards. Then the strange-looking old man in his baggy double-breasted summer suit, his large, pale head entirely hairless as if he had recently undergone cancer treatment. The choir and congregation sang "Guide Me O Thou Great Jehovah" and then people filed out into the glare of the afternoon. The TV cameras were there and when Fielding looked down to the parking lot, he saw a cameraman filming Sandy and Lucille as they were being helped into the limousine behind the hearse.

Imogene Banks gave him a perfect consolatory smile. "A terribly sad day, Dan."

"Yes."

"How are you feeling?"

"Lousy."

The others joined them on the lawn and everyone seemed uncomfortable and eager to be away. Sy Hollis gripped Fielding's hand.

"You're going out to the cemetery, aren't you, Dan?" He had put on sunglasses, and it was hard to read the expression on his face.

"Yes," said Fielding, "and I'd better be going because I'm parked several blocks from here. I think they'll be starting soon."

"Right," said Hollis. "I don't know the way so we'd better get to our cars. We'll see you there."

Fielding worked his way through the crowd that was still milling around on the lawn and on the steps to the street. Dresses and skirts were being pressed against women's legs by the wind, and an older man lost his hat. It went skimming across the parking lot and a younger man was running after it. Fielding hurried on towards his car.

The cemetery was on the other side of town, just off the highway, and only about thirty people were gathered by the grave. The TV folk had apparently decided not to film the burial scene. Maybe, thought Fielding, it was a little too close to the bone for television. Under the bare trees the leaves were thick and still wet from last night's rain. The priest stood by the open grave, her greyish hair blowing across her face as she held the fluttering pages of the prayer book in both hands. The coffin rested on the apparatus that would lower it into the earth.

"*In the midst of life we are in death*," she said.

How true that was, Fielding thought. About this time a week ago he and Denise were eating dinner in a Lebanese restaurant in Soho. They had flown to London from Frankfurt that afternoon, and it was on the plane that she asked him about his weekend plans. When he mentioned his jaunt to Devon, she said it sounded like fun. She had never been in the English countryside. Would he be interested in some company? He didn't like to say no to her, but Devon was special. Devon belonged to Claire and him and so he had said . . .

What had he said? Some nonsense about walking the footpaths and how one had to be used to them. In fact, he wasn't planning to do much walking at all; there simply wasn't the time. He could remember her shrug. She knew he was lying. But in the little restaurant, after two or three glasses of wine, he had changed his mind. Asked her if she were still interested, and of course she was and that was that. She had taken his hand across the table and smiled.

"Should I buy a walking stick in the morning, Daniel?"

"Not necessary," he said.

Forasmuch as it hath pleased Almighty God of his great mercy to receive unto himself the soul of our dear sister here departed, we therefore commit her body to the ground, earth to earth, ashes to ashes, dust to dust, in sure and certain hope of the Resurrection to eternal life, through our Lord Jesus Christ; who shall change our mortal body, that it may be like unto his glorious body, according to the mighty working whereby he is able to subdue all things to himself.

Fielding was listening carefully to the serious, old words, to the stately lustre of this High Anglican language from over four hundred years ago. Yet to believe such words at the beginning of the twenty-first century seemed to him preposterous. The coffin had disappeared into the ground and Fielding read the words on the tombstone above the open grave.

CLIFFORD JOHN CROWDER

1938–1998

Beloved husband of Lucille Anne

1945–

People were now returning to their cars. Sy Hollis was talking to Sandy Levine, the wind stirring his hair as he stood beside her in his big-belted trench coat. Martha Young surprised Fielding by rising on her toes to kiss his cheek. She was not usually demonstrative.

"We're heading back now, Dan. Will we see you Monday morning?"

"Yes, I think so, Mart," he said.

"That's good. You look tired. Try to get some sleep this weekend."

"I'll try," he said, watching her join the others who waved to him.

His colleagues liked him. They were polite and considerate, but they were also surprised and puzzled, disappointed too, perhaps, by his involvement with Denise Crowder. It had changed their estimation of him in unaccountable ways. He could see it in their faces. Sy Hollis walked over and for a moment neither of them said anything. Then, looking around, Hollis said, "I'll bet this is a pretty little place in the summer."

"I would imagine so," said Fielding.

Hollis was watching him from behind his sunglasses. "I'll tell you the truth, Dan, you don't look so hot."

"So I've been told," said Fielding.

"Do you want to take some time off?"

"It might be better," said Fielding, "if I just got on with it."

Hollis made his little popping face. "Well, you're the best judge of that. So you're coming in Monday?"

"Yes, I think it's best, Sy."

"Fine," said Hollis, pausing to stare up at the swaying branches. "I suppose you're going back to the Crowders' for a drink?"

"Yes, I probably will."

"We had to beg off. Denise's mother asked us, but I think it's more for the family and close friends."

Fielding was watching Lucille, who seemed to have collapsed into the arms of one of her sisters. Others surrounded her and they moved off, a sorrowing group of women in dark clothes, huddling towards the limousine on the circular drive.

"I think I'll be off then," said Hollis. "Take care of yourself, Dan."

"Thanks, Sy," said Fielding.

Hollis had only walked a few steps before he turned. "I don't suppose you've had a chance to look at Tom Lundgren's manuscript. I'm only asking because he phoned yesterday afternoon. Wanted to know what we thought. Tom understands the difficult time you're going through. He just wondered if anyone else had read it."

The wind was lifting Hollis's wispy hair as he stood with his hands deep in the pockets of the trench coat. Fielding didn't like talking business at Denise's graveside.

"Can I talk to you about it on Monday?"

"Sure," said Hollis. "I'd just like to be able to say something to the man this weekend. You know what authors are like."

"I've read it quickly," said Fielding. "It needs work, but it's mostly style. The writing is a little stiff and overly technical in places. That can be fixed. It's a book worth doing, I think. I'll call him tomorrow if you like."

Hollis nodded. He looked surprised by this news. "Well, that's good, Dan. Very good. I'm glad to hear it. Thanks." Turning away, he walked towards the car where the others were waiting.

An elderly man in a dark raincoat was kneeling on a mat,

folding the green cloth that had served as artificial grass over the graveside; he was folding it slowly, tucking in the corners as if he'd done this a thousand times. Fielding wondered if this unhurried attention to detail belonged to George Gladstone Senior, and when he asked, the man looked up with his narrow, lined face.

"Sir?"

"My name's Dan Fielding. We talked on the phone last Sunday."

"So we did," said Gladstone, getting to his feet and offering a hand. "My son George said he was talking to you last evening. We appreciate your comments about our service."

"You took a lot off my mind last Sunday, Mr. Gladstone."

"That's what we're here for, Mr. Fielding," he said.

Across the cemetery by a little shed two men were standing next to a backhoe. They were having a smoke and probably waiting for everyone to leave so they could fill in the grave and go home to their suppers. George Gladstone was kneeling again, dismantling the machine that lowered the casket. Standing there, Fielding could see the gouged side of the grave and the dark gleam of polished wood.

When he looked up, Ray Crowder and Kelly Swarbrick were walking quickly towards him, Kelly nestling into Ray, holding onto his arm with both hands.

"Mom wants to know if you're coming back to the house," said Crowder.

"Sure. I would like to say goodbye to your mother and Sandy."

Crowder nodded and the two of them turned and walked back towards the others who were now making their way through a row of gravestones to the circular road where cars were parked. Fielding hurried across the damp leaves and grass towards his own car. He badly wanted to talk to his daughter, and once inside the car, he called home on his cell; as he waited for the connection, he watched the funeral home limousine drive away, passing through the gates onto the highway. Other cars were following.

When Heather answered, her voice sounded faint and groggy as if she had just awakened.

"Heather, it's Dad."

"Oh, hi Daddy."

"Hi. Were you sleeping?"

"Yeah. Just a little nap. I didn't go to school today. Mom thought it would be better if I took the day off. Have a long weekend to myself."

"Yes, she told me last night that you had a rough time yesterday."

"It's not been that bad. Some crappy e-mail from people I definitely despise."

"Delete them," he said.

"Oh, I already have. But you know . . ."

"Yes, I think I do. But you have to expect some of this stuff, Heather. I'm sorry."

"I know. Mom says it will all be over soon. Things will settle down. Once the television stuff is finished and the newspapers stop writing about you and Miss Crowder."

"Well, she's right. Soon there'll be other things for them to write about, and we can try to get back to normal."

"I hope so," she said. "When are you coming home?"

"This evening, though I may be a little late. I'm going to the Crowders' for an hour or so. I shouldn't be long."

"That's good."

"Is your mother around?"

"No, she went to a movie with Mrs. Burton. Something called *The Hours*. Mrs. Burton was going on about it when she came by for Mom. You know how she can be. Anyway, she's read the book that this movie is supposed to be about and she really liked it. She's been bugging Mom to see it. So they went this afternoon. Mrs. Burton said it would be good for Mom. Take her mind off all this stuff."

"Good idea," he said. "Just tell her I called, and I'll be a little later than I thought. I should be home by nine or ten o'clock."

"Sure."

"Take care now."

"You too, Daddy."

By the time he arrived at Lucille's, the house was already crowded with people who sounded as if they were on their second drink. Not festive, of course, but more relaxed certainly, grateful no doubt that the formal ceremonies were now over and a more relenting spirit allowed. He could see a smile or two flickering now and then across faces as people talked. Del was again in the kitchen, and with the help of two other women had prepared a supper of salad and cold cuts; there were also plates of sandwiches and cakes and pies. Lucille was seated on the sofa, attended to by her sisters, dark-haired, good-looking women in their sixties. Lucille was the only one smoking in the house; others had stepped through the patio doorway to enjoy a cigarette on the back lawn. Fielding could see Sandy Levine talking to a young couple, and again he envied her that ease with strangers. It was not difficult to sense people's reluctance to speak to him. He was neither a friend of the family's nor strictly speaking a business acquaintance; he was instead the man who had cheated on his wife with Denise, who had in some manner put her in harm's way. What kind of conversation could you have with someone like that?

The wind was gone now, the sun behind the trees and sinking into the lake, leaving a salmon-coloured sky that grew paler by the minute. Fielding stood near the patio door, with a glass of wine, looking out at the picnic table and barbecue, the guests on the lawn, the early evening sky. Here was an ordinary and pleasant little space in the world, somewhere to come to from the city on a weekend, a place to sit with her mother on a Saturday morning in July, catching up on town gossip, telling as much about what was going on in her own life as she cared to—a place where one day she might have watched her own children playing with their grandmother. People were now making room for Lucille, who had stood up. From outside, others were squeezing through the patio doorway and Sandy smiled at him as she passed. Slowly the murmuring died away as Lucille, standing alone now by the dining-room table, looked nervously around, clenching a tissue in her hand.

"First," she said. "I want to thank you all for coming back to my house to help us remember and say goodbye one last time to Dee. Some of you have come a long way, including my own two sisters, Sylvie and Mathilde, and their husbands, Don and Laurent, who drove from Montreal. And also dear Bonneverre, who worked so many years with Cliff on the *Tilden*. Bonneverre has been a guest many times in this house and he was a great favourite of Dee's. How she used to laugh at his stories and jokes. Remember, Bonneverre?"

The old man was sitting in a corner of the room, and as others turned to stare, he nodded.

"Thank you," Lucille said, "for coming all the way down from Thunder Bay."

There was scattered applause and again the old man inclined his large, pale head.

"Of course I must mention Denise's special friend, Sandy Levine, who has come from New York City. She is going to say a few words, but before she does, I want to first ask Miss Robertson, Dee's favourite teacher, to speak to us."

People paused to sip their drinks, watching as Florence Robertson came forward. Lucille seemed especially proud that the old teacher was now in her house and was going to speak about Denise. Beneath the tightly curled white hair, Florence Robertson frowned, the facial expression of a temperament inclined to constant judgment; Fielding imagined that she had set her features just this way even as a child, quick to find fault with others and produce her little scowl. She was holding pages of handwriting and said dryly, "I very much doubt, Mrs. Crowder, that Denise regarded me as her favourite teacher."

A little scattered laughter as she adjusted her glasses and bent to her task. "Denise Crowder came into my Grade Twelve class in September of 1986. She was nearly seventeen and I was sixty-four and I can assure you that we didn't see eye to eye on many things." There was more laughter, uneven and light. What was the old girl going to say next? "I will be frank. I found Denise pert and wilful and in my opinion much too sure of herself. At the same time, however, I am bound to say that for a girl her age, as I soon discovered, she had a remarkable grasp of English literature. I remember an essay she wrote for me on Edgar Allan Poe. I found it quite extraordinary, and I have to confess that I had serious doubts at the time about it being her own work. That's how professional it seemed to be. But of course it was her own work, and I soon came to realize what a gifted young woman she really was . . ."

As Fielding listened, he could see the sixteen-year-old Denise crossing swords with her flinty old English teacher, the girl standing by her teacher's desk after class to dispute a grade or defend an argument in one of her essays. But Florence Robertson was going on a bit, losing some of her audience—men and women for whom high school may have been nothing more than time spent listening to stuff they hadn't the slightest interest in and could see no point to, a boring interlude between childhood and the rest of life. Still, Florence Robertson finished her speech with a flourish, admitting that "the young lady proved to me how first impressions can be so wrong, and I want to say how proud I was to have heard how she went to work in publishing in New York City. In closing, I can only add that I was and am utterly shocked and saddened by her untimely death. This is a very tragic day for all of us."

There was applause, hesitant at first, and the old woman looked rather startled when Lucille embraced her. Sandy Levine came forward and began to speak of the young woman who had come to her office six years ago, eager to find her way in the publishing world. "Denise," she said, "was young and energetic and confident." Sandy had cleverly tailored her remarks to her audience, knowing that for most of them the world of book publishing would be as remote as astrophysics; yet her words were without condescension and filled with engaging anecdotes. Everyone laughed as she recalled Denise's sense of humour, her unbuttoned appreciation of the ridiculous in life. Sandy mentioned a visit to the office by a pompous author and, in its wake, Denise's devastatingly accurate imitation of the man. When Sandy finished, there was enthusiastic applause, and Lucille, pressing the tissue to her eyes and laughing in spite of herself, said, "Yes. That was Dee. Exactly."

As people again began to mingle, Fielding stepped outside onto the patio, hoping fresh air might help a lurking headache. He would wait until Lucille had a moment to herself and then say goodbye and be on his way. It was dark now, but still mild enough to stand outdoors in a suit. Behind him the patio door was opening again as more guests came out for a cigarette, talking quietly among themselves. To his surprise, Lucille also appeared. She had thrown a sweater across her shoulders, and was smoking and holding a glass of wine.

"I've been looking for you, Dan," she said, "but there are so many around. A good thing, of course. I'm glad, but . . ." She shrugged. "Don't mind me, I think I'm getting a little tight. I haven't been drinking at all these past few years. Not since my husband's death." She stepped closer to him. "Cliff and I," she said, "we used to drink quite a bit. I think it's what did Cliff in. He had cancer at the end, but I think all that drinking weakened his liver." She was almost whispering to him. "Poor fellow. If he was alive today, he'd be sixty-four. But it's probably just as well. He thought the world of Denise. She was his pride and joy. For sure, this would have finished him off."

Around them people had gathered in little clusters and Lucille said, "Let's walk down to the hedge." She had linked her arm in his the way Denise might have done, and they walked down to the end of the garden. Fielding could smell the cedar bushes and the smoke from the cigarettes. Lucille sipped her wine, looking up at the dark sky.

"I enjoyed our little talk last night in Dee's room. It was nice to look at those old pictures with you."

"I enjoyed it too," he said.

They were quiet together for what seemed to Fielding a long time and then finally she said, "I think you are a nice man, Dan, and I can see why Dee liked you."

"Thanks," he said, "but I'm not as nice as you might think."

"That may be so," she said, "but Dee liked you. She'd talk about you when she'd come home on the weekends. How you would say something funny in a meeting that would make her laugh."

How odd to hear this! Never had he imagined that he was making any kind of favourable impression on Denise Crowder at editorial meetings, or at any other time. If she had been sending signals, they had missed him entirely.

"She said you were a little shy, but she liked that about you. Of course, she knew you were married and she'd had problems with a married man in New York. She was in quite a mess there for a while. But she liked you a lot. I could tell from the things she said about you."

He could see where Lucille was heading; she wanted to know more about his relationship with her daughter. How did he feel about her? Did she make him laugh? Had he thought about her when he was at home? Had he considered leaving his wife and daughter for Denise? Was it that kind of relationship, something grounded in genuine feeling? In other words, had they been in love? How could he tell her that it was only a few days in Europe? One of those episodes in life that most people take guilty pleasure in, hoping that deceit will conceal their secret forever. Two weeks ago, he would not have been able to say truthfully that he even liked Denise Crowder.

Perhaps in his silence Lucille intuited something, for she suddenly threw the rest of her wine into the cedar bush.

"Well, what does it matter anyway?" she said. "I am very proud of Denise. Of the confidence and ambition she had. I used to wonder many times, My God, where did all that come from? She was not like the rest of us. I could see that even when she was a little girl, and it used to scare me. I knew one day I would lose her. I don't mean lose her to a husband, I mean lose her in another way. Not really ever understand her. Do you know what I mean?"

"Yes, I do," Fielding said. "I think my father may have felt that way about me."

Lucille seemed not to hear him. "We used to have parties in this house. Good times. Lots to eat and drink, dancing, cards. Friends would bring their kids too. We used to have a ball. But after a while Denise would just fade away. Go to her room and close the door and read. Sometimes her father would get so mad. He'd say, 'Where is Denise? Why isn't she down here with the other kids?' But really he wanted to show her off. Show how smart she was. I could see that. 'She'll never have any friends,' he used to say. And for sure she didn't have many friends. Girlfriends anyway.

"All through high school, the other girls didn't like her. Or so it seemed. They were jealous, I think. Dee could wrap the boys around her finger, and other girls would get mad." Lucille shook her head and laughed a little bitterly. "I remember her saying one day, 'Mom, I'll be gone from this place in a couple of years. I'll be living in cities and I'll just come back to Bayport to visit you and Daddy.' Then in Grade Ten, I think it was, she got a job at Dairy Queen and she worked there in the summers. The best cashier they ever had and those words are from the man who owned the place then, Jack Lambert. He was at the funeral home last night and he told me that again. He said that Dee practically ran that dairy bar over on Lake Street. And she looked so cute in that uniform. The fastest, the smartest at the cash register. Jack told me.

"You know, Dan, I never worried about her making her way, handling boys, anything like that. From the time she was a little girl, I knew she was going to look after herself in this world. She was that independent. When she went off to university, she had her own money. I think her father gave her a thousand dollars, but most of it was her own money."

They heard a commotion from the patio and looked up to see a figure stumbling near the doorway. Kelly Swarbrick was holding onto Ray Crowder and another couple were helping out; there was some laughter over a missed step. Lucille was looking at the lighted doorway and the dark figures.

"I thought he was in the basement watching television with Cala," Lucille said. "He told me he didn't want to hear any speeches."

She had taken out another cigarette and was striking at a match furiously and without success. She seemed at once fed up with the sheer cussedness of life: its enslavement to appetite and old bad habits, its helpless reliance on chance, its thousand natural shocks that threaten to undo us. Fielding took the box of matches from her hand and lit her cigarette.

"Someone's brought a bottle," she said, pushing her arms through the sleeves of her sweater, talking with the cigarette in her mouth. "Someone's given him liquor."

They could see Ray and Kelly along the side of the house walking towards the front.

"Kelly's taking him for a walk," said Fielding. "She'll look after him."

"Kelly's a good woman in her own way," said Lucille. "She takes care of that little girl. I give her all that. But she's not for Ray. She's not the one." Lucille was taking huge reefs on her cigarette, pulling the smoke deep within her, talking as it billowed forth. "It breaks your heart to see her try so hard. Dee could see that early on. First time she saw them together she said, 'This won't last. It's too one-sided. Ray likes her well enough, but he'll get tired of her hanging on him like that.'"

Lucille had stopped to button her sweater.

"One night in the summer Kelly was talking about herself. Ray had gone somewhere. So she was telling us how she quit school and got this job and that job. Met Cala's father. A real bum. Lived with him for a while and then had to get out. She didn't say, but I guess he was beating her. Took the baby with her and went down to Windsor where she got a job as a stripper. She called it exotic dancing, but it's the same thing, isn't it? Then she came back to town and found work in this new call centre. Met Ray. After she went home that night, Dee just tore a strip off her. Said she was tired of hearing that stuff about never having any education. 'Mom' she said, 'I went to school with lots of girls like Kelly. Tits out to here at fifteen and a lineup of boys waiting to get into their pants. Always too busy doing their hair to do their homework. Then ten years later they're whining about never having any education. How many brains does it take to finish high school? And why does she still go around looking like a tart? Those gunslinger jeans and all that hair. Jesus!' Oh, Kelly was scared of her. You could tell the way she looked at Dee when she said anything. I feel sorry for Kelly. She's a good woman in many ways."

Lucille flicked her cigarette across the grass.

"It's getting chilly. We better go in."

They began walking towards the house and Lucille said, "I suppose you'll have to go back to England for the trial."

"Yes, I'll have to be there."

"When do you think that will be?"

"I don't really know, Lucille. The detective I dealt with over there said probably late spring. These things take time."

"Yes," she said. "I imagine they do." She paused. "I was thinking I might go over. I don't really want to, but I feel I should be there. My oldest sister, Mathilde, thinks I should leave it alone. Let the courts deal with this man. She says I'll sleep better if I never lay eyes on him. And I'm not much of a traveller. I've been to Chicago, Detroit, Superior, Wisconsin, places like that. That was on the boat years ago, but you don't see much on the boat except the docks." She stopped. "Cliff and I went to Las Vegas once. It was just a year before he passed away. He looked just awful and I kept thinking he's dying. I'm walking under all these lights, going to these shows where people are laughing at the comedians' jokes, but I'm having a holiday with a dying man. That kept running through my mind as I looked at all those older women in the coffee shops or playing the slot machines. Widows! And I kept thinking, I'll be a widow this time next year. I could never go back to that place now. And England would be sad like that too, I suppose."

They had reached the flagstones of the patio, and in the light from the house she looked haggard. It was all catching up to her as they stood looking in at the people who were talking, using hands to emphasize a point, nodding in agreement as they listened. From outside it looked like just another Friday-night house party.

"What do you think, Dan?" she asked. "Should I go over there for the trial of this man?"

He had been thinking about that. Thinking about her in the strangeness of an English town with its old buildings and narrow streets. In the courtroom watching the bewigged figures with their accents and mannerisms. Trying to make sense of it all. Watching television at the end of the day in a bed and breakfast.

"I can't really answer that question," he said, "but I tend to agree with your sister. I just don't know if you'd benefit in any way from being there. They have the man who did it. He's going to prison. Probably for most of the rest of his life. You might want to think about it a bit more, Lucille. About going over, I mean."

"Yes," she said. "You're right. I have to think about it."

They stood for another moment looking in at the people.

"I'm sorry it all happened, Lucille," he said.

"Well, of course you are, Dan. It's not hard to see that."

They fell silent once more, and then she said, "Well, I better go in. They'll wonder what's become of me."

In the warm, noisy house, people stepped aside for them as they entered, smiling at Lucille, one woman touching her arm as they passed. Sandy Levine was sitting on the sofa next to the old man called Bonneverre. He was telling a story, slicing the air with his large hands. When Sandy noticed them, she said something to the old man, and then got up. She could see that Fielding was on his way. He found his raincoat in the hall closet and Lucille shook his hand.

"Goodbye, Dan," she said. "I'm glad you were Denise's friend."

He had wanted to say something more to her out in the backyard, something about her courage, and generosity, her goodwill. But he hadn't and now it was too late; she had already turned to thank a man and woman who were also leaving.

Sandy Levine said, "If you are ever in New York, Dan, I hope you'll give me a call. I'd love to see you again."

"I will, Sandy. Thank you."

After he closed the front door, he listened for a moment to the murmuring voices from within, and then he walked down the steps and across the lawn. He recognized at once the two figures coming along the street and crossing the dark grass towards him. There was no way to avoid them and when they were only a few feet apart, Ray Crowder stopped and said, "Leaving us now, are you, Mister?"

"Yes," said Fielding. "I was just saying goodbye to your mother."

"But you weren't going to say goodbye to me, were you?" Crowder's question seemed unanswerable and Fielding said nothing. The young man was drunk, but not all that drunk. He wants to hit me and nothing else will satisfy him, thought Fielding, wondering if he should take off his glasses. But that could be seen as provocation, an invitation to fight. He wondered how long it would take the couple in the hallway to say goodbye to Lucille and be out here walking to their car.

"What does your wife think of all this, Mister?"

Fielding considered the question. "I think she's disappointed in me."

"Disappointed." The sneer in Crowder's voice was palpable.

"Isn't that just too fucking bad? The man's wife is disappointed in him."

"Ray?" said Kelly. "Come on, hon, let's go in. Leave him alone."

She had been holding onto Crowder's arm, but now he pulled it away. "Why don't you just shut the fuck up, Kelly? You talk too much. Do you know that? You just talk too much."

Kelly Swarbrick shrugged. It was as if she had heard all this before. Pulling up the collar of her jacket, she walked off, heading towards the side of the house and the back patio. Fielding and Crowder turned to watch her disappear around the corner of the garage and then they faced one another again. "You should have taken better care of my sister, you son of a bitch."

As Fielding staggered back and fell, he worried about his glasses and the drive home. He should have expected it. In fact, he had expected something like this, but it came so quickly, this blow striking his left cheek; his glasses were now askew, hanging it seemed on only one ear. Everything was a dark blur and one side of his face was numb. Above him Crowder was cursing but the words seemed to come from afar, and there was also shouting and the sound of running feet. The grass felt damp and cold on the back of his neck. He recognized Lyle Parsons' voice.

"Jesus Christ, Ray, what the hell have you done?"

Fielding could not make out Crowder's reply, and now there were other voices too and he imagined people spilling out of the house, eager to see what was going on. Something to talk about tomorrow. And how quickly it would get around the town and become a part of the folklore surrounding Denise Crowder's death. But Lucille would be furious with her son. A large figure was kneeling beside him; he could hear the panting and smell the faint sourness of Lyle Parsons' breath.

"Are you all right? Can you get up?"

"I think so," said Fielding, "but my glasses. I've lost my glasses." He was now leaning on his elbows and behind him someone was fitting the glasses around his ears. He could see the shoes and legs of those standing above him. Slowly he sat up and Parsons helped him to his feet. Light-headed, he was only half-listening as Parsons told everyone to go back into the house. It was all over and there was nothing more to see. Ray Crowder was between two men and they were walking away towards the side of the house. One of the men had his arm around Ray's shoulders and was talking to him.

"Are you going to be all right?" asked Parsons.

"I'm fine," said Fielding.

"Are you sure you don't want to go back in the house for a while?"

"No, no. I'll be on my way."

Together they walked across the lawn towards the street and Fielding's car.

"You're lucky," Parsons said. "If he'd been sober, he'd have put you in the hospital. I was watching from the front window."

"Thanks."

"You've got a long drive ahead of you. Think you can handle it?"

"I can handle it."

"Did you drink anything tonight?"

"Not really. Maybe half a glass of wine."

"Well, you should be okay then."

They stood under the street light regarding one another warily, and Fielding wondered how intimate Lyle Parsons and Denise Crowder had been all those years ago. Perhaps more than he had at first imagined.

"Well, take care of yourself," said Parsons.

"Thanks. You too."

He got into the car, grateful to be sitting down again, and watched Lyle Parsons walking back along the street, a big-shouldered, bulky figure, turning into the Crowders' drive-way. Fielding's left eye was beginning to water and he pressed a handkerchief against it.

As he drove along the streets of the town, Fielding glanced at the windows of houses and the lighted television screens. On the main street, he saw a boy and a girl. They were Heather's age, and they were eating pizza from a box, laughing as they walked along the wide, empty street. When the street became the highway, he passed the hamburger and the coffee places, the roadhouse with its half-filled parking lot, the heavy throb of the music briefly insistent even within the car. He passed the Moonbeam Motel where that morning he had finished reading *A History of Water*, and soon the town was behind him, the headlights tracing a path through the dark-ness of the countryside. Looking out, Fielding was moved by the terrible finality of death. Denise Crowder was under earth and leaves, and all that was left now lay in the memories of those who had known her. But memories reside in conscious-ness, and in time the dead are conveyed gradually to its fur-thest reaches, returning only when summoned by keepsake or song, on anniversary dates, in dreams.

—

She was watching television in the study, and after he opened the front door and took off his coat, he felt the abrupt silence of the house as she turned off the TV. A moment later she was in the hallway watching him hang up his coat. It wasn't until he walked towards her that she noticed his face.

"My God, what happened to you?"

She was standing by the entrance to the kitchen in a bathrobe, her arms folded across her chest.

"I got punched in the face," he said, stopping in front of her. "I was careless. I knew it was coming. I just didn't see it."

"Who did this to you? The brother?"

"Yes, Ray took a poke at me on the front lawn as I was leaving. He was a little drunk."

"Jesus."

"I don't really blame him. He thinks I'm responsible for what happened. He got it off his chest tonight. His mother will be more upset about this than I am."

Claire was frowning as if she didn't want to hear anything more about the Crowder family.

"You'd better let me have a look at that," she said, going into the kitchen.

He followed her, narrowing his eyes against the brightness, and sat down at the table.

"How's Heather?"

"Heather is fine. She's sleeping." Claire was at the sink running cold tap water over a cloth. "She's doing a lot of sleeping right now," she said, returning to the table and standing over him. "I'm just wondering if she has a touch of mono. I'm taking her in to see Janet next week."

She had taken off his glasses and was now pressing the cloth against his face, probing the cheekbone with her fingers.

"When I talked to Marlene this morning, she told me Janet wants to see you again. You never told me that."

"No," he said. "I went to see her Wednesday afternoon. My blood pressure was running a little high."

"You never told me that either."

He felt a little sleepy under the touch of her fingers.

"Does that hurt?" She was pressing lightly on his cheekbone.

"A little. Not too much."

"I don't think anything's broken. Did Janet prescribe something when she saw you?"

"Some little white pills."

"Lorazepam, probably."

"Yes, I think that's what they're called."

"You better take one of those tonight so you can get some sleep."

"Yes, I will," he said.

She had moved behind him. Closing his eyes, Fielding leaned his head against her stomach, and felt her fingers on his face. It was enough. For now it was enough.